Scott's Tulsa

A Wyatt Scott Novel

BY

S. L. Chalmers

Table of Contents

My thanks to Terry Collins for editing, suggesting, encouraging, and supporting my writing through many years. My supreme thanks to him for being a fantastic friend. I miss our laughs and conversations.

CHAPTER I

THE MAY ROOMS

The windows of Tulsa's infamous May Rooms lay dark, save one frame of the top floor. On the alley side against that casing's lighted and drawn blind, a female silhouette stood peering deep into the room. A male profile rushed into the tableau; his malevolent intent, even in two dimensions, became clear. The two shapes roamed and twisted in and out of the window's panorama. The male departed, shade right, while the woman recoiled, drawing closer to the window. His image reoccupied the scene charging like a rogue rhino, while brandishing the outline of a club. Her arms' shadows crossed her facade in fear and defense as her primal instinct sought protection from the onslaught. He drove forward with the bludgeon looming larger in aspect than in hand. He struck. The weapon smashed into her head. She wavered. A second blow, crueler than the first, crumpled her body out of view. As the cudgel's specter repeatedly came and left the screen, without slowing and without pity, he struck and struck again. His worst done; the marauder retreated beyond the beamed light.

The illuminated scene waited in blank anticipation for the assailant to complete his unspeakable purpose. Without the shade being raised, he lifted the pane, which framed the violent tableau. The blind fluttered out of the opening, ruining the projection, and ending the shadow performance. It rippled above the alleyway, a cautionary banner waving unheeded to the empty sidewalks and city streets. Before it could calm, a naked woman, beaten and bloodied, sailed out. She tumbled, silent and lifeless. Four floors of gravity's influence caused her body to rupture with a splat on the old brick surface. Blood seeped from her head, collecting on the mortar. It flowed north and south before encountering new paths to flow east and west. Despite the warm night air and the June heat caught in the pavers, the flowing blood congealed and altered the tiny rivers of crimson into extensions of the brick-red facade. The summer breeze swept down the alley. The neighbors slumbered and didn't see. The pigeons saw and didn't care.

* * *

The May Rooms supposedly rented rooms, but true vacancies came about as often as snow in Key West. The police, the city officials, the business community, and those in need of sexual relief knew the true business of the May Rooms. The local girls, who plied their trade on the premises generally had their own rooms to entertain and, more often than not, to live in. The proprietor and madam enjoyed an office and a comfortable apartment off the main parlor. The various rooms took the second through fourth floors, while the basement held a spot for Carl Jefferson, the maintenance man, bouncer, and factotum of the madam, Queena Capps.

In a third-floor room with an oscillating fan gently humming, big-band music streamed from a radio on a wooden nightstand. Except for a few feminine frills, the room presented an unadorned and basic appearance. The dresser supported an old-fashioned hand basin fired with a deep blue pattern on a white glaze. A pinkish washrag kept it company. An open wardrobe displayed exotic outfits and an unusual array of hosiery – sheer, colored, and fishnet. A bed, a closet, and seemingly out-of-place male clothes draped over a chair, completed the bed chamber.

Paulette, a pretty, brunette whore in her early twenties, lay bare, partially, but not strategically, covered by a white sheet. Her few years in the profession had yet to impose decay on her looks or figure. She possessed a pretty, if naive, smile and a complexion that glistened a little owing to her modest application of makeup. The clothes on the chair tattled that she entertained a man in her room, and her expression disclosed the companion could not be mistaken for an ordinary john.

"Are you mad at me, Wyatt?" blurted out Paulette.

"No. Why?" replied her guest, Wyatt Scott.

Standing near the bureau, his frame showed toned muscle, no scars, and little strain. Tall, athletic, and thirty-three, Scott carried the lacerations and misfortunes of his life inside. A whirlwind tour of big-league baseball brought him overseas barnstorming in nineteen thirty-four and huge disappointment a few months later. Afterward, he studied languages and history during his west coast, postgraduate days only to be caught up in the draft where the army exploited his talents in the OSS. His parents' deaths in a car accident brought him home to Tulsa. An association with his old high school baseball batterymate brought him to his occupation – private detective.

"It's...you were...so urgent tonight." Paulette dropped her eyes from Scott avoiding emphasis on her metaphor.

The radio music stopped. The announcer broke in; "You are listening to KTOO Tulsa. The time is ten o'clock."

The brief delay, from switches being switched, gave way to the familiar three-note motif of the radio network. A coast-to-coast announcer from New York confirmed it. "The National Broadcasting Company welcomes you to music live from the Starlight Room." On cue after his prologue, soft tones of muted trumpets and quiet strings flowed from the radio.

Scott moved slightly closer to the bed. "It's not you, Polly. I keep thinking about a *solved* crime. Somebody got away with murder in Alaska. I'm not sure who and I have no idea why."

Paulette reached for Scott, but he strayed to the side of the bed. She stretched out her arms like a child seeking reassurance. He resituated himself within her reach. She caressed his head and hair with her yearning undeniably exposed. He didn't recoil, yet he didn't reciprocate her attention or even glance in her direction. The wall took his stare, while his consideration focused much farther away and three years distant in time.

"Things were not right in Alaska," swore Scott. "Sticks in my craw."

A knock on the door interrupted them. Paulette withdrew her hands, freeing Scott. He stood up scrutinizing the offending wooden barrier. He edged toward the chair supporting his clothes. Paulette kept her gaze on the door. A second knock triggered her to sit up.

"Mr. Scott. When you get your pants on, come to my office. I need to see you." The footsteps of Queena Capps trailed off as she departed down the hall.

Paulette giggled. "Queena don't know it, but she'd like seeing you with your pants off."

"Just for you Polly." Scott grabbed his shirt from the chair and slipped into it with an aggressive flourish. "Do you know what she wants?"

Playfulness and joy fled Paulette's face. She lost her smile and glanced away. She pursed her lips, dropped her chin, and inspected the wrinkled sheet. She even feigned a cursory check of her fingernails.

Scott noted the fidgeting. "Is it about Darlene Barnes?" He moved on to his trousers.

She peeked at Scott before averting her eyes. Polly pulled the sheet over her nakedness and tight around her neck. She swallowed, then peered at Scott. "Wyatt, something's going on here." She drew her legs to her body still clasping the sheet to her neck. "Queena's troubled, and it's not just about Darlene's killing." Paulette's fear softened her tone and added breath to her words. "Cora's been gone nearly two weeks. Mary, the new girl, the real young one, hasn't been around in days. And then Darlene...can't help but think they're all connected."

Shirt tucked, and trousers zipped; Scott sat in the chair to work on his socks. "Connected like someone is systematically killing Queena's girls?"

"It's worrisome is all," sighed Paulette. "Are you going to work for Queena; check on the missing girls?"

Scott slid a foot into one of his wingtips, then followed with the other. He looked at Paulette before tying either. "Is that what she wants?"

"You know her," complained Paulette. "She only tells us to work the johns faster."

The left shoe tied; Scott wound the bow on the right one. "Could be she wants to hire me about the girls...could be about the time I spend with one of them." He flickered a sly grin as he made his conjecture. Scott stood and retrieved a ten-dollar bill from his wallet.

Watching his action, Paulette rose up. The abandoned sheet fell away. Her breasts jiggled. "You don't have to pay." Her wide-eyed, girlish gaze did not belong to her circumstances, her occupation, or her commonplace demeanor toward everyday clients. Wyatt Scott brought affection and hope to her eyes that others did not. Her hope languished in her storybook world where a sullen shamus and a veteran whore could be the sweet couple next door. It did not reside in Tulsa, in Scott, or in reality.

Scott dropped the bill on the nightstand. He petted Paulette's bare shoulder. "I know." He ambled toward the door picking up his pace as he neared it. He grabbed the knob, flung the door open, and left, closing it silently and summarily.

Wyatt Scott made his way down the stairs. The parlor's décor expressed comfort rather than the stale cheapness of most houses of the night. The lighting glowed low and soothing from a glass chandelier and several floor lamps. Easy chairs, wooden chairs with cushions, soft couches, hard couches, plush chairs, and wicker ones, which were out for the summer and generally replaced leather ones due to the heat, provided ample seating for the customers and the working girls of the house.

The parlor hummed with carnal tension and whispered euphemisms. Suits and ties mostly waited for their ladies of choice, while a few patrons delighted in the girls' competition for their business. A pair of men wore no coat or tie, but if they were laborers, they knew enough to be clean and well-mannered. Three robe-swathed girls competed for business in hushed tones with prospective clients. One flirted with a laugh, while the others advertised with a smooth leg peeking from her robe's slit or a pert breast daring to escape its halter. A console phonograph spun a Benny Goodman tune to set a cordial mood and ease the wait. Scott reached the door to which he had been summoned and entered the realm of Queena Capps, the madam and owner of the May Rooms.

Leaving the door ajar, Scott found Queena pacing near her fainting bed. Closer to fifty than forty and trying to look provocative in her night robe, she smoked like a stack. The lighting seemed brilliant after coming from the subdued hues of the parlor. An overhead, dome light, a couple of floor lamps and the lamp on her desk reflected off the jazz-plaster walls. Other than her tan lounger, the room, like Queena, was all business.

"Can't say I appreciated the visit, Miss Capps." Scott stopped just inside the doorway.

"I apologize, Scott. I'm not my right self lately." She puffed on her cigarette; in and out so fast she hadn't time to savor the smoke. The cigarette miasma billowed from her pacing figure like a forming storm flowing across the room.

Not one to deal in niceties or circle a problem, Scott drove to the point. "Do the police know about the missing girls?"

Queena jerked her head to see Scott. Her eyes narrowed. The right corner of her mouth twitched a smirk before it drooped to a frown. "Paulette should keep her mouth shut unless she's working a prick." She took a deep drag, held it, then blew the smoke toward the ceiling. "No, the cops most certainly know nothing beyond Darlene being tossed out the window. I pay them a lot of money not to care or get curious. But after her murder, they're bound to stumble into a few things."

Miss Capps sat down on her lounger but did not recline. She wore too much makeup, but not garishly promiscuous like the working girls. Her powder and paint spoke of a failing battle against time. Even as her upper body suffered from gravity and aging, her legs defied them and still held the firmness of her youth. She stretched them out resting her feet on the edges of her high heel pumps; footwear which spoke to Queena's vanity and disregard for comfort.

Scott pulled the single, plain, wooden chair from near her desk, spun it toward the couch, and straddled the seat with the back forward and his arms on top. "What will they stumble into?"

"Nothing...something. I don't know what – and that worries me." Queena inhaled again. She leaned toward Scott but swiveled her head to exhale the blast of smoke away from him. "Think you can help?"

"Tell me about the girls."

"Shut the door." Queena waved her smoking hand in the door's direction.

Scott left his chair, grabbed the handle, and peeked both directions beyond the frame. Satisfied no one loitered nearby, he eased the door shut and reclaimed his chair. "It's clear; no wandering souls or rabbit ears." He took a small notebook and a sharp pencil out of his inner coat pocket. He nodded to Queena to begin.

Another exhale and Queena started. "Cora went AWOL about twelve days ago. That's the last we've seen of her. She worked steady but day-by-day. Worked at Vandevers part time too. The gal had fantasies of a rich guy taking her away and making her the missus. Good with men, but she's not really a working girl at heart. Maybe she did find a guy and run off with him before he could get wind of her past." Queena dabbed her cigarette ash in the ashtray next to her chaise lounge. "Mary is new, from Kansas. She came by way of a friend of mine, who works Lawrence and college boys. Been here less than a month. Pretty thing, real pretty – could do well in the business. Naive and likes daddy figures, but that's a policy to bring in top dollar."

"Don't know either one of them, I guess." Scott printed the names on his pad.

"You haven't been Queena's customer long enough to know the girls." She raised her head high and rolled her eyes down at Scott. "Just since your girl left for California."

Scott stopped scribbling his notes. His narrowed eyes, and a piercing stare formed his reply. Unaffected by his visual rebuke, Queena sucked her Lucky and blew smoke rings, which drifted until they fell apart.

"When did Mary go missing?" Scott's gaze reverted to his pad.

"Four, five days ago." Queena snatched a new smoke from a gold case next to the ashtray. She lit it with the remnant of her old one. She crumpled the stub in the center of the ashtray; its bent vestige standing rigid with her lipstick ringing its tip.

"After Cora, a missing Mary didn't worry you enough to call me if not the cops?" grilled Scott.

"Whores don't give notice like secretaries. The young ones wander off, fall for some guy, up and leave. And I told you; Cora was never a real worker."

"But after Darlene, you figure there's a connection?"

"Something's off. Darlene was well worn and coarse as burlap, but she was smart. Cora had a date with a new john. He claimed she never showed. He took a date with Darlene as consolation." A puff and re-puff busied Queena without a true inhale.

"You hear from that john again?" Scott stood. He put a foot on the chair and used his thigh to support the jotter while he logged Queena's testimony.

"No, not my point though. Rumor had it Darlene wanted to start her own house, so maybe she saw him again." Queena sought refuge in another deep draw.

Scott finished his note and left the chair. He strolled and contemplated. "And Mary?" He sauntered toward Queena to receive his answer.

Queena forced the smoke out before she spoke. "Other than being new, she worked as a usual in-house girl. Left for dinner one night, and we haven't seen her since. She did spend time with Darlene." She flicked an ash in the tray. Miss Capps stared at the assemblage of crumbled butts as she seemed to formulate her next comment. "At first, I thought maybe Darlene wanted to give Mary advice, take her under her wing and all, but maybe she tried to work her off-the-books."

"I see." Scott scribbled, paced a little, then paused. "They all live here?" Scott's pencil awaited the reply.

"Not Cora. Had a place west of the river, Red Fork, maybe farther out. I don't collect addresses."

Scott worked his way around to Queena. "Okay. Tell me I'm hired, and I'll see what I can find."

"Wyatt, I'll double your usual fee if you can locate my missing girls." Her grim features tightened further. "Find Darlene's killer before the cops do, and I'll triple it. But you bring him here to me." Queena took another drag. She sneered as she exhaled. "I'll dispense a little whore-house justice, personally. If I slip up and get caught, no amount of jail time could wipe the smile off my face."

Queena gave a sample of the smile she would wear. She sucked in another puff and glared a provocation at Scott. Scott put away his notepad and returned the stare in kind.

CHAPTER 2

ROUTINE AND NOT SO ROUTINE

On June mornings in Tulsa, one could often see a fire-engine red, convertible LaSalle winding along Riverside Drive. The vestige of Wyatt Scott's big-league bonus from the Philadelphia Athletics, the flamboyant nineteen thirty-four Cadillac had spent more time in his late parents' garage than on the road. Through college at Oklahoma, graduate school in California, and five years of army war service, it saw Scott fewer than a dozen times. The upshot being that it looked and drove like its odometer reading and not its fourteen years of car tags.

This morning, the trees lining the boulevard along the river seemed fresh even though sandbars and driftwood rivaled water between the banks. Scott left his hat in the seat and his tie loose to feel the air whirl around his head and through his hair. Being a few degrees cooler than the concrete and brick city streets, the jaunt invigorated Wyatt more than last night's visit to the May Rooms. The wind held from the south keeping the acrid and sulfur odor of the Sinclair Refinery largely at bay. It promised to be a fine day – a warm June day and weeks from the late July furnace Tulsans had come to expect.

Scott hung a left on Thirty-first Street then shifted north by taking Cincinnati. Once he slipped into the Pythian Building, he'd see how things figured. If there were no messages or problems, the morning would be a one-two-three inning. He smiled at the prospect, planning to enjoy a long lunch at the Tulsa Club and maybe make some time for lonesome, old Bugler.

He slid the convertible into the alley half a block down from the front entrance to the Pythian. The spot afforded a discrete, back way into the building through a delivery entrance. He didn't need to sneak in. Avoiding Johnny or young Evie didn't matter since they knew he came and went on no set schedule. The procedure helped Scott avoid the building's lobby and the sketchy crowd that frequented the Western Union office. Irregular hours also kept problem clients and adversaries conjecturing on his methods and even which case he was working. His final reason for parking in the alley, and perhaps the most salient, was to avoid the parking meters that had become the scourge of downtown Tulsa. He detested the city's nickel-by-nickel extortion for daring to leave one's vehicle to conduct business.

* * *

Scott spent the entire day in his office. He made notes about Queena's missing whores and Darlene Barnes's murder. He calculated that it was too soon to get anything out of the police, and the newspaper accounts were long on sensation and short on details. With a rough plan sketched out by his second cup of coffee, he settled into a routine and boring few hours. He sifted through bills, while only once reminiscing about his baseball days and only three times grumbling over Alaska. He hadn't felt hungry at noon, and a brief walk turned up no sign of Bugler. The clock ticked so slowly it occasioned him to tidy up his desk in the afternoon before capping the slow day with a splurge steak dinner at Bishops. Before heading home, he took an evening cruise in his LaSalle, looping south and east out of the city. Cottonwoods, elms, oaks, and underbrush pushed in on the two lanes. The green foliage in every direction made the drive shaded, refreshing and best of all, cool. He spent high octane fuel waiting for the sun to duck toward the horizon and brainpower on past problems.

After raising the top and locking the LaSalle for the night, he made his way through the Sophian Plaza and up to his apartment. Once through the doorway, oblique light from the hall exposed a tiny ring of carpet while slats of dim, streetlight patterned the furnishings and floor. The summer heat lingered inside and offered him no relief from the corridor. As he shut the door extinguishing the hall light, a distant lamp clicked on revealing a specter from his past.

A civilian now, former Colonel Fielding, sat easy on the couch. Just north of fifty, Fielding retained a slim figure, gray temples, and a wrinkle-free mug. Attired in a dark suit, tie, and polished, black shoes, he admired a framed photo of then army Captain Scott with two other soldiers. He shifted the frame from one hand to the other before looking up.

"How have you been, Wyatt?" Fielding tapped the photo before setting it in its place on the end table.

Scott walked to a stuffed chair separated from the couch by the lit lamp. He remained standing while glaring down at Fielding. "So, two out of three dead. You looking to complete the job?"

"You know I had nothing to do with what happened to those two. And you know I want you on my team." Calm confidence surrounded Fielding.

"I am fine right here." Scott sat on the arm of the stuffed chair. "How's Moe? Does he have to work for you now?"

"Mr. Berg always had top support at OSS, and never fell under my regulation since he worked in Europe, and we worked the East. But now, the new civilian agency wants younger personnel." Fielding slid his arm from the couch to his lap. "He's retiring."

"Pity. Moe was good."

"Good enough to recommend you."

"Yeah, I forgave him that." After a moment's consideration, Scott swung to a less laudable subject. "You still have your gunsel, Pierce?"

"Pierce does work for me as a civilian agent. I'll give him your regards."

With as much sarcasm as he could muster, Scott retorted, "Sure, much regard for Agent Pierce." Scott leaned toward Fielding. "Why the visit?" His tone made it as much an accusation as an interrogative.

"Major changes in the game. You remember Venona?"

"Uncle Joe's encrypted love letters to America, of course. We got a lot of it in two and a half years."

"We cracked it, all of it, after you left. I can't tell you everything, but it's huge. We know why the messages weren't sent to consulates or embassies." Fielding let the statement dangle without offering the implied payoff.

"We speculated Moscow was running some game, even spies. You knew that." Scott stared at the man he blamed for all the misfortune in Alaska. "Brock had enough to make an educated conjecture. Did you get more than Brock found?"

"Yes. Spies all over the country. Real, genuine, commie operatives, not HUAC characters," declared Fielding.

"Figures. Stalin was always as dangerous as Hitler." Dialing down his interest, Scott slid into his chair. "Still, Fielding, it's not my game."

"Should be. You're good at it."

"I haven't changed my mind," asserted Scott as he crossed his arms.

"Scott, what are you doing with your life?" The former colonel leaned forward.

"I'm cruising through it in my LaSalle."

"Your old car and your old life. Do something important with your time; leave Tulsa and help your country." Fielding spread his arms in a welcoming plea adding to his petition for Scott's services.

"I'm fine here." Scott unfolded his arms, leaned forward, and placed his palms on his thighs. "I'm not throwing in with you."

"Your folks are dead. Janet got tired of waiting and left for California. You've no girl this side of the May Rooms. It's time you moved on." He dropped his arms and sat spreading them along the top of the couch cushions as he rested his case with cold, hard facts.

"I don't want to chase commies or search for guilty secrets you dropped in the Alaskan snow." Scott bristled. Had he been from a distant, red-sun planet, his eyes would have burned holes in Fielding.

"Wyatt, my boy, *you* are my guilty secret." Fielding smiled.

"No, I'm just the one soul who won't kiss your ass."

"Yes-men are a dime a dozen, and that makes you valuable." Fielding sat forward once more and looked directly at Scott. "You could be in Japan or China, or pick up German along with your Japanese, Mandarin, and Russian. Work Berlin under the airlift; work Tokyo or Peking. There's even a fresh game afoot in this new state of Israel. This silly detective life of yours is beneath you." Fielding reclined and once again stretched his arms along the sofa. "If you had your youth and your arm, I'd encourage you to go back to baseball, but P-I work, half the time for your Indian pal, the stuff's bullshit."

"Bullshit like your spread in Alaska? I don't want any part of your plans. You leave me alone, and I promise to spend the nickel to call if I run across a commie."

Fielding collected his hat, let out a sigh of defeat, and stood. "Keep a nickel handy, you may need it sooner than you think." Fielding walked to the apartment door. "Scott, you're wasting your life."

"Take a long walk in the snow," Scott blurted out.

"Whores get murdered all the time. The cops will find a pissed-off bumpkin or a pimp with poor management skills, and he'll be their guy. They don't need you squandering your talents on their problems."

"You're well informed but snooping into my business just squanders the taxpayers' money." Fielding's knowledge about his work stunned Scott but he refused to let it show.

Fielding nodded slightly as he pulled on the doorknob. "Nice seeing you, Wyatt."

Fielding left, quietly closing the door. Scott reached to the floor lamp and switched it off. He shifted left, then right, before easing back into his stuffed chair. The faint slats of streetlight enhanced his sour mood. Fielding brought hidden baggage with his visit. Scott realized he would have to unpack it and sort it through again. Sifting through those memories and frustrations would probably take more than one scotch. Luckily, the bootlegger had delivered a full bottle of Cutty Sark the day before.

* * *

A train of nearly endless nights rumbled through the army camp, carrying senselessness in its boxcars. It offloaded crated, boxed, or canned insanity for officers and enlisted men alike. The deliveries were regular, the depression relentless. It was winter in Alaska.

Repeated decorative attempts could not conceal the transitory nature of the Quonset hut. Bare bulbs dangled from their electric wires causing dancing light and kaleidoscopic shadows every time the door opened, and the wind blew. Ice-glazed windows filtered the scant light from the ephemeral hours of winter sun, requiring the lightbulbs to shine round the clock. The building, put up in days and outfitted even faster, afforded recreational escape for those in Alaska, who were fighting World War II through airwave intercepts, decoded messages, and translations. OSS and OIS warriors lived safe from Japanese or German fire, but bitter cold, boredom, and lack of light created casualties, nonetheless.

Tommy Dorsey music flowed through the single room, rolling across the barrel ceiling before sliding down both walls. Behind his bar, a bored enlisted man watched the three officers, who kept him from closing down and going to bed. First Lieutenant Paul Brock, the youngest of the trio, and Captain Roger Harris sat with Captain Wyatt

Scott at a table far from the door. Even indoors, the men remained bundled against the Alaskan cold. A mostly empty bottle of scotch, Cutty Sark to be specific, sat at the triangulated center of the men's three glasses. While rare, humor, reminiscences, and tall tales could push out the cold, cheerlessness, and gloom. On this night, the liquor and camaraderie held sway over the darkness and drudgery.

Calming a laugh, Roger Harris put down his drink to gesticulate his point. He raised his arms above his head and spread them wide. "So, Hiroshi caught you and Berg dead-to-rights near the ships in Tokyo Bay, and he believed you two were just sightseeing?"

Chuckling at a story of his own adventures, Captain Scott corrected Harris. "No. No. Nothing so prosaic as sightseeing." Knowing what was coming, Scott snorted a little as he continued. "Moe told Hiroshi we came to Tokyo Harbor to piss in the ocean because we pissed in it in San Francisco." Scott sipped whisky to clear his laugh.

Always the serious one, Brock could not accept the levity without cross-examination. "And this security chaperone bought it?"

"Let him finish, Brock," scolded Harris with a grin. "I've heard it before, but Moe Berg is a force of nature."

His whisky glass returned to the table; Scott continued. "Hiroshi asked Moe 'why.' He told him without the slightest chuckle we were trying to see if the two streams of piss would meet in Hawaii." Scott raised both hands, seeming to perform a double oath of honor. "It was so preposterous and offensive to Hiroshi's sense of decorum that he just asked us to get a cab to take us to our hotel."

Brock lost his seriousness and joined the laughter. "I'd like to meet Berg."

"I'd like to meet Hiroshi." Harris reclaimed his glass. "There's a bridge I'd like to sell him."

Scott grabbed the bottle and poured the amber fluid into his glass, where it rose dangerously close to the top. "Gentlemen, let me fill your glasses, and we'll have a tall drink to poor Hiroshi."

The other two pushed their glasses toward Scott, who poured them full as well.

"Hiroshi, may you find yourself looking up at a Yankee bomb," offered Harris.

"Hell, that's too easy. May he get stuck listening to our radio crap in a place as cold, dark, and bleak as this," countered Scott.

"Damn right!" agreed Brock. "Let his ass freeze off."

The trio raised their glasses and drank in unison.

CHAPTER 3

The Pythian Building

Scott, wearing his light blue summer suit, stood facing a wall covered by framed photos of uniformed baseball players. The simple, domed, overhead light reflected off the glass of several pictures, forcing Scott to shift and circulate slightly to view them all. Framed ribbons, programs, and a Babe Ruth poster carried Japanese symbols. Photos of a young Wyatt Scott in his Athletics' uniform shared space with the likes of Lou Gehrig, Babe Ruth, Lefty Gomez, Jimmy Foxx, and a group picture of the 1934 Japanese All-Stars. Wyatt made it into photos but not the official roster. He was only allowed to make the trip because Athletics owner and manager, Connie Mack, thought he could learn from the all-stars.

Scott appreciated the personal photos from the barnstorming trip more than the historic ones. Smaller less glamorous snapshots of him with his trip mentor, Moe Berg, and their Japanese guide and chaperone, Hiroshi Ishikawa, brought venerated recollections. Farther down the wall, pictures from Alaska brought merciless memories and the taste of last night's scotch. Those had lost their sway after he opted to conjure happier recollections of his baseball sojourn to Japan.

"He wants to see you."

Scott shifted to perceive Evie Hall, the secretary of his friend, high school batterymate, and local lawyer, Johnny Grayhawk. Posing in the doorway and perfectly up to date in her knee-length skirt, matching jacket with padded shoulders, sheer nylons, and pumps, Evie was a young, cute, but not beautiful woman. She carried herself beyond her years and combined extra pluck to promote a formidable personality. Scott moved to his swivel chair behind his wooden desk, black phone, and old desk lamp.

"Reminiscing about Japan?" asked Evie.

"Considering how things change in fourteen years." Scott sat in his chair but continued scrutinizing the wall of photos even as the distance and oblique angle made them impossible to discern.

Evie meandered in front of the desk but did not sit in the guest chair. She stared down at Scott. "Guess so. I was six."

Scott looked toward her giving up on his memory wall. "Grown up now though. And already dressed for a night out," quipped Scott.

"Nope. Work ensemble. We're high class in the law office. Come Friday night, I'll show real pizzazz." She ran her hands flirtatiously down the outline of her body.

"Hot date Friday?"

"You offering?"

"I couldn't keep up." He smiled at Evie – a smile which had trouble deciding if it were avuncular or condescending. "So, what's Johnny got for me?"

"He didn't say. He's finishing up with that odd-duck heiress, Ruth Brown." Performing for her audience of one, Evie sashayed toward the door. She turned placing her hand on her side like an impatient grammar school matron. "Oh, and Johnny wants you to shoo Bugler away from the building."

"Poor old Bugler; Johnny's only allergy."

"And I'm just his messenger." Evie dropped her arm and gruffly sighed out her frustration. "Wyatt, please just have Bugler stroll along before you see Johnny." Evie paused a moment being her young self before reclaiming her tough-woman persona and swaying down the hall in her tight-fitting skirt.

Wyatt grabbed his hat from his desk and left his office, pushing the door with two fingers and letting it fall closed. He grabbed the main banister with his right hand, swung around to take the stairs, and accelerated down the steps to the ground floor. He pushed through the doors to the sidewalk outside, knowing whom he would find.

A short, shabbily dressed, older man, Bugler, paced near the curb of the art deco Pythian Building. Topped with a Tulsa Oilers baseball cap, he was seventy if he was a day, yet his spry gait and slim figure belied his years. His nickname predated those, who knew him now, since none were alive during the Spanish-American War. As Scott emerged from the building, Bugler burst into a grin and stepped smartly toward his friend.

"Hey Wyatt. Dja' see that looker what visited crabby Johnny? I seen her somewheres before." Bugler scratched the top of his ball cap. "Cain't quite stick mah' thumb on the wheres."

"You know I'm not in the skirt market," reminded Scott.

"Jus' the same, lookers ain't around ever' corner." Bugler nodded agreeing with himself.

"I suppose not," replied Scott with an accompanying smile.

Bugler rubbed his stubbly chin and meandered around to his basic interest and foremost enjoyment. "Say, you goin' to the ballgame? Playin' San'tone. Tommy Tulsa's pitchin'."

"Tommy Warren?" Surprised by the news he had not heard, Scott reflexively expressed his perception. "I thought he gave up baseball and became a deputy sheriff."

"He got furlough," clarified Bugler.

Scott laughed at the term. "You mean they gave him a leave of absence to play ball again?"

"Playin' ball again, yep. Pitchin' like he always done. Second best one ta' ever come outa' Tulsa."

Scott nodded and smiled at Bugler's oblique compliment. "Fans probably like it. But that's a lot of comebacks for one player."

"He had a start out of town and did all right." Bugler made the case for Tommy Warren, who was indeed a Tulsa fan-favorite.

"You'll just have to tell me how he does. I can't make it today." Scott looked away to avoid Bugler's disappointed visage. An electric trolley slowed as it clanked down Boulder Avenue. Both men watched as sparks flew from its connecting rod and the live overhead wire. It sped up when no riders moved to come aboard. Scott glanced back at Bugler and proceeded with his task – looking to move Bugler away with as little disappointment as he could. "But you give me your score pad tomorrow. I trust you to keep score better than the papers."

Bugler perked up at the compliment and nodded his agreement.

"You bet. I don't give no glove-bounce singles. Ya'd swear them sportswriters was mule-kicked worse than me."

Scott, as a loyal friend and staunch supporter, could kid Bugler about his injury where others avoided the old man, if possible, and the subject of his injury in its entirety. "I guess Oklahoma mules kick harder than Cuban ones."

Scott's humor and subtlety were lost on Bugler. "Naw, I was funnin' 'bout them. They wasn't really kicked. Jus' ain't got no baseball brains and dunno nuthin' 'bout the game."

Scott smiled at Bugler's seriousness. Landing on a plan to placate his old buddy, he reached into his pocket and produced a quarter. "Since I can't make it, give me a full rundown without reporter garbage." He handed Bugler the coin. "Get a Coke and coneys from the Greek before you head to the game."

Bugler eyed the quarter in his palm, then slipped it into his pocket. He tipped his hat and started walking before he twisted around to address his pal. "I'll let ya' know sure." A grin, another hat tip, and Bugler ambled toward the Coney Islander.

Scott made his way back into the Pythian Building loping up the stairs and passing by his small office on his way to the much larger one of Johnny Grayhawk. He hurried through the outer office, where Evie stood filing with her back to his passing. Without a word to her, Scott made his way through the private door.

A grander and more professional office than Scott's, the place had an aristocratic feel even as it seemed a bit forced. Upholstered guest chairs, a dry bar, shelves of law books, and western art conferred an aura of class. A softer, domestic feel came from several framed family pictures of Johnny's wife and two children. Behind the desk, Johnny Grayhawk presented his usual dapper self, wearing an expensive three-piece suit despite the summer heat. In his thirties, Grayhawk had perfectly cut, dark hair and the facial features of his native Osage heritage. He looked up to see his longtime friend march in.

"I took care of your Bugler phobia." Scott removed his hat. "He's on his way to the ballpark via the Greek's."

"I don't have a phobia," sighed Johnny. "It's hard enough getting the high-pay set without them wading through a ragamuffin baseball encyclopedia."

"No sympathy for a war hero?" Scott smirked with his sarcastic tease at Johnny.

"I've always felt sorry for him, but we both know he was kicked in the head by a supply mule, not shot charging up San Juan Hill." Mild exasperation twinged Johnny's face.

Scott smiled and shook his head at Johnny's defensiveness before he flopped in one of the stuffed chairs. "Johnny, Johnny."

Grayhawk paused to let Scott rearrange himself in the chair. "Before I get to our new business, could you do me a favor?"

"Okay, give it to me."

"Next week, the Junior League is giving their big charity ball and Ruth Brown always attended with her grandmother. With her grandmother's passing, she needs an escort."

"And these facts are a prelude to me taking her to this thing?" Scott cocked his head and squinted at Johnny.

"Yes, exactly."

Scott responded by crossing his arms. The gesture served as his initial comment on the suggestion. "She hasn't got a boy her age for this?"

"Formal, ritzy dance – a classy guy with a tuxedo is required." Johnny laid out his case like a courtroom summation.

"All right, sure," Scott acquiesced despite his eyes glaring in the negative. "Only for you, Johnny Grayhawk. What's the new job?"

"Assuming you are free or can at least add another case, I have a good paying one for you."

"Good pay is nice. What have you got?"

"A well-known, well-to-do, Tulsa socialite wants a very, very discrete man to find something. *Something* is all she told me, so I guess the details would fluster her girlfriends. I have her phone number. She snuck in here once but won't come anywhere near again." Johnny raised his eyebrows. "She probably doesn't want to be seen dealing with an Indian lawyer." He smirked. "I suspect the main reason she chose me was because all the white ones would know her and her husband." Johnny shoved a folded paper across his desk toward Scott. "Call her after eleven this morning and make arrangements to meet someplace out-of-the-way."

"Hmmm, I'll have to find a spot where no society gal, businessman, or their domestic help would go." Wyatt stood and pocketed the paper without looking at it. "Such a mystery spot may not be in the county."

"I have faith in you. And when you do find that elusive spot, drop Bugler there so he doesn't discourage my classy clientele." Johnny beamed with a Cheshire-cat smile.

Scott grinned and headed for the door. "Watch out what you wish for, Johnny. Some of those fancy manicures hide poison under the nails."

He marched out of Johnny's office into the outer office where Evie dealt papers on her desk. She watched Scott make his way to her. No expression surfaced to betray her thoughts. Scott stopped directly in front of her. Her eyes made their way up his necktie, past his lips, and landed on Wyatt's eyes. She said nothing but shifted in her chair signaling her readiness to listen to what he had to say.

"Evie. You have a free moment? I need a favor."

Her blank expression broke into her dour-matron look. "With what Johnny pays me and what you don't, all my moments seem free. Whatcha' need?"

Scott extended his hand with a couple of bills. "I want you to buy yourself something nice."

"This is new." She took the five and the single, then shuffled them in front of her eyes. "I must have two more wishes right?"

"Wish all you like, but that's all the money you get."

"As long as it spends. There are a couple of things I have been eye-ing." She looked beyond Scott apparently shopping in her imagination.

"Okay, but eye at Vandevers and make it perfume or a scarf. I'm looking for a girl who used to work there. She probably left suddenly. I need you to get her address." Scott paused to let his mouth catch up with a sudden thought. "She might have an alias."

"Alias? So, why not check on Miss Alias yourself?"

"If you were a woman, would you give a stranger another woman's address?"

"I am a woman in case you've gone wacky. And no, I would not." Evie let slip a coquettish smile. "They might give you their address though." When she failed to get a wink and a nod or at least some flirtation in reply, she quickly revived her business countenance. "Okay, I'll go shopping," she agreed.

* * *

Bugler sat askew on a trolley seat. He liked to ride the trolley. It ran all the way to Sand Springs and back to downtown Tulsa. He couldn't ride his bike that far, but there were nice folks on the trolley, friendly and willing to share a few words, words about baseball. He snagged a folded newspaper from the seat across the car. He sifted through the segments, dropping them to the floor, until he clutched only the sports section. He ruffled and shook the saved portion of the paper before squinting at its contents. Finding the box score from the previous day's Oiler game, Bugler pulled the print close to read the numbers and nuances of the play.

"Dang! It weren't no hit by Papsky," he corrected the paper's box score. Bugler glanced up from the paper to see a young boy in seersucker shorts staring at him. The boy gaped at Bugler, while his mother remained oblivious to both and content to observe downtown Tulsa from the window.

Bugler felt compelled to answer the boy's stare. "The third baseman had more leather on that grounder than covers a cow." He affirmed his comment with a noggin nod. The boy stuck his tongue out in reply. Offended by the gesture, Bugler offered his thoughts. "You'll make a newspaperman someday, sonny."

The trolley slowed. Bugler knew the spot. He dropped his sports page and swirled into the aisle. As the trolley stopped, he 'begged pardon' past everyone till he swung out the door.

On the street, he reconnoitered the lady shoppers and suited businessmen hurrying along the sidewalk. More children appeared on the streets now with school out for the summer, and they ran with little heed for anyone or anything in their paths. Just as preoccupied with their desires as the adults, they doubtless looked for ice cream, candy, or the picture shows to begin. He didn't hate children; just thought they fit better in school or on a baseball field. Bugler started walking, reflexively keeping pace with the general foot traffic. The trolley pulled away.

Bugler made it down the sidewalk to the first stoplight. Its red hue had forced a group of pedestrians to congregate until it signaled safe and legal passage. As he waited, his interest swapped from the red bulb to a young, pretty woman also waiting for the light to change. It took him a moment, but he recognized her as the looker he saw go into Johnny Grayhawk's office. Having seen her come and go from the Pythian Building where he waited so often for Wyatt Scott, he felt they must be friends.

"Howdy." Bugler touched the brim of his ball cap as any gentleman would. "You goin' ta' see Johnny the lawyer? I seen ya' there. I stood out front a' th' buildin'. My pal, Wyatt, works with Johnny sometimes. He does the dangerous work, not the grumpy lawyerin'."

The looker ignored Bugler before grudgingly peeking in his direction. "That's nice you know Mr. Grayhawk." Her small courtesy done; she refocused on the indolent red light.

"Ya'oughta' visit my pal, Wyatt. He has a red car, and don't have a steady girl," explained Bugler with the facts he saw as most important.

The looker expelled her agitation with a hard sigh. "I'm sure your friend and his car are delightful." She clutched her purse tighter and glared harder at the intractable red light.

"Best ballplayer ever come outa' Tulsa too," added Bugler with pride and conviction.

"Yes. Even better." She scowled at the stoplight.

Bugler pulled at his ear and stared directly at her. "You don't go ta' th' ballpark, but you've been somewheres else than at grumpy Johnny's place. I'm not catchin' it though."

The light changed to green. The looker hurried across with the suddenness of a sprinter. Bugler tagged right behind her. After stepping up the far curb, she opened her purse, and without breaking stride, her gloved hand withdrew a quarter. "Here. I'm sure you could use some lunch." She extended her hand and kept walking.

Bugler kept pace while he stared at the quarter. The moving offer vexed him. The looker stopped. She stood in front of The National Bank of Tulsa Building. Holding the quarter like bait on a hook, she wiggled it at Bugler. He gazed at it, but his eyes caught the bank building and its glass front behind her. He peered through the bank's huge frame window catching sight of his mechanical phobia.

"I really must go," explained the frustrated woman.

Bugler ignored her, staring instead at the bank entrance. "Ya' gonna' ride on that X-calator?"

"What? I have business at the bank." She reached in her purse and brought out another quarter. She offered both to Bugler with a hand jiggle and coin rattle.

The clanking of silver-on-silver jostled Bugler's awareness. He stared at the pair of coins.

"Well?" Impatience sprung from the young woman.

Bugler took the coins and touched the tip of his cap. His frustrated patron hurried into the bank building. Watching her enter the bank, Bugler caught sight of the dreaded escalator before jerking his body around to avoid observing it anymore. He sauntered away, considering the coins in his hand as he did.

"Lookers with money don't grow on trees," he offered up to no one in particular. A few steps along, he stopped dead. He worked his brow. His memory light brightened setting off a laugh. "I knew I'd seen that looker 'sides at Johnny's place." Having told a crow and two pigeons of his recollection, Bugler moseyed down the sidewalk admiring his two quarters and whistling *Take me out to the ball game.*

CHAPTER 4

Day Work, Night Work

Vandevers had been a Tulsa department store since the heady, boom days of the nineteen-aughts. Its namesake and founder built his own building on Fifth Street just east of Main in nineteen twenty-four. A six-story beaux arts beauty out of which the Vandever family operated, yet it still couldn't fulfill Tulsans' demands for their wide variety of goods. The next-door Thompson Building rented its lowest two floors to Vandevers to expand its retail space. With the Depression a distant memory and war shortages a thing of the past, Tulsans wanted to buy, buy, buy – none more than Evie Hall.

Evie strolled down a short aisle filled with handbags on display. Large leather bags in browns and blacks, small cloth and silk purses, crocodile and alligator materials called to her. She slowed to give them all a chance to pick her as their new owner. Regrettably, that beguiling department did not fit her charge nor her secretarial salary. She sighed a little as she left the section making her way to her target, the perfume counter.

Behind the counter, a woman of her age and generation smiled at Evie as she approached. Although properly outfitted for her department store role, she could not reach Evie's look of business sophistication. Cognizant of her responsibility to Scott, Evie also smiled to gain the salesgirl's trust.

"May I help you?" asked the young woman.

"I hope so. I'm Evie." She extended her hand across the counter.

The girl took her hand and shook it. "I'm Shirley."

"Shirley, I need to buy some things for my boss; presents for him to give to a deserving gal." An embellishment Evie considered factual as she certainly considered herself a deserving gal.

"What were you thinking?" inquired Shirley.

"Perfume or maybe a scarf."

"I have scarves over on the side." Shirley pointed around the corner of her counter domain. "And you can see all the swell..." She caught herself and offered another smile as recompense. "We have a collection of elegant perfumes." Shirley swung her hand directing from one end of the counter to the other.

"I see you do." Evie nodded and looked through the glass at the distinguished bottles from France.

"May I offer you a sample smell?"

"No. I think I will hold off for now." Evie peered down the aisle where she adored the handbags. "Some of those purses sure look swell."

"Oh, I can sell purses too." Shirley perked up noticeably. "One of those would help with my quota."

Evie lit up after receiving justification for a grander purchase. "Now you're cookin' with gas." She stepped away from the counter and ogled the purse section. "Let me lay my peepers on those beauties."

Shirley came around the counter joining Evie on the customer side. "We'll stroll the line together and I can let you get the feel of any you like."

As the pair launched for the handbag displays, Evie began working on her rationale for the shopping trip. "I shopped here before, and there was a girl that helped me name of Cora Duncan. You know her?"

"I did," remarked Shirley as they entered the handbag section. "She left."

"Yeah. I heard she took a powder."

Shirley nodded. "Strangest thing." She shook her head. "Probably because of her boyfriend. She got in trouble once over him."

"The recent boyfriend?"

"Only one I ever knew her to have, Jake Barlow. Cora was never khaki wacky, but she liked this one even though I don't think he had any moolah." The young salesgirl dropped her facade of sophistication after Evie's reversion to slang gave her license to do the same.

"Yeah, I never laid my eyeballs on the guy like you. Was he a dreamboat or a sap?" quizzed Evie.

"Not a dreamboat. That's for sure." Shirly wrinkled her brow. "Seemed honest and I think he liked Cora. Might've been the jealous type, though."

"Lot of those. Think they own a gal if you kiss 'em once." Evie pointed at a handbag. "Let me look at the brown one."

Shirley eased to the edge of the display and reached up. She grabbed the purse and held it in front of Evie. Unclasping it, Shirley displayed the inside to her.

"I don't mean to be a gossip, but could you tell me about poor Cora?" Evie took the purse and began to examine the inside.

"Oh, I never like to gossip," affirmed Shirley. She watched Evie examine the handbag. "Still, poor Cora had some troubles. Then she's up and gone with the wind."

"Yep, that is *so* odd. I liked her, and she seemed real nice when she waited on me."

"Cora was nice enough. I just hope she's okay."

"It just makes me wonder," pressed Evie.

"Yeah. She left here in such a strange way." Shirley reached for the tag. "Evie, you know this purse is on sale?"

"The poor dear." Evie closed the handbag. "On sale, you say?"

"Yes. Marked down to nine, ninety-five."

"Then, let's take this handbag to the cosmetics counter, and I'll shop some more while you tell me more about Cora's boyfriend and if he caused her troubles." Evie strolled toward cosmetics. "I could use a scarf for sure and maybe I'll sample some of your perfume too."

* * *

Evie strolled into Scott's office wearing a new scarf and toting a new handbag. She swiveled left, then right, modeling her shopping triumph. Scott watched like a bored husband at a dress shop, not interested, but not wanting to rankle the model. She dipped a little. She writhed a little. She twirled her new purse around her hand before shifting it to her shoulder and extending her arms to twirl. Her spin complete, Evie beamed with pride at her successful mission. She stopped moving altogether and froze her pose apparently waiting for a torrent of compliments.

"Pretty scarf. Did it come with the information I needed?" offered Scott for better or worse.

"And then some," replied Evie undaunted by the lack of praise. "But you owe me six more bucks."

"For what? A scarf was plenty."

"No, it wouldn't do. Shirley, the salesgirl, was still short of her quota for the day. So, if you really needed that address, it required a purse sale too. So, ipso, dipso, all Johnny lingo, you owe me for this purse." Evie brandished the purse hanging off her shoulder like it was a hunting prize she garnered on safari.

"What did you find out?" Scott stayed strictly on point.

"Corabell Duncan worked at Vandevers about eleven months. She was well-liked but kept her private life private. She didn't run around with the other girls after work." Evie stepped closer to the desk. "Her sales were good – had an eye for accessories and men liked her." Evie handed Scott a slip of paper. "Here's what you asked for."

Scott grasped the note. "Thanks," he said before peering at the message.

Evie spun the purse behind her and put both hands on his desk. "I've got more." She leaned toward Scott. "Shirley told me that Cora had a fella' name of Jake Barlow; said he bugged her at work. Once he made such a scene their manager broke it up. The guy stormed out and poor Cora got a warning." Evie straightened dropping her hands to her side. "Then, out of the blue about two weeks ago, she called up and quit. No notice, no reason, bupkis. She didn't even come around to pick up her last check. Bonkers, huh?" She gazed at Scott like he might explain it.

"Thanks, Evie. You did well." Scott rose from his desk. "You did *really* well." He grabbed his hat off his desk and scooted toward the door. He had an address and his first solid lead on the murder in the May Rooms. At the door, he donned his fedora and grinned at Evie.

Evie stood flat-footed with her mouth agape in front of Scott's desk. "What about my six bucks?"

"Charge it to my expense account." Scott ducked out and hit the stairs without closing the door.

"You don't have an expense account," yelled Evie. "You owe me six smackers!"

* * *

Scott climbed out of his cherry-red LaSalle and eyed the ill kept, simple, frame house. He sized up the dwelling as he had done its Red Fork neighborhood as he drove through. The place had the look of working-class out-of-work. Poor paint, loose shutters, and a dried lawn with the hot Tulsa summer just beginning, left little doubt the occupants had no interest in keeping up appearances.

He made his way to the porch where the locked screen door forced him to knock on its fluttering frame. No toys on the porch completed the picture for Scott. He rapped the screen door harder. After a long wait, a woman wearing an apron over a summer dress cracked the main front door a tiny bit and peeped around it. The cheek below the single eye showed the hint of a healing bruise.

"Yeah?" The question came with a scowl.

"Cora Duncan?" inquired Scott.

"Who wants to know?" She peeked a little further into the gap revealing both eyes and more of her brown hair in need of a combing if not a wash.

"I'm Wyatt Scott. I'm a private investigator. A few minutes of your time is all I need."

"A few minutes, yeah. I bet that's more than you need, but I don't do that anymore." Her leery tone grew harsher. "I'm married!"

Scott disregarded her implication and pressed on. "You heard about Darlene Barnes; I expect. Queena told me you two were close." He took particular note of her face for any signs which might belie an evasive response.

"You got me mixed up with someone else." She began to close the door. "Jake, my husband, will be here shortly, and I have to have supper on the table when he gets home."

Scott read her like a headline. She couldn't get away fast enough. "Miss Duncan, I'm working on the murder of your friend. You are Cora, perhaps you're married. There's no smell of food cooking for a Jake or anyone else." He caught her lying at least by omission. Scott glared at her before changing his approach and his expression. "I understand you're scared, but a bad man is out there killing working girls. He will keep on killing them."

Scott stared at her through the rusting mesh of the screen. Cora Duncan stood as indifferent as the door. It was a standoff. He considered his limited options. Scott pulled his business card from his pocket.

"Here's my card. If you get the guts to help, give me a call." Having given up on her after stomaching her obdurate comportment, Scott stuck the card between the screen door and its frame. It looked like a tiny flag of surrender, but for the sake of the missing girl and justice for Darlene, he hoped it had a future beyond Cora Duncan's trash.

"Don't hold your breath gumshoe!" She yelled out and slammed the front door with a thud of finality.

Scott made his way to his car. He slid into the LaSalle, cranked it over, and started down the street. An older, dark sedan parked on the far side of the street, started up and followed the LaSalle. The driver, a young, working-class guy, kept his distance as both cars left west Tulsa.

Once over the Arkansas River, Scott steered toward his office. The light wind made it a rare summer day. The conditions allowed the sulfurous discharge from the Sinclair Refinery to linger and issue into town rather than be blown north like the usual June days. It didn't irritate Scott, but it distracted him from the older sedan growing closer as he veered off Denver.

Wyatt Scott parked his LaSalle in the alley near the front of the Pythian Building – his convenient spot to obscure his unmistakable vehicle. It also saved him from the parking meter problems that inhabited the front of the building. He switched off the car, engaged the brake, and left it to cool its tires on the red bricks. He began to stroll through the alley shade toward the sunlight of Boulder Avenue.

After just a few paces, the dark sedan from west Tulsa roared into the alley; the metal equivalent of a charging rhino, it bore down on Scott. Still the agile athlete, he dived to the nearer wall as the sedan swerved in but could not claim him. Jumping to his feet, Scott watched the car bounce across the alley's road bricks and skid onto Boulder. Its tires screeched and left dark, rubber lines on the clean gray street. Too late to do more, Scott glared at the fleeing car as it barreled south on what he suspected was a circuitous route back to Red Fork.

* * *

Scott waited in his convertible with the top down, and darkness settling in. He arrived at dusk and had been lingering at the Riverside Drive-In movie theater for thirty minutes – fifteen minutes past the scheduled rendezvous time. The new, parked-car theater, launched in February, was the second one in Tulsa within the year. The fad had spread across America as more people had cars and for some reason were loath to leave them. The faint flicker of the distant screen splashed the windshield and Scott's eyes. He didn't recognize the actors and hadn't bothered to read the movie title on the ticket booth. Scott scanned the dark lot, where a boy with a hot dog ventured toward his presumptive parents' car. No one else moved in front of him.

A spark of color in his rearview mirror prompted Scott to focus there. An overall-clad, plaid-shirt wearing, hayseed-looking woman made her way to the passenger door. A pulled down farm hat covered her hair but not her face – a face once beautiful but now yielding to time.

"Mrs. Folger, I presume?" asked Scott forthrightly.

She nodded. "Wyatt Scott?" came her curt reply.

He nodded. "Would have expected more Daisy Mae than Lil Abner."

She opened the passenger door and sat in the seat. She craned her neck around looking at the other cars and the empty spaces. Apparently satisfied, she pulled the door closed very quietly with both hands. "And I would have thought the top up would have been more appropriate for discretion," scolded Mrs. Folger.

Scott accepted the rebuke with a smile. Mrs. Folger stared at the screen. Scott redirected his eyes from Folger to scrutinize the drive-in lot for himself. Noting only reflections of the film's changing light and faint sounds from the speaker on the pole, he reverted his attention to her with a little irritation.

"Mrs. Folger…"

"You are the second Wyatt I've known," she interrupted without looking his way. "I met Wyatt Earp in Hollywood. He worked as an adviser on a western where I played a small role as a schoolmarm. Randy ol' coot – couldn't keep his pistol in his holster."

"You were an actress?" His surprise manifested without his approval or control.

"I am an actress. I just don't work at it anymore," she replied coolly.

"I see. Perhaps Tulsa Little Theatre is your venue."

"I'm on the board there." She paused but continued to stare straight ahead. "Clifford, my husband, prefers me to be on boards and not *on-the-boards* – Much more fitting for Tulsa society."

"So, is your problem associated with acting or the T-L-T folks?"

Mrs. Folger sat for a few moments before finally twisting toward Scott and shaking her head.

"Fine. What is it that concerns you enough to come to Johnny Grayhawk and need me?" Exasperation bled into Scott's voice.

She duplicated his exasperation in spades. "Mr. Scott, I am dressed in costume, hiding on the last row of a drive-in theater in the care of a stranger. Pardon me if I am reluctant to bare my soul. I have to decide if I trust you." She resumed her gaze at the movie screen and her expression shifted to dispassionate, if not quite calm.

Scott observed the flowing characters hundreds of feet distant. He still did not know the film and didn't care to learn more. He spent his attention on Mrs. Folger, looking at her profile. There seemed to be a game being played. Scott did not like it. He glared at the side of her head, light and shadow dancing on it as she pretended to watch the movie.

"Mrs. Folger, please decide soon about your trust." Scott sucked in a deep breath and sighed it out. "While I have all night, I hoped to sleep through part of it."

Folger lowered her chin to her chest. She looked down at her feet without a glance at Scott. "I am being blackmailed." She mumbled more than spoke.

"Blackmailed. By whom?"

Mrs. Folger jerked her head up and swiveled her neck, scouring the lot. Secure for the moment that no one heard Scott's declaration, she finally looked directly at him. "There's more than one, I believe. A little gang of blackmailers banded together to cash in on people's misfortunes."

"Do you have their names? Have you met them?" Scott rushed his questions having broken through her resistance.

"I paid a woman once, a rather generous sum, in fact. It happened some time ago. Things were quiet until I ran into her downtown a few days ago."

"So, she asked for more money."

"Not exactly. She made oblique comments about meeting next week, but she walked away without being specific."

"What is she blackmailing you about?"

Folger jerked her head to face Scott. She narrowed her eyes. She didn't breathe. "That is none of your *goddamned* business! I will not be compromised again."

"Don't get overwrought. I'm on your side." Scott tried to soothe her indignation. "I just want to know what's going on to help stop it."

Mrs. Folger renewed her viewing of the movie screen. "My reputation is important to me. I expect to keep it intact. I'm looking to you to find these people and keep me free from scandal."

"Okay." Scott eased into his next question having started a fire with his last one. "You said they were a group, but I take it you've only met the one."

"That's right. She always says 'we' when she makes her veiled threats."

"Could be a ploy to keep you from going after her, but I'll assume she has accomplices. Her first contact, did she call?"

"Thank God, no. She approached me in Miss Jackson's. She said she knew about my past and would never do this, but she had financial problems. She told me to meet her at the same spot, same time, in one week." Folger fidgeted, glanced at Scott, then revisited the movie screen.

"And you did."

"I did. She never mentioned an amount. I gave her two one-thousand-dollar bills. She thanked me more than once and said it would get her out of trouble. At the time, I thought it all over."

"When you met and repeated the meeting, what time and what day?"

"Around noon, and it was Thursday."

Scott glanced around the lot mulling the problem. "She probably has a job then. So, you want me to find this woman and convince her to forget about you.?"

Mrs. Folger dropped her gaze from the screen to her feet once again. "Yes." She reached into her overall pocket and pulled out three bills. She scooted toward Scott and extended them to him. "Here's two hundred, fifty as a start. I'll give you a lot more if you can end this." Her anxiety seemed clear despite all her efforts at control.

It was a lot of change up front, but she was rich and snobby – Scott gripped the bills. Mrs. Folger let them loose and unlatched the door. She stepped out, grabbed her large hat, then scanned the expanse more keenly than a fox being hunted. She shut the door without her previous caution and stepped briskly away. He didn't bother watching her reach her car, while he wondered how much strain such a wealthy socialite might cause him. He could use a spare two-fifty and the promised greater sum, even if his cost ran higher. Scott fired up the LaSalle. He figured taking a cool drive would beat the hell out of the hot gravel and a bad movie at the Riverside Drive-In.

CHAPTER 5

WHORES AND BOOTLEGGERS

Mornings at the May Rooms consisted of sleep, Carl assessing the damage from the preceding night, and Queena Capps drinking her coffee while checking her books against the previous day's receipts. The whorehouse girls did the sleeping. Carl went about his business without complaining even though the film of smoke, spilled liquor, and on occasion, nastier fluids, required daily mopping, cleansing, and disinfecting. Queena complained, frowned, rechecked figures, complained some more, and recorded the tally. The sequence obeyed its routine – constant, orderly, and relentless.

After completing her work, Queena lounged on her day couch drinking a fresh cup of coffee laced with sugar and doused with cream. She finished her books with her usual grievances but somewhat greater satisfaction than usual. She barely budged when Wyatt Scott pushed through her office door. He defiantly left it ajar. She allowed a smile to break the powder and paint of her face in spite of the intrusion. Scott marched sullen and determined to find what she knew.

"Wyatt, Paulette's not here," explained Queena with playfulness in her tone and a sly hint of sexual innuendo.

"I'm here to see you." Severe features and glowering eyes supplanted Scott's usual placid countenance. He stopped directly in front of Queena looming over her reclined figure like a shadow of his distrust. "I have questions."

With Scott towering over her, she pivoted to a sitting position before pushing herself up to stand. She wiped her expressions clean, presenting only business in her face. "More questions? I hired you for answers."

"I'm not sure why you hired me." He raised his volume. "You really didn't know about Cora?"

"What about her?" She sharpened her tone in reply.

"She's alive for one thing."

Queena swayed slightly, then flopped on the couch. "Thank God!" Her relief at the unexpected news trumped her coolness.

"You want me to believe you really care about the girls?" Scott's cup ran over with sarcasm and incredulity.

"I just want to know they're okay." Queena took a breath, then glared at Scott. "And I don't giv'a shit what you think."

Neither seemed ready to follow through on sharing their stories. Before thought or conversation could persevere, the front door buzzer sounded off, halting the exchange. Queena squinted through her door to the parlor. "Carl's in the kitchen and I need to see who the hell came in this early. Sit tight! I want some particulars about Cora."

Scott shrugged his acceptance. Queena gathered herself, repositioned her bosom and bra, then marched out. Her receding footsteps grew quieter as they traversed the parlor toward the front door.

Waiting played a necessary part in private investigations, yet it annoyed Scott. Stakeouts caused him more anxiety than dangerous encounters. He shuffled around Queena's office observing the minutiae of her décor and personal treasures. Trinkets covered the shelves of a portable bookcase, the bottom of which had smoked glass doors and a lock. Movie posters played stand-in for artwork, but a photo of a young Queena Capps at a jazz club drew a snicker of surprise from Scott. The old madam had been a torch singer. He had just assumed she too had started selling her female favors at a youthful age and evolved to management.

The indistinct voices from the parlor rose in volume pulling his attention toward it. Scott could see nothing of the commotion through the narrow proscenium of the door. He shifted his ear searching for greater distinction in the utterances. Scuffling sounds came through followed closely by a body striking the floor. Scott bolted out of the office with the quickness of his baseball days.

Queena lay gasping on the floor, her arms hugging her stomach. A young man in workman's clothes stood over her clinching a lug wrench. He spied Scott and moved toward him with malicious intent. Scott stood his ground sizing up the fellow.

"You! You sonofabitch. I figured to find you here. You're tryin' ta' take up with my Cora," shouted the fellow.

Scott held out his arms showing his palms. "Hold on, chum...."

The man raised the lug wrench and swung it wildly at Scott. He stepped aside from the swing, which left the attacker off balance. Scott then delivered a one-two to the belly and jaw. The guy dropped to the floor. His eyes did not roll back, but they did float in their sockets. Scott grabbed the lug wrench and flung it aside. It bounced and cartwheeled toward the front door.

Carl Jefferson, Queena's unofficial house marshal, rushed in with a dish towel hung over his shoulder. A very large Black man still in his thirties, Carl was a formidable human being. Taller than Scott and a well-constructed two hundred and forty pounds, few individuals ever tested Carl. He placed a hefty foot on the downed fellow's head. "Stay down." He looked to Queena. "You okay, Miss Queena?"

Queena nodded. "Just clipped me." She collected herself a moment before rising to her feet.

A pinkish hue, from the increasing pressure of Carl's foot, manifested in the man's complexion. Queena straightened her hair, brushed her blouse, and fixed her stare on the face beneath Carl's shoe. She moved to stand over her attacker. "S-O-B sucker punched me with that tire tool." She pointed toward the offending weapon before she kicked the downed intruder in his side. He groaned and pulled up his legs. He started wiggling with Carl still holding him to the floor. The big man applied a bit more pressure to let the fellow know who was in charge.

"Don't try son. You ain't brung enough." Carl shifted his attention to Scott. "Mr. Wyatt, you bringin' trouble to the May Rooms?"

"I know better, Carl. I suspect this fellow is Cora's husband, Jake Barlow. If you give me a hand, I think we can clear this up." Scott stepped over to Barlow's side.

Carl lifted his foot off Barlow. Queena slid into her detached managerial persona, looking more annoyed than angry, she scrutinized the process. Scott and Carl jerked Barlow to his feet. Carl stood him up straight and held both his shoulders secure with fingers developed on a farm but repurposed for life on the rough side of the city.

"Can you drive, Carl?" asked Scott.

"Sure can."

"Good."

Scott sized up Barlow, then belted him with a haymaker right. Barlow's eyes rolled up as he wilted into Carl's grasp. Queena glanced from Carl to Scott as Carl eased the unconscious intruder to the floor.

"Guess I won't be asking him any questions." Queena put her hands on her hips and glared at Scott.

"I've got a handle on it, Queena," replied Scott. "Just need to secure him for a little visit to Cora. You have any rope or twine?" asked Scott to both Queena and Carl.

"Package a' twine in the kitchen," replied Carl.

"I'll get it," said Queena as she made for the kitchen.

* * *

Carl steered Jake Barlow's car into the drive at Cora (formerly Duncan) Barlow's house. Right behind him, Scott stopped his LaSalle along the curb in front. Through the living room window, Cora peeped out. Seeing her man's car driven by a stranger must have motivated her. She rushed from the window. Without delay, she threw the inside door wide, shoved the screen door clear, and charged onto the porch.

"What are you doing with Jake's car?" screamed Cora.

Scott set the brake on the LaSalle and circled around to its trunk. Carl climbed out of Jake's car and trotted toward the LaSalle. Scott kept his eye on Cora. She stared darts at him.

"We brought it back home." Scott popped his trunk as Carl reached the Caddy. "I brought Jake too," added Scott with delight and derision.

Carl and Scott reached into the trunk, lifted the bound Jake Barlow out, and stood him on the street. He wobbled, but Carl held him rigid. Shock restrained Cora for a moment before she bolted down the porch steps and ran to Jake's side.

"What have you done to him; you fake flatfoot?!"

Scott left Jake to Carl's care and intercepted Cora just where her scruffy lawn met the edge of the street.

"If you hurt him...." Cora raised her arms as she confronted Scott.

"I showed him why you and I have nothing in common," interrupted Scott. "Since he had to fight with me and not a woman, he managed to finish last."

Carl gripped inflexibly to Jake's shoulders. Scott seized Cora's smaller shoulders and stood her rigid to avoid her kicking feet. The moment persisted. Carl deferred to Scott's leadership, while the two detainees conceded their lack of choice. All parties breathed into a more composed state.

"Tell her you are okay, Jake," requested Scott while maintaining his hold on Cora.

"I'm fine, Cora." He looked at her to start, then ducked his head away as embarrassment swept down his mug. "Couple a' punches is all."

Scott pressed Cora slightly away and dropped his grasp on her. She rushed to her man and rubbed his swollen cheeks. He looked down and did not bring his eyes to meet hers.

"If you just tell me the truth about the night you were supposed to meet Darlene's john, I'll deliver you two lovebirds once more into wedded bliss." Scott appealed to Cora but drenched his statement with two coats of sarcasm.

"I don't know a thing." Still holding Jake's face, she glared at Scott. "I only took the date 'cause Darlene said the guy didn't want sex. She said he liked to tie girls and maybe beat 'em where it don't show." Mrs. Barlow raised her chin and added her version of respectfulness to her explanation. "We needed the money, and I didn't want to cheat on Jake."

Cora rekindled her attention for Jake and stroked his hair. He finally looked at her, even as his body drooped a little in Carl's grasp. She kept her focus on him. His eyes strayed to Scott, then to his feet. Without a hint of fatigue, Carl continued holding Barlow up. Scott shut the trunk lid and leaned against it.

The trunk's thud brought Cora's notice to Scott. She took a deep breath before imparting her version of events. "Jake came home early and found me dressed up. He got mad." Cora halted seeming to plead Jake's case to Scott. "That was that. I never made it to the date. I never saw the guy. Sure, Jake got rough. He had a right." She looked toward Jake. He raised his eyes to her. "He loves me," justified Cora.

Jake squirmed a little. Carl wrenched him to look at Scott and straightened his posture in the process. Scott stood impassive to the domestic confession. He waited for Cora to continue.

"I quit for good the next day. Quit Vandevers too. Ain't that right, Jake?" Cora sought out her husband's confirmation.

Jake nodded.

Scott moved from the trunk toward Barlow. "That right, Jake? She never went out and you never went after the guy?"

"Cora never met'em," confirmed Jake. "I got sore with her, same as I got sore at you. I love her, see." Jake made a half-smile to Cora. She hugged him despite his bound hands and feet; as much of him as she could with Carl's thick arms and large hands still grasping him.

"I didn't know who to fight. I never saw the guy." Barlow finished his confession. "When I saw you drivin' away, I thought you was him…and you went to that whorehouse, it all added up." He squirmed a little; his righteousness affirmed, at least to himself. "I got steamed up is all."

"Damn!" Scott took out his pocketknife and cut the cords around Barlow's ankles, then those on his hands. "Go on!" Exasperation spewed out with his words.

Cora threw herself into Jake's arms as Carl dropped his hold and stepped out of the way. Scott folded his knife and jammed it in his pocket. The two lovebirds hugged and kissed. Scott bristled.

Carl noted Scott's frustration. He eased to Scott's side. "Mister Wyatt, don't know if I am talkin' outa' church here, but this whore don't seem ta' know nuthin'."

"You're always right to speak your mind to me, Carl. Too bad for us, you're right." A shake of his head admitting defeat and a sneer of frustration confirmed everything Scott could add.

Carl glanced down at his shoes. He scuffled one foot against the other. "They's a thing you might mean ta' know." Carl raised his gaze focusing on Scott. "I don't know 'bout this one or the young whore, but that Darlene Barnes sure as rain did work them johns behind Miss Queena's back."

"I heard there's rumor about it. You know it as fact?" quizzed Scott.

"I do. No loyalty and no class neither even as whores be judged. Knew her to get dirty knees in th' alley." Carl wrinkled his nose. "She'd pick off a john if he looked like extra money; short Miss Queena on it. I know sure 'bout a banker, don't know his name. She met him outa' the house. There's the bootlegger, Bob Shanks, she gabbed 'bout dealin' with him, and she visited that KTOO Joe radio fella' too." Carl slowly shook his head. "Others sure enough, I just can't peel off any more names."

"Does Queena know about these johns or about Darlene working off book?"

"Can't say. I didn't tell her...probably should've, but there's so much cathouse goin's-on a fella' can't shove it all out there." Carl's expression showed concern before switching to consternation.

"Don't worry on it, Carl. I'll see what I can dig up about Darlene and tell Queena." Scott moved to the driver's door. "Hop in."

The reconciled couple sauntered toward their house with arms draped around one another. Carl eyed them. He tossed up his hand apparently not believing their bliss to be lasting. Scott paid them no heed. He pulled open his car door, slid behind the wheel, and slammed it shut.

Carl climbed through the passenger side door and squeezed his sizable body into the seat. "You be sure ta' tell Miss Queena what you find. I know you to be a fair man, but see I'm loyal to Miss Queena, even if I don't yap ever'thin' I see."

"I'll do my best Carl. We're on the same side." Scott started the LaSalle. "Do you know where Bootlegger Bob lives?"

"Prattville, I heard."

"Good. I'll take you to the May Rooms and then look the boot-legger up."

"He don't deal out of his house – angry man. Heard tell of visitors bein' run off with a gun or worse," warned Carl.

"I'll keep it in mind."

* * *

Scott swung his LaSalle just off the dirt road and in front of a dusty path. It posed as the walkway to a house, which appeared allergic to paint. Its sturdy frame supported a gnarled and coarse exterior. Only tiny specks of white adhered to the support posts, while the planking consisted of bare, weathered boards. The boondocks neighborhood grew underbrush at the expense of grass and only the occupant's footsteps wore the seedlings enough to keep the front yard clear of growth. The porch pitched slightly forward toward the cracked concrete steps. Galvanized washtubs outnumbered chairs three-to-one. Clutter consisting of boxes, bottles, crates, and barrels covered either side of the door. Scott made his way up the steps of the dwelling he presumed housed Bootlegger Bob Shanks.

His first knock on the door garnered no response. He rapped again with more vigor. After a phlegm-filled, guttural cough arose from inside, a stocky, baleful looking man opened the door. Stubble testified to his sloth, and the loose dungarees to his disregard for fashion. His face showed no scars, but it might have been because he moved nimbly. He stood several inches shorter than Scott, but his stocky frame made fisticuffs even money. A former professional athlete like Scott aside, the man looked to be more than a match for his usual customers.

"I don't deal out of my house, so get the fuck off my porch," growled Bob in a rough, throaty voice, which suited his appearance.

"I'm not looking for trouble or liquor," replied Scott. "I'd like to ask if you know Darlene Barnes."

"Don't guess so. Now you can leave," barked the reputed bootlegger.

"She worked the May Rooms."

"A whore then; still no, and *now* you can shove off." Shanks looked to spit, but to keep the screen door closed, he swallowed.

"Ten bucks, no liquor, just answers," countered Scott.

"And who are you that's offerin'?"

"I'm Wyatt Scott."

"Okay Scott. Let's see the color of your cabbage," dared Shanks.

Scott unfolded his wallet and removed a ten-dollar bill. He held the currency near his waist, neither offering nor withdrawing it. Bob leered at the ten-spot. He pushed through the screen door and stepped onto the porch.

Scott stepped away to give Bob more room. He tended the bill, casually stroking it with one hand then the other. "Did you ever deal with a working girl named Darlene?" asked Scott.

"Nah. May...be. Not at the May Rooms though. Met a whore at a roadhouse I supply."

"Thirty, brown hair, not too long, her face a little worn looking?"

"Sounds about right," agreed Shanks.

"So, what about her?" quizzed Scott.

"She sucked my pecker in the car outside the roadhouse."

"Not the info I'll pay for." Scott drew the ten into his palm. "Did she mention her work or any johns?"

"She claimed she did special work and wanted a sawbuck. I tol' her she weren't so special and half-a-sawbuck was plenty. Then she come around to wantin' to make a trade."

"So, you gave her some hooch for sex?" questioned Scott.

"Naw. Started thata' way, but she really wanted pills."

"Pills. What kind?"

"Morphine, codeine, pain pills," replied Shanks coolly.

"Where the hell do you get those?" More than a little surprised at this info, Scott shifted his feet to regain his thoughts.

"That's outside a' ten bucks, but easy to figure – a doctor who likes his booze."

"Good enough." Scott nodded and settled in on his query about Darlene, the dead flying whore. "Your roadhouse gal, she say why she wanted the pills rather than cash or booze?"

"I wasn't dealin' with her ta' talk, and she didn't get much chance doin' what she did." Shanks smiled a little at his wit.

"Before then. When she asked for pills." Scott grabbed the end of the bill with his left hand and creased Hamilton's likeness in front of his chest.

The bootlegger watched the ten-dollar tease. He looked up at Scott to offer more of his story. "When we made the deal first time, she talked about preferring pills to booze because they helped with the pain. I figured her guy had some kinda' real big pecker."

"Yeah, must have." Scott smirked. "You never saw her at the May Rooms?"

Bootlegger Bob shook his head.

"When was your last car seat visit?"

"Ten, 'leven days ago. Don't think she's been 'round my route since." Bob ran his hand through his hair to stimulate his memory, but nothing more came of it.

Scott took a step forward. He held the ten-spot out to the bootlegger. Shanks took it.

"Why the interest in this whore?" Bob massaged his stubbled chin as he eyed his new patron. "You ain't a cop payin' ten bucks, and you're not the whore's beau neither."

"Somebody killed her. Another somebody paid me to look into it."

"Private peeper then; I get it. Thinkin' I kilt the woman?"

The bootlegger was as blunt as a lead pipe working on a porcelain doll. "Don't see a good reason you would. Am I missing it?"

"Nope. If it was your whore-gal in mah' car seat, ours was strictly a whore and pecker relationship. Nothin' in it to rise to murder." Shanks grabbed his screen door handle. "If you need hooch, we could deal some more."

"Thought you didn't deal out of your house."

"Special cases I do. A gutsy Pinkerton might be handy down the curvy road." Bob cocked his head as a signal for a reply.

"Fresh out of business cards, but I'm in the book," declared Scott with neither enthusiasm nor disinterest.

"Hang on. I gotta' bennus' card." Bob stepped into his house. He reappeared with a bottle of Coke.

"A Coke?" Scott noted the bottle then scrutinized the man.

"Recapped. Two shots of Weller; not local crap. Never get noticed by cops or in-laws." Bob grinned at the quality and cleverness of his product. He raised his arm and tendered the bottle to Scott cap first.

Scott took the spiked bottle of cola. He admired the recapping – it looked as authentic as the day it left the bottler. This concluded their business and added Scott to the select company, who had coaxed Bootlegger Bob to deal from his house. Wyatt didn't figure to secure such a prize from his next visit.

CHAPTER 6

INVESTIGATIONS AND BREAKFAST

Scott strolled down the hall of the KTOO radio station studio. A poster hung on one side declaring big band music live and direct from New York. On the opposite wall, another ad touted the Lewis Meyer radio show. The man's jovial face fit his happy book reviews and prairie philosophizing. He projected a blend of folksy and urbane Tulsan despite being an oil inheritance child and a Jewish man from Sapulpa. Back on the right-hand wall, the national news broadcast from NBC shared artwork space with the local Tulsa news schedule. Beyond it, a print of a smiling, middle-aged woman advertised for a cooking show, which Scott had never heard.

A bit farther along the hall, the poster Scott hoped to see emerged. KTOO Joe, it proclaimed. According to the poster, Joe spun the discs Tulsa craved. The rendition included the cheerful visage of the celebrity, a vinyl disc on a player, and splashes of song titles and artists names printed around the edges. Wyatt checked his coat pocket for the sheet of typing paper and his pen. It was a longshot notion, but if he conned Joe into an autograph, he would have a handwriting sample and fingerprints to compare to any note the police might find or anything he could uncover at the May Rooms.

Scott took a side hall following the sign pointing to the station's studios. Glass walls replaced the upper half of the plaster as he made his way down the corridor. Each studio exhibited clear line of sight to the hallway. The doors enumerated the studios logically starting with number one, which stood empty and dark. Number Two had the lights on, yet looked as deserted as the first studio. Three, reportedly Joe's studio as recounted by the downstairs receptionist, had a resident standing near a revolving turntable. Scott opened the door and stepped in.

"Are you Joe?" Scott sized up the man who resembled the poster of the radio personality. His hair appeared neatly cut and neither long nor short. Clean shaven, his face carried no scars or distinctive marks. His clothes appeared to be a younger style than his age called for, but less flamboyant than Scott expected. The image did not fit Scott's view of a local celebrity.

"Not my real name, but my radio name is KTOO Joe. And who are you?"

Scott strode close to Joe stopping beyond arm's length. No need to crowd him without feeling out his thinking. He offered a tiny, but friendly smile to Joe. "Wyatt Scott. I'm a private investigator looking into the murder of Darlene Barnes."

Joe remained expressionless. "Okay." He traded his blank look for a more quizzical one. "I don't know a Darlene Barnes, so why are you asking me questions?"

"I'm checking anyone who might've had contact with her, even if they didn't know her name." Scott paused to allow a response. When none came, he added; "She was a prostitute."

Joe narrowed his eyes. "Even less likely to know her then." He stood taller raising his gaze. "I'm in demand from real women. Being a radio personality may not be movie-star renowned, but in Tulsa, it's got no competition. I get calls. I get skirts asking *me* out. And I don't have to hustle women let alone buy them."

Undaunted by the immodest disclaimer, Scott continued as he had done with the bootlegger. "Darlene worked at the May Rooms."

"That place I have heard of – whorehouse with little pretense." Smugness permeated his tone. "Seems like your time would be better spent talking to the ladies that work there or getting a list of their customers."

"Already done the former. Not a good business practice for the owner to keep records of visitors to such an enterprise, so that suggestion falls flat." Scott didn't hide the smirk Joe's suggestion spawned.

Retreating a little from his conceit, Joe backed off. "I guess you know *your* business. Mine is gabbing to the Tulsa folk and finding songs they want to hear." He waved his hand to his stack of records.

Scott looked toward them, then brought a new question to Joe. "You're not on the air till later. What are you working on now?"

"Play list. Selecting records, songs, for tonight's show." Joe stepped to a stack of records. He shifted the stack and set the top one on the console. "This one by Sinatra has girls squealing. It will get plenty of play."

"He does seem popular." Scott moved past Joe to the stack of records. He tilted the top one to read its label. "Do any of the record companies encourage you to play certain songs?"

Joe crossed his arms and sharpened his gaze. "You asking if I get payola?"

"Just hear things run that way."

"Not with me!"

Scott figured he hit a nerve. "I have no way of knowing about you. Folks just believe it's part of the industry."

"Look, shamus, I get paid pretty well by the station. My commercials, endorsements, and appearances pay me another real nice chunk." He gestured with both hands from his chest to his belt. "These clothes don't come from Clarke's store racks."

"I believe you." Scott nodded. "I have no interest in your income or work whether broad or narrow. The murdered working girl is my case."

"I got that earlier. As I said, never knew her, never heard of her except maybe in the paper for being murdered." Joe narrowed his eyes and shifted more weight to his right causing his left hip to rise.

"I got ya', Joe." Scott pulled away from the console and the radio celebrity. "One more question and I'll let you get back to selecting your records. Did you know a girl named Cora or one named Mary?"

Joe wrinkled his forehead and pursed his lips. "No. Don't think so." He relaxed his expression as he made a conjecture on the names. "If they were fans, who showed up at a record store, I might've signed a record or some autograph without knowing them or remembering them."

"Might've been fans. I don't know. Both are May Rooms girls," stated Scott without elaboration.

"Well, other than the place's rep, I don't know it or the girls working there."

"Thank you then." Scott plastered a sycophantic smile on his face. "I wonder, Mr. Joe, if you would help me out with my niece. She loves your show and if she hears I met you and didn't ask for your autograph, I would be in Dutch with her." He reached into his pocket and brought out the folded paper and his ink pen.

Joe stared at Scott. His celebrity ego apparently ruling his actions, he took the pen and paper. He bent to the desk surface near the stacked records and signed with a flurry. "Here." He handed the autograph and the pen to Scott. "Wouldn't want to disappoint a true fan."

Wyatt went beyond thankful to unctuous. "This is great! She'll just love it. Thanks, again." With his huge grin almost hurting his cheeks, Scott removed his business card from his coat pocket. He handed it to Joe. "Anything comes up about those whores, call me. You're out and about in town. Some fan fella' might blab to you."

Joe took the card glancing at it before he slid it in his pants' pocket. "I generally associate with female fans, but if I do hear something, I'll give you a call."

"All I could ask," replied Scott.

Joe nodded.

Scott made his way to the door and left the studio. He didn't have a good gauge on KTOO Joe other than how much Joe loved Joe. Retracing his path along the studio hall and then down the main one, he calculated his next move. Wyatt realized he had few other trails that were not already run or exhausted by the police. Visiting Carl Jefferson and hoping for new leads or at least a more defined one on the banker seemed his best bet.

* * *

Scott drove his LaSalle down the graveled driveway to the small frame house that had become Wilton's café. And just in case any visitor felt uncertain as to the building's use and proper place, the sign over the door read *Wilton's Café* in bright red lettering. Scott knew it well as a frequent patron. A few tin advertising plaques dotted the front as decorations and gave Wilton a tiny stipend for the space. Cola, beer, a local gasoline station, and a local grocer accounted for the outside displays.

The warm June morning accounted for the screen door being the only barrier to Wyatt's entry. Before he hit the first step, the smell of bacon, thick enough to taste, poured onto the porch. Scott's attention shifted toward breakfast and coffee momentarily diverting him from his meeting with Carl Jefferson, which remained the true reason for this visit to Wilton's.

Stepping through the door, Scott paused to let his eyes adjust from the bright morning sun. Bacon and sausage sizzling gave his ears the data his nose gathered outside. His pupils sufficiently widened, he made out the interior counter, stools, and wooden tables. Two men in overalls sat at a table, while a man and woman took up another. Two fellows at the counter worked away on their plates, while a third sat waiting for his food.

Wilton took pride in his diner. Always spotlessly clean from his hard work and devoid of violence from his shotgun under the counter, the place displayed a single decorative motif: film posters. He did not afford his female customers any male stars, but they could imagine themselves to be Ethel Waters, Ella Fitzgerald, Lena Horne, or Wilton's favorite, Mina Mae McKinney. Wilton claimed the lovely women added class to his eatery.

A gaunt Black man, whose appearance was counterintuitive given his high fat menu, Wilton stood with his back to the door, while working on a plate. He wore white pants, a white shirt, and a white apron with a tiny streak of bacon grease. As he flipped sausage then eggs on his grill, his rubber-soled shoes tapped out a rhythm to fit the sizzle and pop of the grease. Scott sat on the end stool away from the other diners leaving the gap for Carl and hopefully a little privacy. Wilton delivered the prepared plate to the unfed man at the counter. The proprietor noted Scott and dipped his head before starting his way.

"Hey, Mr. Scott." Wilton flashed the huge, toothy smile he always offered. "What can I get ya'?"

Scott offered his meager version of a smile in reply. "A cup of your strongest coffee. I'll order breakfast in a bit. I'm meeting Carl Jefferson."

"Fix ya' right up." Wilton turned for a moment to grab his pot. With it in his right hand, he pulled a mug from under the counter with his left and poured with panache.

The squeal of Wilton's screen door hinges signaled a new customer. Wilton looked toward the squeak and nodded. "Here's yer' man, Mr. Wyatt."

Scott pivoted to watch Carl Jefferson's mountainous figure approach. "Thanks for meeting me, Carl."

"My pleasure, Mr. Wyatt. 'Specially since you offered breakfast." Carl smiled as he sat next to Scott. "Wilton." He nodded to the proprietor.

"Mr. Jefferson." Wilton spread his oversized smile for Carl. "Always good to see a man with an appetite. What are you thinkin' for breakfast?"

Carl rubbed his chin. His contemplating process apparently complete, he rested both hands on the counter. "Bring me one of them ham steaks of yours, some grits and red-eye gravy, couple a' biscuits." He raised his arm and pointed behind Wilton. "And a mug a' coffee there."

Wilton nodded, reached around, and grabbed the pot. "What'll you take, sir?" he asked in Scott's direction, while he poured Carl's coffee.

"Carl's order sounds good to me. Double it up," replied Scott.

Wilton stepped to his stove, whistling a little as he did. Carl sipped his coffee. The other patrons ate away, oblivious to the large man and his white friend.

Scott tapped on the counter as a preamble to addressing Carl. "First, I appreciated your help with Jake Barlow."

Carl slurped a little coffee then replied, "He was troublin' the May Rooms and Miss Queena. Jus' my job. I thank you for finishin' up with the problem."

Scott stirred his coffee without adding anything to it. He stared across the café without focus, while he considered his approach to Jefferson. He knew the man to be straightforward, so he thought it best to get down to business. "Carl, I hoped there might be something else you can tell me about Darlene's johns. Bootlegger Bob doesn't seem likely. He didn't have much interest in Darlene outside of quick work in his front seat."

"Don't suppose I know a bunch more. Just heard about the three I tol' ya' she was supposed meetin' outside the house, likely others though."

"KTOO Joe claimed he didn't know her or ever hear of her. I can see why he wouldn't like to admit he saw her even if he did. I think he fancies himself a ladies' man," detailed Scott. "I have to believe lying about visits to a whorehouse is as common as rolling back the odometer on used cars."

"Yessir, not many customers linin' up to give testimony 'bout the pleasures of the May Rooms," opined Carl.

"They are not. You mentioned a banker. Can you give me anything about him? What bank or what he looks like if you don't have a name."

"Not sure on the bank. It's one a' the ones downtown. I heard no name."

"Uh huh." Scott nodded. He swigged his coffee while considering questions to help jog Carl's memory. He watched Wilton work on their breakfasts, but inspiration hid out of sight.

"Think he's a baldie though." Carl broke the silence with an unprompted clue.

"Why so?" questioned Scott.

"Heard talk of Darlene with a banker. And some other whores claimed she got onto a chrome-dome john that mighta' been that banker. May be no more'n just whore gossip but could be the truth. Waitin' in the cathouse gives time for flappin' their gums 'bout things."

"That's a help. Suppose NBT and maybe First National fits the bill. Now, I just have to find a bald banker with a guilty conscience," mused Scott.

"Not sure any a' them financiers got a conscience guilty or not," offered Carl with more resolution than passion. Carl looked toward the skinny proprietor and snapped his fingers. "Wilton, can ya' get me a glass a' water?"

While Scott harbored no great friendship for the elites, he knew most bank employees just did a job, a little cleaner than grease monkeys, but not much more authoritative. "Money makes the world go 'round, so gotta' have bankers. Gotta' have whores too, Carl. The rest of us just have to make our way best we can."

"Ain't it the truth." Wilton placed the water in front of Carl, who eyed it before taking a huge gulp. He caught Wilton's eye once more before the man could get to his griddle. Carl wiggled his coffee mug in lieu of asking for a refill.

Wilton noted Carl's request and moved smartly to the counter. "Fillin' ya' up, Carl." He charged the mug. "Say, I heard that cousin a' yours got trouble again."

Carl barely glanced up from his coffee. "Yeah, Cousin George had a little run-in with the law, but I hear tell he bought his way out."

"George, who runs the roadhouse toward Rentiesville?" jumped in Scott.

"That's him, all right," affirmed Carl.

"Get him on liquor violations?" queried Scott.

"Naw. He pays his bribe regular. He got in a fight with some fella' thought George was after his girl. Course, he was, but the fight got a local sheriff involved."

Wilton chuckled. "Yep, that's George. Never met a ginchie dilly he didn't want." He paused a couple of seconds before amending his state-ment. "Never met a butterface he didn't want neither."

"Hope it works out for George," added Scott.

"Usually does with that rascal. He's one lucky sucker." Carl shook his head regarding his wayward cousin.

"Yessir. Him all-over bein' lucky," jumped in Wilton, who then scooted away to check the food on his griddle.

"Let me know when he's out and operating. I might drop in the roadhouse again," mused Scott.

"Don't see ya' down ta' the roadhouse since Miss Janet left."

"No. Don't go too many places since then, Carl. Stoppin' by diners or driving down Riverside is my social life."

"I know ya' see Paulette now and again, but not near the same as Miss Janet. I doubt Paulette ever come ta' the roadhouse either."

"No. I doubt she or the folks there would be comfortable."

Carl nodded in the affirmative. "Shame about Miss Janet all around. She was good people, sure enough."

With the conversation speeding into uncomfortable territory, Scott looked toward Wilton. "How's that breakfast coming? Ya' got a couple of hungry fellows."

"Jus' be a minute," replied Wilton without moving from his preparations.

"Sorry I don't have more for ya' Mr. Wyatt. I'll listen 'round the May Rooms closer for your investigation and for Miss Queena's sake. That Darlene Barnes got gossiped on for some time – might be more on her disloyalty. The lil' girl lookin' blonde one, she's too new. Never heard no tell about her at all. Miss Queena probably knows most on her. Mighta' jus' left. Kinda' child lookin' and young. Coulda' gone home to mamma."

"Just looking into Darlene for now, Carl. After breakfast, I'll go banker hunting at some financial institutions."

"If ya' shoot'em, shoot twice. Even with that big gun ya' carry, them damn bankers probably like the vampires and hard to kill."

* * *

The National Bank of Tulsa Building measured the tallest in Tulsa eclipsing the Philtower. Its beaux arts style came in second in downtown Tulsa to the high number of art deco buildings built largely during the oil boom of the 1920s. Having started as the Exchange National Bank, Harry Sinclair and J. A. Chapman kept it afloat until reorganization in 1933 when the name changed, and Wyatt Scott graduated from Central High.

A classic building at three twenty South Boston, Scott banked there because his parents had. After their deaths, he kept their account, safe deposit box, and a small number of shares in NBT. He entered the cool, marble lobby scouting for bald headed employees. He knew a teller or two and figured that to be his most productive starting point.

Scott made his way along the tellers until he found Robin. She went to Central High with him, Johnny, and the class of thirty-three. Her husband had been killed in North Africa leaving her with a little girl and his GI insurance. Scott spoke to her whenever he conducted banking business, but that remained the extent of their meetings. At her teller cage, Scott smiled and took out his checkbook.

"How are you, Robin?" asked Scott.

The diminutive woman with black-frame glasses and her hair in a bun smiled upon seeing him. "I'm fine, Wyatt. What can I do for you?"

Scott popped the top off his ink pen and scribbled out a check. "Just need a little spending money." He tore the check and handed it across to Robin.

"Okey-Dokey. Money is our business." She pulled open her cash drawer. "How do you want this?"

"Tens and twenties will do." Scott put away his checkbook and pen.

Robin collected three twenties and four tens to make the hundred he wrote out. She dealt them out for Scott to see. "Twenty, forty, sixty, seventy, eighty, ninety, and one hundred." She pushed the stacked bills forward to Scott. "Anything else, I can do for you?"

"Thanks, Robin." He collected the bills and slid them into his inner coat pocket. "There is a little something else." Scott paused, smiled, looked around then studied Robin. "I met a banker who wanted me to do some work. At the time, I was too busy. I thought now that I'm clear, I would check in with him. Trouble is, I can't remember his name." He looked down, then up with sheepish eyes. "All I've got is he's bald headed."

Robin chuckled. "Oh, we have a few of those. Have you got anything more to narrow it down?"

Seeing his ruse had worked, Scott forced a grimace of memory recovery. "Well, he might work in loans."

"Okay. That narrows it. Two men fit. Mr. Parkland and Mr. Thompson. They're both on three, but opposite ends."

"Parkland and Thompson. Thanks a million, Robin." He spun toward the elevators and marched away.

"Nice to see you, Wyatt," she called out to his receding figure.

The third floor held the class and architecture of the ornate lobby but spoke of business and efficiency rather than opulence. With two choices, Scott veered right to see the first of the separated bald men. Doors along the way displayed individual names or specialties. He passed by a Mr. White, a Mr. Clark, a door showing 'Small Business,' and one claiming 'Auto Loans.' Nearing the end of the long hall, he reached a door proclaiming, 'Mr. Thompson.'

Scott entered the office to find Mr. Thompson seated behind a handsome, mahogany desk bearing a brass placard reiterating the name stenciled on the door. By Scott's reckoning, the window behind him looked down on Boston Avenue making it a more prestigious space than those across the hall with an alley view. Pushing himself to a standing position, Mr. Thompson revealed a rotund figure more reminiscent of Humpty Dumpty than of a serious banker.

"Mr. Thompson, I am Wyatt Scott. I've come to ask about a woman who came to you for a loan."

Thompson stared blankly at Scott. His expensive, three-piece suit fit his round belly so snuggly the outline of suspenders puckered his vest. The vast expanse of his pants circumscribed his stomach like a textile equator on a globe.

"Darlene Barnes came looking for a loan to start her business," stated Scott.

"Barnes. I have never dealt with a Barnes. When did this occur?" Looking more quizzical than blank now, Thompson seemed to be searching for a lost memory.

"Yes. Darlene Barnes. Maybe a month ago."

Thompson shook his head and sharpened his look. "I have a rather good memory, and no Barnes has approached me. And I can assure you no woman has approached me for a loan, ever." His definitive denial softened his look. "You must've confused me with another loan officer. There are many of us, as N-B-T is the largest bank in the state."

Sizing up Thompson's expressions for signs of mendacity, Scott concluded the man was being truthful and likely never met Darlene Barnes. Calculating his withdrawal, he started with a meek smile. "I see. Sorry to bother you. My information must have been scrambled." He eased toward the door. "I will leave you to your hard work." A quick nod and Scott made his exit before the corpulent loan officer could question him.

From Robin's information, Scott knew his other option lay far past the elevators and close to a block away with the building spanning Boston from Third Street to Fourth Street. He broke into a trot along the marble floor. His pace mirrored his home run trot, the single one he had in the big leagues. Pitchers batted infrequently and were not expected to hit, yet he caught one on his bat's sweet spot and pulled it over the left field fence in Comiskey Park. The polished floor reminded him that cleats in clay held firm, while leather on marble did not. He slowed to a fast walk after sliding as he passed the elevators. He found Parkland's office three doors from the end, but on the west side. A view of the brick alley seemed the best its window could offer.

As he walked in, Scott tried a new strategy on Parkland. "Hello, Mr. Parkland, I am Wyatt Scott."

Parkland looked up from his commonplace desk. It flaunted its clutter and its user's sloth like an alley-sot brandishing his paper bag and empty bottle. Loan application forms filled a tray facing away from the banker toward the client chair. Scott lifted one by its corner and dropped it in front of the bald man.

"Uh, umm, yes. What can I do for you?" He stared at Scott searching for a placard to remind him of the name.

"Just jot down my name on this loan application and we can go from there." Wyatt calculated this process would get him the same writing sample and fingerprints his autograph ruse managed with Joe.

Parkland took the paper. He flattened it and held it down with his left hand. Taking a pen in his right, he stared at Scott. "A bit abrupt Mr. Scott, but I will begin with your name." He wrote in a designated blank space. "What is the purpose of this loan?"

With two fingers carefully pinching the corner, Scott pulled the page from Parkland's grasp. "We can get back to that. For now, we need to talk about a mutual acquaintance, Darlene Barnes." He opened his side coat pocket and stuffed the paper down using the flap to avoid touching the page.

A shocked Parkland jumped to his feet. The name chased the blood from the man's round head. His plain, brown suit bulged a little and his belt barely held on the last punched hole. He stood mute, blinking rapidly, perhaps hoping Scott would disappear by some magic intent. Beads of sweat popped out transmuting his face into a dew-covered melon. The blinking halted, replaced by a mesmerized stare. The deluge of perspiration began to run creating a tiny habitat of rivers in wrinkles with whisker stubble diverting flow left then right. The profuse excretion coursed to its crowning, soaking the man's collar before Scott could get the conversation out of first gear.

"Darlene Barnes. You met with her." Wyatt pressed the matter. "What do you know about her murder?"

Parkland dripped without responding. He watched Scott stand implacably staring at him. He drooped in his chair. Apparently realizing his mug flowed with sweat, he withdrew his handkerchief and wiped his jowls. "I, uh...I don't know anything about her or her murder."

Scott stepped to his desk. He narrowed his eyes and placed both palms on the desk before he leaned into Parkland. "You knew her all right. Now tell me the whole story or the police will visit your bosses looking for you."

If Parkland played poker, he might fold four aces out of fear of a straight flush. He shut his gaping mouth long enough to swallow hard. "Barnes wanted a loan." He relaxed. Whether from dehydration or relief of tension, his perspiration stopped flowing. "She wanted fifteen hundred to rent some rooms and start her own whorehouse." He blurted out the detail quicker than pulling his hand from a hot stove.

"Okay. See it didn't hurt a bit. Now, give me the whole story and don't sugar-coat your part." Scott stood erect maintaining his glare.

The banker sucked in air and blew it out. "I told her that kind of loan would never fly, but she insisted I could hide the true intent. She told me she would set me up with a dream girl and have free sex each week until she paid the loan off." Parkland rattled off his account of events like a guilty kid recounting his raid on the cookie jar.

"Then you took her up on it and finagled the loan." Scott eased his posture endorsing the candor of his suspect.

The ashamed banker nodded. "I met her at a motor hotel on Eleventh Street. She met me out front of a room, then she talked me into going in." He wiped his forehead once more, then circled his neck. He brought the wet handkerchief to his lap and grasped it with both hands. "There stood this beautiful, naked, young girl with a tiny tummy and wonderful melons." His voice cracked, making his vivid, personal description. Whether his tonal break came from excitement or guilt, couldn't be discerned.

Scott waited. He tried to look as nonjudgmental as his nature would allow. He didn't speak and literally bit his tongue to ensure his silence.

The pause allowed Parkland to gather himself and continue. "Barnes started taking off my clothes. I was in a trance. Before I knew it, she pulled down my underpants and shoved me on the bed. The girl called me daddy and said she had to have me."

Scott grinned. The middle-aged, chubby sweatbox believed a whore telling him what he wanted to hear. It didn't surprise him. It remained disgusting to imagine, nonetheless.

The honesty and excitement wore off. Fear and worry took their place on Parkland's mug. "I...I...uh...don't tell my wife...please."

"The young whore, was she blonde?"

Surprise at the question, stunted his response. "Uh...yes."

"Natural blonde, not bleached?"

"Yes, natural."

"Did you get her name?"

"No. I ran out of there in five minutes."

Scott smirked at the admission of the man's stunted sexual stamina. "After you got the loan for Barnes, did you see her again?"

"I never completed the loan. It takes time to run things around and through the departments. She died from that fall before I could get it through. To be honest, I was relieved. Nobody checks on a loan that doesn't go through."

"Were you relieved enough to throw her out the window?" Scott asked the question knowing the flabby man couldn't fight off Darlene Barnes, let alone lift and toss her from a window.

"No! If someone killed her, it wasn't me," pleaded Parkland.

"Did you see the young girl again?"

"No. If she works at the May Rooms, I wouldn't go near there. I might be seen," he added by way of explanation.

"So, that's the whole story. You aren't hiding any little embarrassments or others involved?"

"I never met anyone but those two. I didn't see either of them again. You can go to that May Rooms and ask the young blonde. She'll tell you I didn't meet them ever again."

"I might just do that." Scott wanted to see if the banker's expression would betray knowledge of the missing Mary. It reported blank fear as guilelessly as the timid man might ever present. "I'll keep this between the two of us." Scott took out a business card and placed it on the desk. "You remember *anything* else, you let me know." Wyatt didn't wait for a reply. He pivoted toward the door and left the banker alone with his thoughts, fears, and soaked shirt.

CHAPTER 7

A Beaten Whore

One of Carl's huge hands held Queena's door for Wyatt. After he strolled through, Carl let the knob go and eased back into the hall. The atmosphere in Queena's office was anger mixed with cigarette haze. Clinging to her like a London fog of nicotine and smoke, Queena materialized as a ghostly apparition behind an out-of-focus desk. Scott noted the young whore on Queena's fainting couch securing an icepack to her eye. He found the chair in front of the madam's desk but stopped behind it, taking a breath of tolerable air before entering the clinging cloud of fumes.

Quenna Capps's eyes blazed phosphorus white as she seethed behind her desk. Scott took closer note of the young woman with the icepack. Facial bruises, a swollen jaw, and a shiner worthy of a street fight highlighted her face. The madam puffed furiously at her Lucky. The only sound came from muffled music seeping through the walls as it emanated from the May Rooms' parlor. The young working girl kept a sheepish eye on Scott but made no sound.

"Lizbeth, tell Scott here the whole story of this sonofabitch beating on you," demanded Queena.

The girl cleared her throat and swallowed. She took a breath, then sat upright on the fainting couch. "He come here before. Asked 'bout me going to see him for something special." She looked at the floor. "I asked what he wanted and where he wanted." She swallowed once more making a harsh, dry gulp.

"You want some water, honey?" Queena broke in after noting the girl's difficulty.

Lizbeth looked up at Queena. "No ma'am. I'll be okay."

"Keep on then."

"He tol' me to come out ta' Sapulpa where he was at." She cleared her throat. "Tol'em I couldn't go outa' town. Then he told me a motel out on sixty-six headin' west was possible. I figured that might could work okay. Then I ask'em what he wanted and how much extra." She stopped talking and looked down at the floor.

"Lizbeth! Finish your story." Madam Capps glared for the first time as her patience waned past silence.

"Yes'am." The youthful whore flinched from Queena's scolding. "He wanted some rough action, and he'd pay forty dollars."

"Well, that's a lot for a little whore. Although not enough to offset the foolishness for a gal to take such a stupid risk," interrupted Queena before she smashed out her cigarette.

Scott dragged the chair away from Queena's tobacco fog and finally sat down nearer the victim. He pondered a moment gazing neither at Queena nor the young woman. Deciding on his course, Scott spun to the girl. "You met the guy here, right?"

"Uh huh." She glanced at Queena, then lowered her gaze to the floor.

"Was he strictly your customer or did he visit other girls?" Scott caught Queena's eye hinting to her to analyze the coming response.

"He made the rounds a little. Came to me special though." Lizbeth looked directly at Scott as she made her declaration.

Scott caught the tiniest of nods from Queena confirming the reply. "You think he made this kind of offer to any other girls?"

"No. He didn't say nuthin' ta' me the first time neither." More than a little defensiveness rippled through her answer.

Scott thought for a few seconds before continuing. "Where abouts in Sapulpa does the guy live?"

"Don't know. Never made it closer than the motel, and he never let on where he lived."

"Did he try to tie you up or ask if he could?" Scott pushed into the darker realms of her dalliance with the rough side of the trade.

"He wanted to. I tol' him I didn't trust that. He said he was payin' for rough, so he wanted to be rough." She looked up and sniffled. "He hit me. He did it till I fell down. He tol' me to get up and come over to him. That's when I flew out the door and ran." Her head slipped down as Queena and Scott followed her every movement.

"Okay," said Scott. He visualized the scene considering its faithfulness.

Queena peered at him with a question in her eyes. Scott affirmed her look before ending his conversation with Lizbeth. "That's all I need, Lizbeth. If Miss Capps is finished, I suppose you should get some more ice and take to your bed."

The young whore looked to Queena for confirmation. The madam nodded her acquiescence. Lizbeth eased from the lounger and slinked from the room.

"Did she bring in any money?"

"I didn't ask," replied Queena. "Sounded like she ran out before she got paid."

"Yeah...sounded like."

"Can you find this shitass?" asked Queena.

"Probably. I would like to talk to any other girls who had a visit from this john."

"I can arrange that." Queena coughed, then stretched for another stick. She fired it up and blew a smoke ring of satisfaction. "I want to get him. I want to visit him with Carl and get the truth out of him."

Scott stood. "Let me find him and take a run at the *truth* before you get poor Carl in trouble with the law."

Queena pulled the Lucky Strike from her mouth as she leaned over the desk toward Scott. "You find him. I'll pay for that. You get any answers, and I'll listen. If I need more answers or real justice for my missing girl, you steer clear."

"Let me talk to the other girls, and we'll see where things lead." Scott walked to the door. "When you have the ones who met the guy, you can put them on the phone or have them visit me."

* * *

Scott nosed the LaSalle into one of the parking spots in front of the *Sapulpa Feed and Seed* store. The establishment's sign hung above a large, storefront window, which detailed products by painted letters. Alfalfa seeds and two brands of chicken pellets competed with protein supplements for cattle and oats for horses. From the outside, aisles and shelves were visible, but no humans could be detected.

He had talked to two girls from the May Rooms, who knew of the man Lizbeth maintained she met for rough sex. Both expressed surprise at the notion of his wanting anything off the main menu. They separately confirmed the fellow, Andy Donald, leaned closer to timid than belligerent. Each had mentioned his propensity to have the shortest of passionate visits before he spent his ammunition and hurried away. One told Scott that she believed him to be married. The second girl couldn't say one way or the other about his marital status.

A tiny bell above the door rang as Scott entered. Dressed in his suit and tie, he didn't look like a customer, but he didn't need a ruse to obtain the facts he sought. He strolled down an aisle with implements and utensils before coming to an empty space with a counter, a cash register, and a gentleman in khaki pants and a white, short-sleeved shirt.

"Can I help you?" asked the man.

"I'm looking for Andy Donald."

"I am Andy Donald. I am the owner. What can I do you for?" He grinned at the wit of his out of order syntax.

"Fine, Andy." Scott smiled but narrowed his eyes. "You can tell me why you like beating up whores." Wyatt did nothing to hide the menace behind his words.

"What?" Donald froze, while his mouth gaped wide enough to fit one of his cattle protein bricks.

"You heard me." Scott clenched his teeth and stared holes through the feed store proprietor. "Why did you beat on Lizbeth from the May Rooms?" He calculated shock and directness would evoke a response leading to the truth, be it an aggressive or an apprehensive reply.

Still stunned, Donald recovered enough to close his mouth. After a long swallow, he veered straight into mendacity and evasion. "Don't know what yer' talkin' about. I am a married man."

Scott moved pugnaciously closer to the counter and the man. "I know. You have two kids too." He paused a moment to let his research sink in. "Your wife and those kids might want to know why you hired a whore to beat on her."

Andy Donald's expression melted into fear. "Don't tell!" he blurted out before looking around to see if he had indeed uttered the words.

"Then..." Scott stepped to the counter and leaned toward Donald. "...answer my question!"

"I never paid that little whore to beat her. She stole my money!"

"She did what?" questioned Scott.

"Once I was outa' mah' pants, she grabbed my wallet and run out of the room." He motioned with his hand and arm to represent her getaway.

Scott didn't retreat but relaxed his intensity. "Go on."

"She ran out and I caught her." He swallowed, which seemed to be his nervous habit. "When she scratched me, I slugged her. She wouldn't let loose of my wallet though. I had to hit her three, four more times 'for she let loose of it."

"You didn't start with rough stuff in the room?"

"I didn't have no reason to. I just wanted ta' wet my pecker, you know." He looked at Scott for affirmation but continued when none came forth. "I was gonna' be in Tulsa and I don't like goin' in the May Rooms for fear someone'll see and tell my wife."

"You've been there before more than once," countered Scott.

"Yes. And the last time, I saw a woman my wife knows right across the street. She didn't see me, but I can't chance that again."

"Okay." Scott gave Donald more breathing room and let calm claim his face. "Why risk chasing after your wallet when you were going to pay her forty bucks anyway?"

"Forty!" I was payin' her ten like usual. I had to get my wallet 'cause it had the store's receipts for deposit at the bank. I figured to head on to Harvard and the F&M after I had my quick poke."

Surprised by the declaration, Scott began to see a motive for Lizbeth to concoct a story to cover her betrayal of Queena Capps. "How much did you have in your wallet?" His tone tilted to neutral if not a tad sympathetic.

"More'n two hundred. It was a week's receipts and all," explained the repentant john.

This version of events played with veracity. Scott considered where to take things. Not wanting to let Donald off without some recrimination, he offered thinly veiled advice. "I think you better keep your pecker at home awhile. If you do sneak out to Tulsa, try the New Fox hotel or maybe a spot down route sixty-six. The May Rooms will be too dangerous for you to try again."

The proprietor of the *Sapulpa Feed and Seed* nodded his silent acquiescence and appreciation for the advice. Scott left the man and his feed store. In all, Scott knew more than the police about Darlene Barnes, but he didn't know anything to get him closer to her killer. Queena would not like his report on the feed store owner. Lizbeth would like it less.

CHAPTER 8

MURDER-SUICIDE

As night drew down in Tulsa, a new round of problems brewed for Wyatt Scott. East of downtown, the direction Tulsa first grew during the nineteen-twenties, a brown brick home, with a relatively new owner, shrouded a deadly play. Inside the house, drab prewar trappings coexisted with slick, nineteen forty-eight contemporary furniture. A corner lamp bathed away strips of darkness but shone too faint to surmount the primacy of nightfall. The console radio faintly imparted *Take it or Leave it*, the audience encouraging the player to leave it and gamble for more. The home's owner, Mildred Fuller, in her mid-forties, secretarial in garb and arrogant in demeanor, displayed the shadow of a smile. From her side, she lifted and offered an envelope to a guest.

Disbelief disrupted her countenance. Mildred's expression shifted to wide-eyed fear. She raised a defensive hand. "This is crazy! You're not the kind...."

A shot scorched from the revolver of her shadowed guest. Another followed. Thrown against the furniture before she could utter another word, Fuller crumpled to the floor. Blood, thick and crimson, oozed from her chest singularly interrupting the black-and-white tones of the throw rug where she lay. The radio show proceeded on. The contestant chose to leave it, and the audience cheered. Mildred Fuller never heard the contestant's choice or the audience's approbation. Her dead eyes stared down the length of the throw rug.

* * *

Scott stopped the LaSalle on a wide driveway of crushed river shells, light brown with white flakes. The drive fronted a cabin in Osage County, north of Tulsa. The dwelling sat in a rough circle of cleared underbrush and saplings. A controlled fire more than likely explained the vegetation void. Scott's pursuit of Queena's whore-killer was on hold for an errand Johnny Grayhawk needed him to run. In an effort to resolve the estate case of Agnes Belcher for her heir, Ruth Brown, Johnny needed some land documents he believed the cabin owner might have.

An unattended car sat cold and quiet to the side of the cabin. It presumptively belonged to the cabin's owner, Jackie Martin. The mid-morning sun hinted at afternoon heat, while the cloudless sky promised to keep the humidity at bay. Abandoning the LaSalle, hat in hand, Scott quick-marched up the cabin's steps to the wooden porch. No sounds filtered through the cabin door even as a jaybird on the roof complained about the new interloper below.

Scott knocked. He waited and knocked more vigorously. He tried the knob – it turned. He pushed the door open. Just inside the door, Scott froze. A body, slumped in a dining chair, shocked him. A gun lay on the floor beneath the man's hand. A disturbing sight for anyone, but a thunder-striking memory for Scott.

* * *

Captain Wyatt Scott rushed into the Material Storage Quonset hut of his OSS unit outside of Nome. The winter sun cast a blue hue across the hut's crates, bags, barrels, and assorted equipment. It also added to the pallor of Lieutenant Paul Brock's body as it rested on the floor. His limp hand partially covered an Army Colt. Pooled blood surrounded Brock's disfigured head. His dark, viscous blood congealed from the wind blowing through the door. Scott's commanding officer, Colonel Fielding, stood beside Brock's body. Scott paced past Fielding and circled around Brock.

"What do you think you're doing?" chided Fielding.

"It's not right. Just not right," replied Scott.

"It isn't. Still, he's not the first and won't be the last," lectured Fielding.

"I mean the set up; the scene; the suicide. It's not right!" Scott's agitation increased the speed of his pacing. The chill grew from moment to moment.

"I know he was your friend. But Alaska takes a toll on everyone." Fielding's plea sounded as genuine as the man could utter.

Scott heard the words, but they froze with the wind and shattered on the body of his fallen friend. "Alaska is shit for all of us. This is not how Brock handled it!"

Coming up behind Scott, Fielding's assistant, Lieutenant Pierce, leered at Scott. Fielding noted him. Scott remained oblivious while his fury raged.

"It's not your concern, Scott," admonished Fielding.

"It is! You're going to cover it up. Call it what it isn't, aren't you?" accused Scott with renewed vigor and disgust.

"I'll act in the best interest of the camp. I suggest you calm down and do the same. Lieutenant Pierce ..." Fielding looked at Pierce behind Scott. Scott spun to see Pierce. "...escort Captain Scott to his quarters and keep him there until I say otherwise."

Pierce sneered and grasped Scott by the arm. Scott shoved Pierce backward. Pierce caught his stumble before falling, but Scott cleared his grip. Scott stared again at his dead, young friend, then stomped away through the cold, Alaskan afternoon.

* * *

Whether a second passed or ten minutes, Scott couldn't tell. He rejoined the moment and reentered the summer of nineteen forty-eight along with the scene before him. A single room contained kitchen, dining, and living areas. A half-empty bottle of whiskey and a glass, two-fingers full, sat on the table. A wall phone hung steps away. Scott circled the table. He stooped to look at the dangling arms, limp legs, and the revolver on the floor. The setting articulated the tint of suicide. Yet, the minutiae colored outside the lines. He didn't like it. There was no note, but more importantly, a suicide doesn't leave whiskey in a glass, then shoot himself. He downs the last dram – a final taste of life.

Scott pushed off his knees and stood next to the suicide fiction. He donned his hat and set about his paying job. He rapidly searched the cabin's few drawers and cabinets for the documents Johnny had hoped he could retrieve. Beyond magazines and random personal letters, he found nothing.

He made his way to the wall phone. Scott flopped the receiver handle for the operator's attention. The switchboard reached and a connection made, Scott asked the operator for the Osage County Sheriff's Department. A quick, curt description of what he found, and his location, completed his contact with the sheriff's office. The old, raspy voice of the dispatcher promised a deputy as soon as possible.

Having made the report and with nothing other to do than wait for the sheriff, Scott left the cabin. He sat on the porch's steps, fiddling with his hat and wondering how much time he'd lose because he stumbled on a body. After only a couple of twirls of his summer fedora, he spotted a car pulling into the drive. Too soon to have gotten word from Osage County and out of its territory, a Tulsa Police car pulled up and skidded to a stop on the shell surface. Two plainclothes, Tulsa Police officers, Lieutenant Morgan, and Detective Art Cleveland, stepped out of the car and approached Scott.

"Scott! What the hell are you doing here?" cried Morgan. "Where's Martin?"

Scott stood up. The Tulsa Police arriving made no sense. "Why are you and the Tulsa department here? I just called the Osage County Sheriff."

"Why would you do that?" countered Morgan as he continued to approach Scott.

"I called them, Lieutenant Morgan, to report a dead man. The remainder I'll explain to the sheriff."

Morgan halted. "Smart-ass." Aware of Cleveland's presence, Morgan glanced at him. "Watch this wisenheimer. I'm going inside to take a look."

Detective Cleveland nodded to his boss. Morgan climbed the steps and entered the cabin. With the belligerent Morgan gone, Scott came down the steps to Cleveland's side. Scott knew of the politics of the Tulsa Police Department but figured Cleveland to be a square guy. His being a couple of years younger than Scott and in his generation rather than Morgan's staid, older cohort, gave Scott freedom to be direct with him.

"What are you doing here Art?"

"Martin's a suspect in a Tulsa murder," explained Cleveland.

Before they could get any further, the Osage County Sheriff's car skidded in beside the Tulsa car. The Sheriff, Merle Berry, fifty-five and an archetypal rural lawman, popped out of his car. Tulsa and Osage County folks referred to him as Mulberry, but not to his sourpuss face. The sheriff wore his khaki Osage County uniform, brown boots, and his belt and holster with his old S&W forty-five revolver hanging on his right hip. He clutched his county issue, doughboy-looking hat in his left hand.

"Damn. Cheap som'bitch. Crap shells'll ruin mah' new tires. Don't know why they let folks use them old ground-up shells stead a' good gravel. Sure ta' cost more for tars' than's saved." He slammed his door and embarked toward the porch.

Having voiced his complaint to the ether, Berry strode up to

Cleveland and Scott with his right hand on his holstered gun. "I am Sheriff Merle Berry. I'd be obliged if you two gentlemen would identify yourselves. I wouldn't want to shoot the wrong fellow."

Morgan emerged from the cabin as Berry glared at Cleveland. "Ain't gonna' be no shootin', Berry. That's Cleveland; he works for me."

Shocked to see Morgan, even with a Tulsa car there, Berry confronted him. "What the Sam Hill you doin' here Morgan? This is mah' county."

Morgan stopped near the steps looking down at Berry. "Simmer down Berry. Looks like our business has a common thread."

Knowing Morgan and having Cleveland justified to him, Berry moved on to Scott. "Who're you fella'?"

"I am Wyatt Scott. I made the call," he replied simply.

"Why're you here? You have BIA. b'ness?" questioned Berry.

"No. Martin had some papers that Johnny Grayhawk, the attorney, has needed for days. I came to see Martin about getting them."

Berry raised one of his wild-haired eyebrows. "What papers? Where are they?"

"Some Osage tribal records, but I didn't find any papers at all," admitted Scott.

Frustrated with the meaningless questions and answers, Morgan jumped in. "He don't matter. Go in and see for yourself. Dead guy in a chair. Chest wound. Arms hanging down. Gun beside him. Suicide."

Ready for more substantial facts, Berry stomped up the steps. The porch creaked and complained from the heavy march of the sheriff's boots. "Okay, Morgan, show me." Morgan tugged on his collar and reentered the cabin. Berry followed. The pair disappeared through the cabin door shutting it behind them.

Clear of his overbearing boss, Cleveland transformed into Detective Cleveland. "What did you see?" His quick speech and New York accent surfaced a little stronger with his enthusiasm.

Scott liked Cleveland. He'd known him for a few months since he came to Tulsa from New York. His accent still made Scott chortle at times, but he thought Cleveland an honest and true detective. He also felt sorry for him being under Morgan's thumb and an outsider by default among the Tulsa officers.

"Shot like Morgan said. He's been dead a while," answered Scott with brevity.

"You been around suicide before?"

"One...during the war. This has some of the same wrong feel to it."

"Wrong, huh. A suicide still?" Cleveland frowned as he asked the question.

"Could be. Not airtight."

Before Cleveland could reply to Scott's clipped comment, Berry and Morgan emerged from the cabin door and stepped out onto the porch.

"So, what brought you out here in the first place?" Berry asked Morgan.

"We have a murdered woman in Tulsa, Martin's girlfriend from what we can tell. We came to question him about her killing." Morgan put his hands on his hips signaling Berry it was his turn to pass on information.

"Well, it's Martin all right. He's a Bureau a'Indun' Affairs man around here." Berry rubbed his chin again. "You think he killed this gal, huh?"

"Main suspect – only one really. Now he goes and kills himself. Lays out one-two-three." Morgan bobbed his head to his numerical count.

"The suicide is spring water clear. I give ya' that," conceded Berry.

"I guess we came a little late for answers, but this way cuts a lot of legwork and legal crap." Morgan affirmed his statement with a wink to Berry.

Cleveland slipped by the conversing pair. He pushed the door open quietly and all but tiptoed in the cabin. Scott saw him, but the other two remained oblivious. He watched the two older lawmen praise one another and corroborate each other's simple conclusions.

"Well, it's murder-suicide then. Killer dead by his own hand, saves wear-and-tear on Ol' Sparky," declared Sheriff Berry.

"So, we agree. Martin kills his woman, then guilt causes him to shoot himself." Morgan raised his eyes to Berry seeking agreement. "It makes a tidy package, and we all look good before supper."

"I'll get the coroner out from Pawhuska ta' put the stamp on it," confirmed Berry.

"Good by me." Morgan nodded his concurrence.

Cleveland slipped out of the cabin, but Morgan spied him two steps onto the porch. "Who told you to go in there?"

Detective Cleveland tried to deflect Morgan's ire. "No harm intended. Thought I could see what it looked like and learn crime scene observation from an experienced investigator is all."

Morgan chuckled and eyed Berry. "Cleveland here is a New York college boy. He's new and wants to be a real G-man 'stead of a plain, ol' Tulsa detective."

Berry laughed and Morgan joined in. Cleveland looked at the cabin then to Scott in a signal subtle enough that Morgan and Berry never saw it. For Scott, it was as straight forward as one-for-fastball and two-for-curve. They had something to discuss later.

Berry strolled to his car and reached through the open window for his radio microphone. He jabbered at the Osage County dispatcher, but the wind and birds drowned out the actual words. Cleveland stood quietly by Scott. Morgan took one quick look at the outside of the cabin before heading to his car.

"Come on Cleveland, we're done here." Morgan didn't check to see, but Cleveland followed obediently.

Scott thanked the stars that Berry did not like paperwork or procedure. It meant he could make it to Tulsa with only part of his day ruined. Voicing his concerns about murder rather than suicide would leave him vulnerable to a longer conversation with Berry and the risk of a trip to Pawhuska. He needed to report the errand's failure to Johnny, so he opted to keep his thoughts to himself and preserve a free afternoon.

* * *

The next morning, Scott sifted papers at his old wooden desk. They held little interest for him, but bills had to be paid, and new letters might have checks inside, and there was always a chance one envelope might be from California. Several parcels through, the pile comprising invoices stacked imposingly high. The check stack remained nil. The two seemingly personal letters were nothing more than advertisements in Trojan-horse envelopes.

Before Scott could consider which bills to pay, the office door opened revealing a cheerful Johnny Grayhawk. He wore one of his usual three-piece suits and looked as perfect as ever. He carried an envelope tapping it against his vest. He danced over to Scott's desk, his cheery face never flagging.

"Here's your service fee for going to Martin's place." Grayhawk laid the envelope square on Scott's desk.

Scott took it and slid it into the top desk drawer. "A failure, not finding what you wanted, but a dead guy instead."

"So, you told me yesterday, and not much either of us can do about it. You did your job for me and the estate."

"Does the estate care about how he bought it?"

"The estate cares about the missing papers. They are still missing, but you did your part." Scott's old batterymate traded in his jovial look for a more quizzical expression. "Besides, the *Tulsa World* told me this morning it was suicide after he murdered his trashy girlfriend. Why the re-hash?" Johnny crossed his arms to await the response.

"The scene didn't fit suicide. Too matter of fact. The place had no preparation, no ritual." Scott punctuated his misgivings with a sweep of his right arm.

"You're a PI, not the Green Hornet. Let the cops call it as they like." He unfolded his arms after giving his advice, then let them drop against his sides.

Scott rolled his eyes. "They always do."

"Just like clockwork," agreed Grayhawk. His comment prompted him to check his watch. He wrinkled his brow and grimaced at the information. "Wyatt, I've got court this afternoon and I need a favor."

"Okay, shoot."

"Could you drive Evie to Ruth Brown's? I'm hoping she can make headway girl-to-girl with that silly little heiress. If I can't get anything from her, I may have to visit Pawhuska. Johnny sighed out some exasperation about the young subject and his problems with her grandmother's will.

"Sure. Tell Evie to get me when she's ready."

"Will do, thanks." Johnny strolled to the door and grabbed the knob but stopped short of turning it. He swung around to offer Scott a question. "Say, how did things go with that Junior Leaguer?"

"Folger?" Scott stared past Grayhawk for a moment. His insight coalesced and he refocused on Johnny. "Hard to say. That dame is a shot of gin poured over dry ice; too cold and too sharp."

Grayhawk mused over the metaphor. "It's just a job. You do not have to like her. Remember, the money spends the same either way."

Scott shrugged then nodded his agreement. Johnny answered by way of a loose salute with his free hand before he pulled on the knob. He left Wyatt to his few remaining papers, his collection of mixed notions, and several remaining questions.

CHAPTER 9

Evie and the Heiress

Evie Hall, professionally dressed as usual in a gray jacket and skirt to her mid-calf, exited her side of Scott's LaSalle. She toted her equally professional, leather briefcase. The grand stone mansion in the Forest Hills addition told visitors that money was no object. Evie gaped at the massive three stories and silently mouthed her count of the chimney stacks protruding above the roof. As she shut her door, her gaze offhandedly caught the front tire. Light-colored flakes wedged in the treads stuck out like ornaments. She bent down to manage a closer inspection. "What are those thingamabobs in your tire?"

Scott, who had trod several steps toward the front door, reversed his path upon her question. He made his way around the fender to view the suspect tire. The discolorations caught his eye at once. He crouched to scrutinize the abnormality. He produced his pocketknife and inserted the tip of the blade in the tread groove. He pried one sliver free. He rolled it between his thumb and index finger before bringing the flake near his eye to subtly assess it.

"Crushed lake shells from Jackie Martin's drive," he explained.

Evie shrugged disinterest. Scott directed her toward the front door. Once more, she gazed up at the stately abode, which slackened her pace. With her gawking and dawdling, Scott passed her by. When she caught sight of him, she sped up to reach his side.

The protracted walk to the door gave Evie an opportunity to quiz Scott about her employer's history. "Wyatt, I know Bugler's fuzzy-brained and all, but what's Johnny's real beef with him?"

Scott glanced at Evie. He smiled at the question since few, if any, knew the story. "It started during high school. Johnny played catcher. Bugler has always been an avid baseball fan. He came to every Central High game, kept a scorepad then just like today. One time, Bugler got so frustrated with the pitches Johnny called, he yelled out the kid pitcher (meaning me) would be a big leaguer someday and he'd be just another Indian in Oklahoma."

"Dang, I didn't think Bugler was that mean," offered Evie, in defense of her boss.

"It was nineteen thirty-two. Not everyone then had the enlightenment of nineteen forty-eight."

"Yeah, enlightenment." Evie scrunched up her face. "Since the war ended, when it comes to jobs, Indians are Indians and coloreds are coloreds and women are both!" lamented Evie.

Upon reaching the front door, Evie took her feelings out on the doorbell button. She jabbed swift and hard with her middle finger, but it did not seem to satisfy her. She piled on with a full-palm slap, which sounded the chimes again before the resonance of the first set died away. She readied another jab as the door opened. In the doorway, an older, Black woman, dressed in a maid's uniform, held a basket filled with papers and old photos.

Evie raised her briefcase as an object of identification. "We're looking for Miss Ruth Brown. It's about Mrs. Belcher's estate."

"And you be?" asked the maid.

"Sorry, I'm Evie Hall. And this is Wyatt Scott. We're from Mr. Grayhawk's office, the executor for Mrs. Belcher's estate."

"Yes. Indun' named Johnny." She swung the door wide and retreated enough for Evie and Scott to enter.

"Mr. Grayhawk is a highly qualified attorney," countered Evie.

"Hope so. He tol' me Miss Agnes wilt' me a thousand dollars." She grinned at her prospects. "Come in. I am Sadie. Miss Ruth's upstairs napping."

Sadie, the maid, motioned Evie and Scott to follow her. Scott gentlemanly deferred and followed Evie through the door. Sadie juggled the basket against her side to shut the door. She regrasped the container, gripping it with both hands.

"Ever since Miss Agnes passed, Miss Ruth sleeps and sleeps," explained Sadie, to the question no one asked.

"I guess she's still getting over her grandmother's death." Evie offered her opinion to coincide with Sadie's statement.

"I jus' hope the good Lord heals her poor heart soon. She's still not right with things."

Sadie stepped past Evie, leading them into the commodious, opulent living room. Early-century furniture testified to the late Mrs. Belcher's heyday. Wood paneling, a mighty chandelier of glass and brass, portrait paintings of the late Mrs. Belcher and her granddaughter, Ruth Brown, several floor lamps, and too many chairs to use at once, fulfilled the room as homage to the oil-boom days. A couch with end tables offered a waiting spot opposite two wingback chairs.

"Sit yourselves. By and by, I'll go check on Miss Ruth." Sadie directed the pair to the couch. She hovered near the end table cradling her basket of papers and photos.

"Thanks." Evie sat on the couch with her briefcase beside her.

Scott remained standing while taking in the lavish surroundings. The room loomed larger than most hotel lobbies. He noted a couple of original works of art by George Catlin – two portraits of Indians. He had no idea if either had any personal relevance to Mrs. Belcher, but it seemed unlikely given the locales and timing of his work. Hanging on the farthest wall near a stone fireplace, Scott could not miss the Thomas Moran landscape. The painting made him think of Thomas Gilcrease, the local oil man and banker, who had been collecting Indian and western art for years. He wondered if Gilcrease, a Creek, begrudged the Osage, Mrs. Belcher, for her paintings.

"Have you been with Miss Brown and Mrs. Belcher a long time?" Evie interrupted Scott's musings with her question to the maid. A novice to field work, Evie labored to avoid any silence.

For her part, Sadie seemed equally happy to end the silence. "Been with Miss Agnes since nineteen and twenty-five. Her old, dead husband died a' that influenza before I ever knew her." Sadie set the container on the end table close to Scott and eased around it to address Evie more directly. "Miss Ruth, since she's born. More particular after her mama,

Miss Martha, and her white-trash husband, Howard Brown, died in a speakeasy fire. That's how Miss Agnes come ta' raise Miss Ruth."

"Sad story all around," offered Evie with a side of compassion.

"Sad for me cleanin' out all Miss Agnes things. Miss Ruth's keepin' some pictures, but the old, old ones with Mr. Belcher or Miss Agnes as a girl don't hold much no more." Sadie nodded toward the basket. Evie and Scott considered it. "Ya' know young folk always movin' on, not thinkin' much about the past."

"You haven't thrown out any Osage papers of Mrs. Belcher, have you?" worried Evie.

"Lordie, I can't look through all the clean-out things," defended Sadie.

Scott stirred the contents with his hand. "No papers in here?"

"No. A few letters, but mostly pictures and such. Old Mr. Belcher in a straw hat. A sweet one a' Miss Agnes with her orphanage friend Drucilla," clarified Sadie.

"In there?" Evie pointed at the container Scott had sifted through.

Sadie relocated to the table and retrieved an old photo of Mr. Belcher. She extended it to Evie. "Here's old Mr. Belcher."

Evie took the photo. "Wow. Mr. Belcher was a geezer.... I mean, he looks a lot older than Mrs. Belcher must have been." Evie fidgeted with the photo after her clumsy expression and unprofessional word choice.

Certainly not offended and more or less agreeing with the characterization, Sadie offered her opinion on the matter. "Yes 'em. She got stuck with a' old man willin' to marry a half-breed." She nodded reaffirming her commentary on the customs of those times.

Scott poked in the basket and pulled out an old photo of two young girls. He examined the faces, then flipped the photo over. Inscribed with wavy scrawl, a reminding note bore witness to the identity of the two, young women.

"That's Miss Agnes and her other indun' friend Drucilla," declared Sadie.

Once more glancing at the photo side, Scott commented on them. "Her friend has stronger Osage features than Mrs. Belcher."

"Miss Agnes might coulda' passed if she wanted, but she always helt' ta' her blood." Sadie smiled and stood straight with apparent pride for her deceased employer and benefactor.

"Scott flipped the photo over again and read the notation out loud. "Agnes and me, nineteen-oh-seven."

"Yessir, her bygone days. Cleanin' up the last couple of..."

"Who is it, Sadie? asked an unseen Ruth Brown.

"Folks from the indun' lawyer 'xecutor. Miss Evie and Mr. Scott is who." Sadie raised her volume to make sure it reached Miss Brown.

A moment later, Ruth Brown glided into the room. Young and comely, her perfectly coiffed hair framed her delicate and symmetrical features. She wore an expensive silk robe and high-end slippers even though it was well past noon. She joined Sadie facing Evie.

"Something further about my grandmother's estate?" she asked, with a soft, artless tone, and an appearance not quite childlike, but bearing an air of innocence.

Evie dropped the old photo of Mr. Belcher on the top of the refuse pile as she stood to greet Ruth Brown. "Mr. Grayhawk still needs your grandmother's headrights records."

Scott placed the Agnes-Drucilla photo on top of the pile. The movement caused Ruth to look in the basket at the photo. Her appearance reddened. Her eyes narrowed. Her lips twitched, and her quiet tone became sharp. "I told you to clear out these old things!"

"Yes 'em," replied Sadie. She grabbed the basket and slinked away like a scolded pet.

Calmness reclaimed her before Miss Brown addressed Evie. "I'm sorry. These things make me sad. What did you need?"

"Your grandmother's headrights or any Osage records," stated Evie, as professionally as she could.

"I told Mr. Grayhawk I don't know about those. Grandmother did not show me anything but her lease with Skelly. It's in her desk." She pointed across the room to a buttoned up old desk with a cushioned, wooden chair.

"Mr. Grayhawk has what he needs from Skelly Oil," assured Evie.

"I don't understand these things. All of those rights were settled with my grandmother. It's all been fine since before I was born." She panned her view from Evie to Scott. "I'm doing my best. There are so many things – Junior Miss duties, the charity ball." Ruth pivoted away for a moment, composing herself. She breathed in and out, in and out, then allowed herself to look at Scott. "Mr. Scott, did Mr. Grayhawk discuss the Junior League Charity Ball with you?"

"He did." Scott scrutinized her emotional swings.

"Grandmother has always been with me before. Then you'll be my escort?" She lowered her head, reprising the soft, shy girl role with which she began.

Unsure about the subject matter, Evie narrowed her eyes at Ruth, then gawked at Scott. More than curiosity steered her mien.

"This all just makes me so sad." A quiver slipped into Miss Brown's voice. Her lips vibrated in sympathy.

"Yes. I can escort you if it helps," replied Scott.

Ruth dabbed her tears with her robe cuff. "It would. If you'll call me, I'll give you the details." She looked from Scott to Evie, apparently seeking feminine empathy. "You just don't know how alone her death has made me." Ruth dropped her head again, seeking solace in her robe's cuff.

"I see." Evie tried to redirect the discussion to the original business. "Miss Brown, what Mr. Grayhawk needs could be hairy...uh...difficult to find. So, if you can locate the records, it would be a major help." She gritted her teeth at letting her conversational slang slip in again.

Ruth sniffled before looking up. "I'll...I'll try."

"Thanks." Evie clutched her briefcase. She shuffled her feet while only progressing inches. "Call Mr. Grayhawk if you find the papers," instructed Evie, as she took a true step forward. "I mean, we want to help."

Ruth Brown didn't move. She gazed at Evie. Her tear tracks reflected light as she attempted a halfhearted smile.

Evie looked to Scott for support. He nodded, giving Evie impetus to move along. "Thank you, Miss Brown. Um...we'll leave then." Evie turned toward the door.

Scott stepped away and nodded to Ruth Brown. He escorted Evie through the hallway. They left the mansion without success. Evie left frustrated. Scott left shaking his head.

CHAPTER 10

Mildred Fuller's Book

Scott puzzled through dead whores and a suicide that forgot to look legitimate. The summer heat presented dismaying strength for June. It lingered into the night as the physical world released the energy it absorbed during the day. The sidewalk pavement he crossed freed its radiant power into the soles of his shoes. Scott worked his way into the alley behind the Pythian Building. The road-brick surface might have been marginally cooler than the concrete street, but his feet signaled no difference to his tired brain and warm brow. Shielded from the streetlights, his red convertible waited in the darkness to take him to his apartment, where floor fans, ice, and liquor would soothe his brain and cool his body.

Scott hopped over the closed door and boarded the last vestige of his professional baseball earnings. He shoved in the key and depressed the starter. The engine growled on his first push. For the second try, he stomped the starter pad harder, which succeeded in turning the engine

107

over and bringing the LaSalle to life. Before he could switch on his car lights, those of a shiny, new, nineteen forty-eight Lincoln Continental wheeled into the alley, moving the opposite way the LaSalle faced. The lights dimmed and the sedan pulled alongside Scott. Even with night settled in, the driver wore sunglasses and a large, colorful, summer hat. This concealment looked more fashionable, but Scott recognized Mrs. Folger portraying a rich woman rather than a cartoon character.

Folger had her window down before she stopped a little short of even with Scott. She leaned on her door, permitting her hat brim to dangle out of the window. "That dead woman, Mildred Fuller, the one in the papers, she was the blackmailer."

Scott considered what Folger said and why she felt the need to reach out to him. "As you stated, she's dead. You're in the clear. Ghosts don't blackmail."

"No, ghosts don't." She looked up and down the alley, showing her paranoia remained as strong in the alley as the drive-in movie. "I'm still concerned."

"How is it a problem now?" A twinge of exasperation slipped into Scott's tone, and the recollection of her dithering and inability to get to the point wrinkled his brow.

"She had a book, a bankbook. I saw it twice." She waited without additional explanation, while her excessive hat brim bobbed from an upsurge in the night breeze.

The added information provoked Scott's interest but sweating in his car tempered his enthusiasm. "Okay, lady, tell me about the book."

"It was small, brown leatherette with yellow pages – a bankbook. My husband owns banks. I know what a bankbook looks like." Her tone gleamed as haughty as her car and clothes.

"I meant the contents." Scott shook his head. "Do you know what's in it?"

"It looked like names and notes. She taunted me with it – flaunting a page, but I only saw her scribble, no discernable words."

"Sounds like you were not her only victim," reasoned Scott.

"I can't be concerned with others, but I do worry about that book." Mrs. Folger fidgeted with the steering wheel. Apparently too warm for gloves, her manicured nails caught some of the distant streetlight.

Scott wanted to go home. Sweating in his LaSalle while conversing with a paranoid society dame figured at the bottom of his wish list. If she still wanted handholding, he could toss Mrs. Folger's mystery bank-book into his working barrel with the dead whore and Jackie Martin's suspicious suicide. He did need to know where he stood with her before he ordered his quests. "So, I'm still on the job, and you want me to find this book. Is that right?"

"Yes. I will pay you twenty times what I gave you before if you bring me the book." While not reaching desperation, the sense of urgency in Folger's voice played like a concerto of dread.

The suddenness of the answer surprised Scott, but the sum shocked him. "Valuable piece of literature. I'll get started."

"Good." Mrs. Folger peeked in her mirror. She put the car in gear but held the clutch down. "See that you do." Her superiority and condescension had made the return engagement every bit as compelling as the original. She freed the clutch and eased her Lincoln down the alley. Scott watched in his mirror as she drove off. He added the bankbook to his list of objectives.

* * *

The Tulsa Tribune obituaries listed Mildred Fuller's address, age, and occupation without mentioning her violent end or any surviving kin. She worked at Douglas Aircraft as a secretary, and her life ended at thirty-nine. The local crime section proved less delicate. It shrieked headlines about her and Martin; the account and their connection blurred with innuendo. Winding through the paragraphs, the evidence and conjecture intermingled to create the news story. While the paper admitted the case had not been officially closed, it more than hinted that Jackie Martin, her boyfriend, killed her before taking his own life. No mention of blackmail or bankbooks appeared in the article.

Scott made his way down St. Louis Avenue into the neighborhood associated with Fuller's address. He deciphered the house number from a mix of moonlight and a streetlight one house down and across the way. A panel truck parked near the streetlight bore a name on the side, *Campion Cargo.* Scott pulled into the driveway, shut off the car, and emerged with a flashlight. Unsure if it had any relevance to his doings, he illuminated the truck's sign with his beam before walking briskly to the front porch.

Scott ignored the police notice and entered the dark house through the unlocked door. His light shaft caught bits and pieces of the room. He poked about looking in vases and behind the console radio. The police left detailed evidence of their hasty search and apparent lack of concern beyond the body and blood. Eventually, Scott reached a desk and his last hope for clues. He opened and closed several drawers, checking their contents and feeling the underside of each. Finally, from under one lower drawer, he removed tape holding a small, thin bank-book. Scott set his flashlight on the desktop, spread the covers of the small book, and bent to read its contents.

Just as Scott opened the thin booklet, a sap slammed against his skull. He wavered and dropped to the floor. His short and distorted perspective along the throw rug allowed Scott to witness a gloved hand scoop up the small book that fell with him. Scott glimpsed its removal before his eyelids settled, and his world dwindled to darkness.

The long days of June still waxed. The sun had peeped over the horizon. The lights were off, but the uncovered windows rendered the room bright. It brightened a bit more as Detective Art Cleveland came in the front door. He advanced to Scott's sprawled figure. He rolled him onto his back and tapped him.

"Scott. Scott. What have you gotten into?"

Wyatt Scott roused. The brightness helped him become aware of his location and situation. The light did not ameliorate his banging head. He squinted and sat up before rubbing the nape of his neck up to his skull. The pain persisted like a hornet with a vendetta.

"What are you doing here?" quizzed Cleveland.

Scott stood, continuing to massage his neck and skull. "Trying to get to know Mildred Fuller."

"A little late don't you think?" Cleveland sized up Scott's condition.

"Somebody else didn't think so."

"You get a look at him?"

"No. Might have been driving a *Campion Cargo* van. I saw one out front. Why are you here, Art?"

"Felt like re-checking the place."

Scott stopped coddling his noggin and looked directly at Cleveland. "After Morgan and Berry finished measuring dicks, you went in. *You* think it was suicide?" The tone stopped short of accusatory, but it left a dare to answer.

Cleveland paused, then tendered an abbreviated head shake. "Something seemed off."

Scott twisted his neck still trying to reorder his loose connections. "Mildred Fuller dealt in blackmail."

"Oh yeah?" Cleveland tilted his head to match his skeptical tone.

"As good a' motive as love scorned."

"Sure. You have any proof?" asked Cleveland.

"I might. I think I will, but I'd like to sort through it after I get my wiring arranged close to normal." Scott stooped and picked up his hat. He shook it, then adjusted the crease in its crown. He eased it on avoiding the swollen bump and keeping the sweatband above it.

"Let's get you looked at," cautioned Cleveland. "I'll run you by St. John's hospital."

"Naw. I know a better place – fix us both up." Scott grabbed his now dimly shining flashlight and walked to the door.

"You sure you can drive, Wyatt?"

"Just follow me, Art." He paused at the door. "You just make sure I don't drive off into the river."

* * *

Cleveland and Scott seated themselves at the counter of *Joe and Mamie's*. Downtown, but in a modest rent area, it looked the part of a small diner, spotlessly clean with a six-stool counter and a kitchen with a pass-through window. Working-class décor ruled the joint. It held a few worn wooden tables and chairs, a vintage cash register, and a countertop radio still weary from dispensing the war news.

A working man slugged down coffee on the farthest stool. The small diner awakened before most of the city, and the rush still remained an hour away. Although neither of the namesake owners could be seen out front, scullery noises emanating from the kitchen suggested their presence there. Scott's color had improved, while Cleveland's curiosity had not waned.

"Just tell me what you were after at Fuller's place," asked Cleveland for at least the third time since they parked their cars.

"Does it matter since your boss has already solved the case?" Even damaged, Scott could muster sarcasm from the boundless bag he carried.

Cleveland chuckled. Before he could drop his rejoinder, Mamie, the second-billed owner, came from the kitchen and reclaimed her behind-the-counter realm. She headed for the newly arrived pair picking up a pot of coffee as she did.

"Mornin' Wyatt. Who's your friend?" Mamie greeted them with her usual affable smile and welcoming eyes. She pulled two cups from under the counter and poured coffee without asking.

"Mamie, this is Detective Arthur Cleveland of the Tulsa Police." Scott made the introduction.

"Detective, huh." Mamie narrowed her eyes and cocked her hips slightly. "You got anything on that prostitute killer?"

Cleveland seemed surprised by the directness. She didn't leave him any room to duck the question. "Nothing new," he answered plainly.

"Shame. What can I get you boys?"

"I think maybe just toast this morning, Mamie," answered Scott.

"Off your game, huh? You do look a little peaked for your usual," quipped Mamie.

Scott sipped his coffee in reply; a quick, truncated sip to save his mouth from the near boiling brew.

"What's his usual?" inquired Cleveland as he worked his way into the diner experience and attempted to learn more about Wyatt Scott.

"Three fried eggs, over easy, ham steak, toast, grits and too many cups of joe – hot and black." Mamie provided an instant recitation memorized from repeated orders without deviation.

"What are grits?" Cleveland looked perplexed about the one food he didn't know on the oversized order.

"Mamie, he's from New York." Scott winked at her as he offered the obvious information known to anyone who heard him speak.

"Yeah, explains the funny accent." She looked at Cleveland to address him. "Hun, grits are dried corn, ground up and cooked in water."

"Hmmm. Corn comes creamed in a can in New York," replied Cleveland not backing down from his heritage. "Well, in Rome...or in Tulsa, I'll take his usual, but I'll need cream for my coffee."

"Comin' up," replied Mamie.

She scooted the creamer crock to Cleveland while he spooned sugar in his cup. She scribbled on her pad and handed it through the window to her partner and cousin, Joe. Cleveland poured the cream before taking a sip to test the temperature and the mix. He followed up with a large sip, his blending apparently successful.

"You saw Mildred Fuller. What did you make of the scene?" Scott stirred his black coffee forcing more steam to rise from it and reducing its tongue-scorching temperature.

Cleveland held his cup near his mouth but kept his next drink in abeyance. "Pretty straight forward. Somebody she knew stood in her living room and pumped two slugs in her."

"Any witnesses?"

"Nothing to hang your hat on. Neighbors maybe heard gunshots or the Lone Ranger on the radio."

"You and Morgan didn't find anything about her being a black-mailer?" Scott squirmed a little on his stool to look at Cleveland.

"Didn't consider it. The boyfriend really stood out as the best suspect. Spent their time at illegal bars and dance halls. I figured he was good for it. Then I saw his body, and you poured gasoline on my doubts," admitted Cleveland.

"So, no motives beyond jealous love?"

"No. Not much to point anywhere else," replied Cleveland defensively.

"And, I guess, no one beyond Jackie Martin?"

"No." Cleveland glanced at Scott, then looked straight ahead. "You said it – doesn't matter much now. I'll finish the paperwork and Morgan'll close it."

"Yeah. Easier that way for Morgan," conceded Scott.

Mamie brought their food, setting Wyatt's toast down first then Cleveland's replica of Scott's usual.

"Thanks, Mamie." Scott gestured his appreciation with his coffee mug. Mamie nodded and went for the coffee pot.

"You eat this every day?" asked Cleveland with a mixture of doubt and admiration.

"A man's got to keep up his strength." Scott nibbled his toast.

"Cleveland dug into his mound of food. "I guess so," Cleveland spit out the words with a grit or two.

Mamie topped off both cups then headed for the solitary patron down the counter. Cleveland continued to work on his full plate. Scott sulked, sipped coffee, and sulked some more.

* * *

Evie Hall opened the unlocked door and breezed into Scott's office. She ritually tidied bits of junk for him since she carried the key Scott gave her boss, although she found the office open more often than not. Evie stepped behind the desk and twisted the window blinds. The morning sun caught her eye before she could check the rest of the office. When she spun around, the added light revealed an interloper. Evie flinched at the sight. The man's physique was angular, thin, and soft. He sported a scraggly mustache, work shirt, and baggy pants. Maliciousness clung to his body like sweat to a cotton picker. He slinked toward Evie.

"Keep cleaning little lady. I was just fetching something for Mr. Scott." He looked around sizing up the room and Evie.

Evie moved beside Scott's chair behind the desk. "I'm a legal secretary. I work for Mr. Grayhawk across the hall. You have no business here."

The man stopped beside Scott's guest chair. He offered a grimy-tooth smile as a peace gesture. "Then you don't either, dolly. So, as one trespasser to another, I'll just be leaving."

Evie pulled out the top drawer. A thirty-eight revolver, Scott's backup gun, lay loaded and waiting for action. "Who are you? What are you after?"

He pointed to the wall of baseball pictures. "I wanted to see if he really was a big-league ballplayer." He began to tender his nasty grin but retrieved it.

"Everybody in Tulsa knows that," scolded Evie.

"Yeah? I'm from out of town," he countered.

"Well, go home then. If he catches you here, maybe half of you makes it through the window to splatter on the street." Evie showed her pluck even as the hair on the backside of her neck rose up.

The intruder lurched forward, both hands on the desk with his mug thrust toward Evie. She reached into the drawer and gripped the revolver. His teeth grew grimier the closer he came. Her eyes narrowed to slits.

"I wouldn't mention our little meeting," threatened the man.

He righted himself and oozed away from her. She relaxed her grip on the gun but didn't let go. He stopped at the office door and pulled a switchblade from his pocket. He snapped the blade out. "Your pretty-girl complexion would look awful with a zipper." His squinted eyes added malice to the threat. He closed the knife. He raised it to his eyebrow and saluted Evie. The man slipped out, closing the door behind him.

She slumped into Scott's chair drawing both hands to her lap. Relief flushed her complexion. A second thought made her dash to the window. Evie spread the blinds to reveal a *Campion Cargo* van on the street out front. The would-be burglar and reprobate dashed into view and entered it.

* * *

Evie Hall sat on the edge of Wyatt's desk. She left Scott's office door open to make sure he did not detour to Johnny's office. Scott came and went as he pleased, but Evie felt sure he'd drag in soon. She resolutely felt the urge to tell Wyatt about the intruder but needed to run down the hall and finish some typing for Johnny. She fidgeted. She inspected her fingernails, left hand, then right. All ten gleamed with nary a chip.

At last, Scott appeared. He stood bareheaded in the doorway. He had shaved and changed clothes since his breakfast with Cleveland, but he still looked rough. Evie scooted around on the desktop but did not stand.

"Half-past noon. Must be nice to sleep in." Her thick sarcasm belied her tender years but underscored her preparation for the encounter.

"Yeah, peachy." Scott more slouched than sat in his chair. He reached for his phone and dragged it close.

Containing herself no longer, Evie burst out with her news. "Well, while you slept in, I caught a thief in here."

"Thief?"

"He didn't steal anything, but he was snooping for something," explained Evie.

"You know 'em?"

"Nope. Smarmy lookin' mug, mid-thirties, skinny with bad teeth."

"Did he say anything?" asked Scott.

"He told me not to tell you about him while he waved a switchblade." She acted out the knife and blade incident.

"That threat failed I see."

"Every time. I don't abide bullies and jerks," proudly proclaimed Evie.

"I'll look into it tomorrow. I've got to check something before I meet Bugler at the ballpark." Scott pulled the phone book from his left-hand drawer.

Evie stood and moved toward the window. She overtly cleared her throat. "If you let me finish, you might learn something, Mr. Detective."

Scott halted his attention toward the phonebook to look at Evie. "Then continue Miss Hall." Scott shifted in his chair to more faithfully watch her in front of the window.

"I looked out of your window..." Evie reenacted her move. "...and saw the dumb cluck get into a business van. It said..."

"Campion Cargo," interrupted Scott.

"...Campion Cargo," finished Evie right on top of Scott's words. She converted quickly from surprise to consternation. "You know this creep?"

"My neck and head met his sap last night. I have yet to meet him man-to-man."

"He's kinda' squirrely," observed Evie.

"No doubt," concurred Scott.

Scott's disdain brought a giggle from Evie. "When you meet this bum, take pictures, I'd like to see what's left." With her world aligned properly once more, Evie departed for the door. She managed to whistle a couple of song notes on her way.

Scott centered his telephone directory on his desk. He wet his finger and flew through its pages. Alighting on what he wanted, he reached for the phone. Before he could dial, it rang. He answered. The caller's voice surprised him.

CHAPTER 11

Big Bills

Wyatt Scott walked into the private office of Osage County Sheriff, Merle Berry. A mishmash of historical and contemporary lawmen watched over the office from their frames; Bill Tilghman holding an apparent place of honor next to Berry's formal, sheriff's photo. Scott stopped behind a wooden chair facing the sheriff. While never being accused of affability, except when eating a free meal at a cafe, Berry produced a cordial expression. Scott removed his hat showing the office, if not the man, some respect.

Supplementary information on the murder-suicide led Scott to make the drive to Pawhuska to see Berry. He surprised Scott when he called with a promise of added information on the case. The revelation came from a more thorough search of Jackie Martin's cabin. The sheriff would not divulge the news over the phone. As he told Scott, he wanted to see his reaction to be convinced he was not part of the blackmail gang.

"So, what did you find, Sheriff?" Scott asked bluntly.

Berry nodded. "Nice of you to make the trip to see us here in Pawhuska." He motioned for Scott to sit in the chair he stood behind.

Scott accepted the directive, and after a detour to the hat rack, he sat. "What did you find, Sheriff?"

"Nothin' outa' tha' ordinary 'cept one thing."

Allowing Berry's slow roll of the information, Scott played along. "And that one thing happened to be?"

"Money hid behind a picture of a' indun."

Scott dug up his mental image of the cabin. "The picture of Sitting Bull?"

"Don't know one indun' from tha' other. But it had...." Berry's dramatic pause fell a little short in time and low on drama. "...twenty-five hunert' dollars in it."

"Likely blackmail money from his work with Mildred Fuller," speculated Scott.

"Might coulda' been," agreed Berry. "I thought you'd like to know about it if you're still barkin' up the tree where he didn't kill himself."

Scott nodded his head. "Thanks, I *am* still looking into Mildred Fuller." Berry nodded but said nothing. "Anything else other than the hidden money?"

"Not sure." Berry stared at Scott. "Whata' you figure about the money?"

"I told you. I think it was blackmail money collected by Martin and Fuller. I am skeptical about their amorous involvement."

"Ya' might be right on that account. But what I mean is how'd you suppose the money was hid and all?"

"A clever person would've put it behind the picture with the backing showing and the money in the frame." Scott narrowed his eyes slightly at the odd question.

"Not so clever; our man hid it in an envelope taped ta' the back," clarified Berry.

"In a hurry or stupid like you said. A wad of cash might make the picture hang funny and give it away," speculated Scott. "That how you found it?"

Sheriff Berry wet his lips. "Since it was five bills at five-hunert' each, the envelope was flat, and nothin' stuck out. Just searched more thorough than some."

"Five-hundred-dollar bills don't come from grocery stores. Victim must've gotten it straight from the bank," surmised Scott.

"I think ya' lit on sumthin' there." Berry smiled his approval. "In case ya' was wantin' to ask, there was nothin' ta' tell about them bills. Not new nor worn, just big bills."

"Size of them still tells a tale. You have them?"

"Yep. Holdin' them and the envelope as evidence now." The sheriff taps his desk suggesting the storage place.

Scott took in the full picture gallery of lawmen. Beyond Tilghman and current sheriff, Berry, there were likenesses of Pat Garrett, Eliot Ness, Jelly Bryce, Wyatt and Virgil Earp, and the added Oklahoma trio of Frank Canton, Chris Madon, and Heck Thomas. "You have some impressive company watching your office."

Berry nodded. "Fine lawmen, one and all."

"They are," replied Scott. "I am thinking Bill Tilghman holds your highest regard."

"All deserve high regard." Sheriff Berry stared past Scott. His mind must have played some memory since a smile slipped into the right corner of his mouth. "Jelly Bryce is one hell of a modern lawman. Still, Bill Tilghman was special."

"Sheriff, your reputation is that of a country boy just thinking about the next election. I would never have known you had such reverence for outstanding lawmen if I had not seen your office." Scott nodded an affirmation to his statement.

Berry sat up and puffed out his chest just a little. "Thank ya', Scott. Sometimes it works better to have them think yer' not too sharp. The bad ones get overconfident."

The sheriff's face made a quick shift from pride to sincerity. "Ya' see Scott, I take this more seriously than most think. I am the duly elected lawman of the largest county in Oklahoma, and I've been told it's the largest in the U. S. of A. There's somewhere around thirty thousand taxpayin' citizens scattered abouts in our twenty-three hunert square miles." Berry went on ignoring his visitor. "Quite a few folks choose to live in some pretty remote stations. They do it for privacy from the law, Jackie Martin in particular. Word on the street, in this case, gravelt' road, is ol' Martin was a dirty agent, who was known to work a favor for an Indian or cause one a great deal of grief, whichever way someone come to pay him. I believe it to be true but can't prove it. The upshot is Jackie Martin dead is a long wished for thing among certain people in Osage County. And if someone steals a pet 'possum in Shidler, it will be given priority over Martin's suspicious suicide, ya' follow?"

The lawman's sandbagging playbook drew a smirk from Scott. "Any more about our dead guy." Scott shifted around on the uncomfortable wooden chair, but it remained wooden and uncomfortable. "Anything out of his next-of-kin?"

"Naw. Jus' like all kin say – 'Didn't know he had any kinda' trouble' is all," replied Berry.

"Still, their statements are factors making suicide less likely," opined Scott.

Sheriff Berry leaned forward. "Don't go messin' in mah' business sa' much ya' cause troubles here in Osage County. Coroner ruled; case closed."

"The family had no quarrel with the investigation and didn't have any concerns when they came for the body?"

"Family ain't comin'. They asked to have the body sent. The ID came off fingerprints and by fellas from the B.I.A. seein' Martin." Anticipating another question, the sheriff jumped to the answer. "Family wants all the effects sent to them. Got a lawyer to round them up."

"Everything but the twenty-five-hundred dollars."

"Right. Tol' ya' that is evidence." Berry cleared his throat. "If ever' thin's on the up-and-up, they can get it when things get sorted out."

"Ruled a suicide. It seems sorted out," declared Scott.

Berry smiled at Scott's twist. "Maybe. Maybe not. All this black-mailing crap you believe – need to keep track a' things till they come home to roost or don't."

Scott extended his arm toward Berry, palm up, before resting it on the chair arm. "I'm just trying to fit the blackmail into this murder-suicide. Not often, but now and then things are not simple. A person can start with Occam's Razor but end in complexity."

Berry smirked. "Don't go showin' off your college at me. Personally, I don't care if it's a full beard, a straight razor, or Gillette Blue blades, it's suicide in the books."

Scott sighed. He considered his tactics. "It just didn't look like suicide. It matters because it could bear on a case I have. I won't make any waves in Osage County." He paused to see Berry's reaction. The sheriff gave a short nod causing Scott to continue. "Would you let me see the money and the envelope? It's a thin lead, but I have precious little now."

"All right." Berry pulled a key from his pants' pocket and unlocked the top drawer on his right. He looked and poked around in the drawer before extracting a white envelope. He placed it on his desk. "Move up close so you can take a good look, and I can keep one eye on you."

Scott hauled his chair close to the desk. He picked up the envelope and examined the address side. There was nothing printed on it, but there were small, embossed letters spelling out 'National Bank of Tulsa' along the very top. Scott dug into the envelope and pulled out the five bills. They were not new, but like most of their denomination, had seen little handling and no damage from transactions. Noting the serial numbers were not sequential, Scott slid them into their envelope. "Check for any fingerprints?"

"Didn't see much good reason. Sure to get a slew of his, some bank teller's, and my deputies' prints."

"You're surely right about that." Scott offered the envelope to Sheriff Berry.

Scott watched the sheriff take the envelope and drop it in the drawer from where he took it. He used his key again and locked the drawer. He completed the sequence by returning the key to his pocket. He looked at Scott signaling the end of the interview.

"Thanks, Sheriff. I do suppose that is something for me to pursue." Scott stood and pushed the chair to its original position. One last direction of thought formed a question. "Nothing about Martin's work figured into this?"

"Indun affairs?" Berry rubbed his chin. "His job don't figure in atal'. He's white. Dead girlfriend is white." He offered up one hand then the other to punctuate his statement.

"It figures if it's part of the blackmail."

"Blackmail victim kills Martin's girlfriend, and he's so sad he kills himself rather than getting his girlfriend's killer? Don't wash." Berry shook his head; stopped and shook it again.

"It does if Martin was murdered and not a suicide," argued Scott as he bent over and spread his palms on the desk.

Sheriff Berry exaggerated a huge sigh. "If, if, if." He reclined in his chair and stared at Scott. "'Cept it was suicide. Looked like suicide, felt like suicide, and most important of all, ruled suicide."

Scott jerked away from the sheriff's desk. "Goddammit Sheriff, you and I and Detective Cleveland all know it was staged. The only one who doesn't know is Morgan and he is just too lazy to look at it any other way. And I reckon you are twice the lawman he is."

"A word son, watch your language in my office. There's no call for that."

"I apologize, heat of the moment."

Berry gave Scott a look of uncompromised determination. "Jackie Martin's death will remain as ruled, a suicide. If by chance you find any evidence to the contrary in Tulsa County, I would be grateful to hear about it. Now, get the fuck out of my county."

Seeing the need to feign contrition Scott lowered his gaze, "I'll stop poking around Osage County about this. I appreciate you talking to me and showing me the evidence." He made his way to the hat rack, grabbed his hat, and tipped it to Sheriff Berry.

"Good luck, young fella'," offered the old sheriff as a parting gift.

* * *

Wyatt Scott waited in the lobby of The National Bank of Tulsa. He watched a pageant of suits with a sprinkle of skirts flowing up and down the escalators. Scott speculated about what made folks adapt so quickly to the moving stairs. He calculated how many people liked modern technologies and would migrate to them simply because they were new. Perhaps, he mused, some were motivated by the claustrophobic nature of elevators or the abhorrence of rubbing shoulders with strangers, which could not be controlled within the confines of a moving closet. His impatience elevated the traditional stairs above both elevator and escalator, unless the latter ran empty, and he could make his way up or down the moving steps as freely as he could the stairs.

"Mr. Scott."

His focus on the escalators broken by hearing his name, Scott looked to see a fortyish man in a plain brown suit – the presumptive head teller he was waiting to see.

"I can see you now. If you would step into my office." He gestured toward a nearby door.

Scott strolled into the smallish office adorned with a framed photo of the bank on the wall. File cabinets attested to the paper-pushing nature of the man's job. A photo frame angled toward the desk chair declared it to be a wife or family photo. A single window, whose direction dictated that it faced the alley rather than Boston Avenue like those of the executives, sported drawn blinds.

The man sat behind his desk. "I am John Franklin, the head teller. I was told you wanted some information relating to our customers."

"Mr. Franklin, I am Wyatt Scott. I am conducting an investigation into a murder and blackmail in Osage County. The sheriff there and the Tulsa Police are trying to sort out jurisdictions, which is fine, but I have a client in the middle." Scott took out his notebook and pencil. "At the scene of the murder, the sheriff found an envelope with National Bank of Tulsa embossed on it."

"We have thousands of those envelopes for all of our customers," stated Franklin defending his bank against an undeclared accusation.

"I understand that. If the envelope were the only factor, I wouldn't have bothered you. Inside the NBT envelope, the sheriff found five, five-hundred-dollar bills."

"I see," replied Franklin. "While the vast majority of our customers would never deal in such large sums or large bills, we have most ofthe Tulsa businesses and many wealthy individuals, who would have use of such bills." After a short pause, he continued. "Were the bills new?"

"No. They were not very worn, but not new," answered Scott.

"With new bills, it would be hit-and-miss looking at withdrawals. But the bills you mentioned could be passed out recently or kept for years by a business or customer. Five-hundred-dollar bills don't circulate enough to wear much."

"I am aware of that. I had hoped you could help me with recent withdrawals, since I think these bills were involved in a blackmail payment," explained Scott.

"I see." Franklin glanced at his file cabinets, then looked to Scott. "If the Osage County Sheriff or the Tulsa Police serve us a warrant, we will be obliged to search and hand over what we find. Otherwise, I really can't give out customer information." He shrugged his apology for following procedure.

Scott noted the timid man's honesty. He thought he might find a clue if not an answer in those file cabinets, but for now he would have to defer. A high-ranking bank official could change the man's mind, but unfortunately while Scott knew several of them casually, he did not run in their circle suitably to obtain such a favor. He stood. "Thank you, Mr. Franklin. I will tell the sheriff of your concerns."

"I hope you understand, Mr. Scott." Franklin stood, then offered a meek smile.

Scott nodded. "I suppose a list of your large depositors would be as unobtainable as recent transactions."

"You're correct. I can't give you those either." Franklin paused and frowned. "Given our bank's size and reputation, you could imagine a list by using the names from the society page, the Southern Hills membership, Petroleum Club, Tulsa Club or any list of the sort with only a few other bankers and a handful of businesses who deal with those other banks being left off."

Scott smiled in reply. "Yes. It would've been a longshot attempt even with a list of recent withdrawals." The blackmailer money could have come from any rich victim – a thought so worthless and common, Scott scoffed at himself for the waste of brain space. He left the head teller's office and drew his notions toward other things.

CHAPTER 12

BASEBALL

The Babe Ruth led barnstorming tour weaved through Japan, playing to capacity crowds in cities all over the country. November twentieth, nineteen thirty-four, found the tour in Shizouka playing in Kusanagi Stadium. Earl Whitehill pitched for the American All-Stars. The Nippon national team put Eiji Sawamura on the mound for his second try at the all-stars.

As Sawarmura dueled Whitehill through six scoreless innings, Wyatt Scott watched the game from the bullpen bench with his friend and mentor, Moe Berg, who had the day off from catching with Frank Hayes taking his place. Berg had befriended the Athletics' rookie, becoming his guide on the voyage to Japan. As the all-stars began the games in Japan, he started teaching young Wyatt the language and customs of their hosts as well as the strategies of pitching and, by extension, those of life.

The elder statesman catcher gazed at the field from a seat which seemed to view what his fertile mind brought forth more than the play unfolding. His current consideration being Wyatt Scott's handling of hitters. "You need to move the ball around, kid. You can't overpower all the big-league hitters, but if you paint the corners, they can't turn hard on your pitches." Berg did not face Scott. He spoke toward the field letting his words drift like the seagulls beyond the fences.

Young Scott challenged Berg to reply. "Changing pitches works too. If you slip up a little on placement, you can fool them off-speed or get them to chase before blowing the high hard one by them." The teenage rookie waited for the veteran catcher to reply to his points.

Berg sat mute. His silence compounded. Finally shifting his view from the field, Berg shook his head. "Think things through kid. Analyze, scrutinize, know your options and those of your adversary. Baseball, business, politics, life comes down to knowing the other guy's thoughts and likely responses as much or more than your clever choices."

"That's what I said. I just keep'em guessing – curve, drop, fast one, nickel curve." Scott twisted his hand fashioning the grips as he spoke.

Berg stood and stepped away from the bench. He looked at the ground and kicked the dirt with his cleats. "Sure, you need more than a fastball, but two pitches placed well beats a dozen types all grooved." He raised up, looking Scott in the eyes. "Besides, you really ought to lay off the nickel curve."

"Heck no. It's my strikeout-Gehrig pitch. Nobody does that, at least not often."

Berg pointed toward the field. "Nobody? The Jap kid out there today is racking up Ks all across the board."

Scott glanced at the scoreboard, which displayed zeros for both squads. "Strikeouts don't matter. They've got goose eggs too, Moe." He pointed at the wall and the line of white ovals hung under each inning.

"Earl's supposed to whip their asses. He's a pro and they are just short guys playing our game. But that Sawamura kid is throwing bee bees today."

"You know his name?" More than a little shock registered in Wyatt's voice.

"Sure. You've got to know the enemy to beat them. Eiji Sawamura. He's a high school kid; even younger than you. I guess you saw him mow down all those top hitters.

Scott looked out on the field seeing Sawamura toe the rubber. He narrowed his eyes at the young Japanese pitcher. "I give him credit so far. A few good innings in one ballgame." He swung to eyeball Moe Berg. "He got bombed in his first game."

"His first game. Seventeen-year-old against the greatest in the world. Seems you had some troubles in a game or two."

"I got through a full big-league season!" Scott's defensiveness bled through his reply.

"You sure did, kid." The avuncular Berg smiled. "And if you keep winning, Connie Mack will put your picture up all over Philadelphia. Still, remember to think things through. See it like the other guy sees it." Berg drew his attention to the baseball diamond.

Wyatt thought Berg more indecipherable than the supposedly inscrutable Japanese. Answering a question with a question or asking more from an answer, created the feeling that Moe could not be satisfied. Looking out on the field, Lou Gehrig stood at the plate. Scott wondered if the Japanese kid could strike Lou out again. Moe Berg, too, stared at this pitcher-batter conflict.

Sawamura had struck Gehrig out in the fourth inning. His fanning being only a part of the Japanese high schooler setting down Charlie Gehringer, Ruth, Gehrig, and Jimmy Foxx in a row, all by strikeout. This feat of whiffing the best hitters and top home-run threats left the crowd as well as Wyatt Scott wondering what would happen now. The next pitch and the next swing brought the solid sound of wood as the answer. A line drive screamed off Lou Gehrig's bat. High enough and hard enough to clear the right field fence.

Wyatt slapped Berg on his shoulder. "He didn't get that one by Lou!"

"No. He did not. The kid is human after all," declared Berg.

The lone run held up. Earl Whitehill shut out the Japanese All-Stars. The teams played another nine games in the series, but none was as close or thrilling for the local fans. Not one of those games included the young Philadelphia Athletics pitcher, Wyatt Scott. Connie Mack, the barnstorming team's coach, never listed him as a player on the team, but did bring his young pitcher on the tour as a guest. Wyatt got to pitch some batting practice, slipping in a nickel curve now and again much to the chagrin of the All-Star hitters. Moe Berg made disapproving stares when he saw the twisting pitch but spent more and more time beyond baseball tutelage, teaching Scott the Japanese language, sometimes with the help of their guide and handler Hiroshi Ishikawa.

* * *

Afternoon baseball kept Tulsa entertained in the summer. The Tulsa Oilers may not have been world-beaters, but they were better than average. Even on workdays, a decent crowd showed up to watch the national pastime. Texas League Park's wooden fences posed as billboards for advertisements. A Coca-Cola advertisement, shaped and painted to resemble its bottle, rose larger than a man in left-center. Beside it, the big clock kept the actual time as well as advertising for Bulova. Both newspapers had a portion of center, while car lots, clothiers, and dry cleaners battled for attention in right field. A children's section, the Knothole Club, provided the only outfield seats from the left-field foul pole to just short of the clock. No more than a hundred or so could fit in the section, but it was a lively place, more so when a home-run ball flew into it.

This fine June afternoon found the double-A Oilers on the field, and their number one fan, Bugler, sitting along the third base line several rows up in the cheap seats. In his lap, his score pad showed every at bat recorded precisely and accurately down to the backward "K" for called third strikes and a rare "K 2-3" for a dropped-ball strikeout with a catcher-to-first putout. Not that Bugler did not cheer for the home team, he did – scoring could be done between batters when the dust settled from a grounder, a hard slide, or the pitcher kicking the mound.

As Bugler vigorously erased then re-marked his score pad, Wyatt Scott sat down beside him. Without looking up from his scoring duties, Bugler admonished his friend. "Five ta' two, Oilers. That's a' update for those what think the sixth inning's the same as the first."

"I had a late start this morning, then a trip to the airport," explained Scott regarding his tardiness.

"Yer' big, red car ain't enough; ya' gonna' fly now?" Bugler eyed Scott and slid his pencil behind his ear.

"Just looking for a character out that way. So, the guys are ahead. How are they playing?" Scott scanned the alignment on the field.

"Not bad since Vincent finally pulled that has-been Dodge and put in the kid, Edwards." Bugler pointed toward Edwards in the outfield getting set for the next pitch.

"Is the kid good?"

"Hits nuthin' but line drives at B P; runs like the wind; and has a' arm like a gun, 'stead a' peashooter like Dodge."

"Well, maybe Vincent wised up enough to keep his manager's job," speculated Scott.

"Never made sense. Worst arm I ever saw. Dodge's best play was tippin' his hat to the box seats, usually the Douglas folks. Sometimes ta' them Skelly Oil or Warren Petroleum ones." A quick spit put Bugler's final emphasis on his disdain for Dodge and his woeful play.

Scott looked at the box seats behind home plate. Only a tiny scattering of fans occupied the prime viewing section. "Not many box seat folks – no Douglas folks at all."

"Probly' don't care to sit where the murdered gal did." Apparently finding a slight flaw in his scorekeeping, Bugler retrieved his pencil, erased a smudge, and entered a tiny number.

"Mildred Fuller? She came to the ballpark?" Scott sat up and shifted toward his old friend.

"Yep. Sat in a suit-guy's box. He'd come with other fellas too," reported Bugler.

Scott glanced toward the empty box before casting his gaze again to the septuagenarian. "You're sure it was her, Mildred Fuller?"

Unlike Scott, Bugler would not take his eyes from the field. A big play could happen at any moment. "Same dame as the Tribune pichur'. I seen her there. She'd even wave at Dodge like he was still worth a wooden nickel 'stead a' warm spit."

"She came often; with the same guy?" questioned Scott.

"Often enough. Same suit-guy what always sat in the box."

"Would you recognize the suit-guy?"

"Likely so, he's one a' yer' drinkin' club buddies." Bugler winced as the Oiler pitcher tossed ball four and the opposition now had a runner trotting to first.

"What drinking buddies?" asked Scott.

Bugler had to fill in the walk on his score pad before he considered Scott's non-baseball question. "Drinkin', eatin' folks. Your buddies at the fancy club where you meet the town money." He watched a foul ball float weakly behind the visitors' dugout.

"The Tulsa Club?"

"Yeah, your place, rich man, Tulsa Club. I seen 'em go in there, though he weren't nuthin' special." Bugler shook his head in consideration of the plain Tulsa Club member.

The benefit of this serendipity was not lost on Scott. He stood and pulled on Bugler's arm. "Come on, we've got fish to fry."

Shocked by the sudden deed, Bugler protested the near sacrilege of leaving before the game finished. "The game's not done yet...and I don't like fish."

"They'll hold 'em. Come on. I need your help." Scott smiled and patted Bugler on the shoulder.

Bugler stood up. Although none too happy about it, he acquiesced for his pal but still needed to complain. "Dang Wyatt. Miss most a' the game, watch half an inning an' skedaddle. You gone Daffy Duck on me?"

Scott ushered Bugler down the steps toward the exit ramp. Bugler had trouble fitting his pencil in his pocket, finally sliding it behind his ear. The crack of a bat forced him to sneak a peek toward the field. It was an easy pop-up. The second baseman put it away, completing the top half of the inning with the Oilers still leading. They would have to finish the game with two fewer fans as Scott and Bugler disappeared down the ramp.

CHAPTER 13

The Tulsa Club

The late afternoon sun filtered between the curtains adding supplementary light to the well-appointed dining room of the Tulsa Club. Scott entered with purpose and made his way toward a long wooden bar with no visible liquor. Soft drinks and juice bottles, per the law of the dry state of Oklahoma, occupied the expected domain of alcoholic beverages. Nonetheless, well-dressed patrons scattered through the club sipped away at illicit drinks. Businessmen wearing suits filled most tables where they smoked away and savored highballs. Decked out in summer fashions, the fewer female patrons gathered around tables festooned with cocktails ranging from colorful and mild to martinis with onions.

A formally dressed, gray-haired man, C. A. Sanborn, the Tulsa Club's manager, met Scott as he reached the bar. "Wyatt, my boy, it's good to see you." Sanborn extended his right hand and clasped Scott's shoulder with his left.

"C. A., it's good to see you." Scott shook the man's hand with familiarity and friendship rather than the usual perfunctory greeting of client and administrator.

"A drink for you, Wyatt?" offered Sanborn.

"I wouldn't want you to *break the law*, C. A.," replied Scott with over-emphasized sarcasm.

"Neither does Mayor Lundy, but you see the martini at his table," replied Sanborn with a wry grin as he tilted his head to a table holding the mayor, a local banker, and two others, who seemed to be discussing business, while in flagrant violation of the state liquor statutes.

"I'll take a bar seat and consider my options." Scott disengaged from the handshake and resumed strolling toward the bar.

He had known Sanborn for years. C. A. kept himself and the club in punctilious order and pristine condition. He managed the place efficiently and the wealthy, self-absorbed members with grace. Few of those members could guess at the cleverness and finesse it took to run a restricted membership, top-quality dining club, which amounted to a de facto speakeasy, in direct contravention to the state's constitution. Scott's late parents were longtime members of the club, which afforded him continued membership as a legacy. He frequented it after college before the draft swept him up. After their deaths and his move to Tulsa, he kept the membership even though most often he chose to break the state liquor laws privately at his own apartment in the Sophian Plaza.

After completing his journey to one of the upholstered barstools, Scott signaled the bartender. John, the regular bartender, hailed from California but bucked the immigration flow by moving to Tulsa in the thirties. He looked almost elegant in his uniform. Beyond being a fine bartender, the man was a talented and clever practitioner of liquor-by-the-wink. He strode smoothly to Scott's spot.

"I'll take a Cutty with ice and a splash, John."

John nodded and worked out of sight below the counter. He placed the tawny liquid and ice-filled glass in front of Scott. "What is your club number, Mr. Scott?"

"Three-three-seven. You don't have it memorized?" Scott teased.

"Routine, you know, Mr. Scott." John winked.

Scott sipped from his glass and sized up the patrons. The women chatted away with adroit consistency. The men blended hushed business tones with boisterous outbursts of laughter from islands of tobacco haze. Not to be outdone, clouds of smoke hovered over the genteel ladies' tables almost as much as the men's, a distinct change from the prewar days. The pitch of the mingled voices being the distinguishing variable between the genders; segregated as they were by choice and inclination.

A muffled telephone ring sent John, the bartender, to the backbar at the far end of his posting, to answer. After a brief utterance into the handset, he brought the black, Bell-issued phone on its extra-long cord, to sit in front of Wyatt. He spun it to face him. Expecting the call, Scott still waited for the bartender's formality.

"For you, Mr. Scott," proclaimed John.

Scott picked up the receiver. "Scott." He heard what he expected. "You're sure it's him? Good job, Bugler," praised Scott. "The coneys are on me tomorrow."

Wyatt hung up the phone. John took it back to its original location at the end of the backbar. Scott scanned across the room and signaled

Sanborn to join him. He complied with his usual grace of motion seeming to glide rather than stride as he approached.

Upon his arrival, Scott asked his favor. "C. A., I would like to ask about some members."

"You know I turn a blind-eye to shenanigans," admonished Sanborn.

"I wouldn't ask you to dish dirt on anyone, but I'm looking for some connections or potential connections, which include some members," clarified Scott.

Sanborn nodded to the modest request. He glanced around the room before offering his knowledge for consideration by Scott. With no one else near, he cleared his throat in preparation for a response.

"Tell me about Catherine Folger." Scott began with his furtive client.

Surprised by the first name proffered by Scott, Sanborn pulled away slightly. "Mrs. Clifford Folger?"

"If ol' Clifford is a bigtime banker, that's the one."

"He is," confirmed Sanborn. "Mrs. Folger is *high* society, Junior Leaguer, rich, and very classy. Her picture is in the society section as often as yours used to be in the sports pages. She's involved in a lot of charity work and volunteering. Her husband, I suspect you know, owns banks in Texas as well as Oklahoma."

"No scandals about either one?"

"I told you, I don't trade in that, but in their case absolutely nothing," affirmed Sanborn.

Scott moved to something more visceral in his next line of inquiry. "What do you know about Campion Cargo?"

"Albert Campion and his wife Charlotte are members. He runs a transport business or such." Sanborn wrinkled his brow a moment apparently calculating the line between factual mention and pejorative commentary. "He has a lot of money but is not part of the Tulsa social elite. They are new to Tulsa." Sanborn paused again. He stared Scott directly in the eye. "You grew up here. You know how they play. For a town less than fifty years old, it still looks down on the new rich, especially when they are *very* wealthy."

Scott nodded his appreciation. "Thanks, C. A. One last favor. Tell me about the next guy when he comes in."

Scott focused on the door. Sanborn did likewise. A forty-something executive wearing a tan business suit entered the Tulsa Club. He glanced around before walking toward the bar and the general direction of Scott and Sanborn. His shoes needed a shine, and his bare head showed his thinning hair a little too slicked up for current styles. Average in every discernible detail, the man poorly fit the upper crust, Tulsa Club, membership.

"Phil Nichols," declared Sanborn. "Works at Douglas. Rarely picks up a check – lets the suppliers take care of them." A twinge of disdain registered in Sanborn's voice.

"No out-of-the-office connection between him and Mildred Fuller?" Scott invoked the routine question.

"The murdered woman?" asked Sanborn with a twinge of surprise.

"Yes. Just covering my bases," explained Scott.

"He's pretty straitlaced; wife and kids." Sanborn's tone about Nichols's family morals sounded clearly positive. His opinion of the man's business dealings remained negative. "Unless the Fuller woman could make him a dollar, I'd say he never gave her a second thought."

"Thanks C. A. I'll see you later."

"I'll be around." Sanborn took the hint. He walked away and passed Nichols without addressing him.

Scott shifted slightly and intercepted Nichols just short of the bar. "Phil Nichols, right? I'm looking for a little information about Mildred Fuller."

Nichols, flummoxed by the request, stopped cold. He looked Scott up and down. No recognition registered, only bewilderment, before annoyance took over from surprise. "She's dead. That's pretty much the final information on her." He took a step. Scott caught his arm.

"Who are *you*?" Nichols snipped, while pulling free from Scott's grasp.

"Somebody who knows about you and Mildred." Scott's tone rang sharp and severe. "But I'm an investigator, not a *blackmailer*." Scott emphasized the last word and raised his voice.

His consternation replaced by concern, Nichols glanced around quickly to see if anyone heard. "She was a...." He looked around again before continuing. "...secretary."

"Not qualified for the job you gave her then," speculated Scott in hopes of acquiring better insight into Fuller's machinations.

"Less efficient than I liked," admitted Nichols. He looked away from Scott's scorn.

"Yes, I expect so." Scott paused to see if Nichols would look at him. He did not. "Tell me, what did Mildred Fuller have on you?"

"What?" The accusation caused Nichols to scrutinize Scott despite his previous inclination to avoid eye contact.

"Enough you had to kill her?" Scott escalated the theme.

"No!" Taken off guard, Nichols swiveled once again to see if anyone could hear before he continued. "Mildred worked her angles you're right, but we had an understanding." He hushed his volume to barely more than a whisper.

Scott scoffed at the admission. "That's more like it. I'll guess her end was helping you get kickbacks and yours was what; higher pay than she deserved and some trips to the ballpark?"

"Who are you?" Nichols eyed Scott up and down.

"I told you. I am an investigator. I'm not with the police. You and your secrets are safe. I only want to know about Mildred Fuller's angles."

"I'm not admitting anything. Got it?" He raised his chin and glared at Scott, taking his first aggressive stance. "But, yeah, she liked the stupid Oiler ballgames. She'd yell like a kid and cuss the umpires like a sailor." He did not hide his dislike of Fuller's coarseness.

"So, who did she blackmail?" Scott vaulted to the important question.

"I wouldn't know, really," he answered flatly. "I overheard bits, no details. One guy may have been at the company," he added with a helpful tone.

"Somebody at Douglas Aircraft?"

"Yes, but I couldn't tell you who." Nichols shifted nervously. His discomfort was more than apparent, but a quotient of fear trumped it.

"You don't have any notion? How about where the guy works?"

Before Nichols could answer, the telephone rang once more.

"She wasn't blackmailing me, so I kept out of it," explained Nichols.

The bartender reached the ringing Bell set and answered it. While Scott considered more questions, Nichols watched the bartender pick up the phone and situate it on the bar beside Scott's drink.

"Mr. Scott, you have another call," advised John, the bartender.

Displeased with the interruption, Scott hurried to his spot at the bar. He picked up the receiver. "Scott!" he barked into it.

The caller growled at Scott. "Stop nosing around Douglas. There's nothing there about your small-time crap."

Surprised, but not shaken, Scott countered, "How do you know this?"

"Because we do," replied the man on the phone. "And because we don't want you screwing things up." He paused, then added, "Drink your drink and go home."

With Scott diverted, Phil Nichols took the opportunity to slip away. Scott didn't notice him slink toward the door. Nichols glanced at the bar, but no one at the Tulsa Club lifted an eye in his direction.

A click in Scott's ear signaled the call's end. Scott cradled the handset. Becoming aware of Nichols's movement, Scott shifted on his stool to see the man easing out of the Tulsa Club. Nichols trod unobtrusively through the door. Beyond Scott and the mystery caller, no one noted or cared about his departure.

Scott shoved the telephone away. He sipped his drink. He rattled the ice. He sipped again. Reflected in the bar glassware, a stocky figure in a dark suit came out of one of the phone booths in the back of the club. His reflection shifted from glass to glass while Scott drank his whisky. The distorted figure disappeared through the club's door. Scott's glass held only ice. He raised it high for John, the bartender, to see.

CHAPTER 14

MRS. CAMPION

Dressed in his light summer suit, but rejecting a necktie, Wyatt Scott weaved his way along a garden path. Behind him, up the lane through which he entered the grounds, the mansion of Albert and Charlotte Campion loomed like a Bavarian castle. Upon his arrival, the servants had looked him up and down before, apparently, deciding it would be Mrs. Campion's option to converse with him or order him thrown out. They directed him to the garden path advising him Mrs. Campion was at the pool, which would appear around a bend and beyond the weeping willow trees. As Scott walked the trail, the garden appeared lush, varied, colorful, and well maintained. Butterflies and bees approved of the summer flowers flowing along both sides of the footpath. The blossoms' singular and mixed odors scented the elongated trail – even so, the walk seemed endless.

The route wound to the garden's end where a tennis court materialized on the right, and a short length of path continued to a huge swimming pool, befitting the oversized nature of the house and grounds. The setting featured a ten-foot tall, stucco fence along the pool's far side and a cavalcade of outdoor furniture which overwhelmed the panorama. A brightly colored, striped umbrella shaded supplementary chairs on the near side and the figure Scott presumed to be Charlotte Campion.

Clad in tennis whites, a wide, straw sun hat, and sunglasses, she reposed on an outdoor lounge with mermaid print cushions. Comely and well-proportioned, Mrs. Campion exuded sex. Standing near her, at attention, her manservant, held a towel and a tray. Walking the final steps along the pool, Wyatt Scott approached her. As she saw him, Mrs. Campion pulled off her sunglasses and twisted her body to size him up. She licked her lips into a coquettish grin.

"Don't tell me, let me guess." She looked away from him as if to think, then directly at him. "Your name is Beefcake, Bill Beefcake." She giggled with delight at her cleverness.

"Wyatt Scott," he corrected flatly.

"Well, Wyatt, sit beside me and tell me your story." She patted the chaise cushion. "Maxwell..." She waved her hand toward the standing servant. He turned his head without moving the rest of his body. "...can get you anything you want. My husband keeps a well-stocked bar including some nasty little numbers like Lillet and Chartreuse." She stared at Scott while again licking her upper lip. "I'll have Lillet." Her stare slid into a leer. "I like nasty. I'm thinking you do too."

Cooler than the water in the pool, Scott replied, "An iced tea and some shade from your umbrella would do just fine." He ducked under the umbrella and sat on a cushioned, wrought-iron chair opposite Mrs. Campion.

Her leering complete, she pushed her sunglasses back in place and motioned to Maxwell. "Maxwell, bring me an ample Lillet and Wyatt here an iced tea." He bowed slightly and nodded before walking toward the garden path.

"Campion Cargo, panel trucks; I suppose your husband has a fleet." Scott stated what was really a question. He fixed his focus squarely on Mrs. Campion's eyes.

Mrs. Campion smirked. "If you don't know, his business is air cargo. He owns or leases planes, lots of planes. Trucks, he has a couple." She waved her hand dismissing the notion of trucks.

"Okay, does he ever drive one of those?" Scott pushed on.

Mrs. Campion laughed out loud. It was a sudden, unexpected, and genuine guffaw. She explained through the smile that lingered – "The chauffeur drives Albert's big Packard. He'll fly any plane, but he doesn't drive at all." She beamed with delight from detailing her husband's shortcomings to her visitor.

"So, he has truck drivers out of the Campion facility at the airport." Scott followed the circuitous path looking for the name of his office visitor and presumed assailant even as his impatience slipped into his tone.

"You've been there?" asked Mrs. Campion.

"Yesterday. I wanted to learn who drives the trucks."

"Then you learned that my brother drives them."

His surprise broke through before Scott answered. "No. I learned the poor cargo loaders barely speak English."

"I wouldn't know. It's not a spot I frequent." She did not try to hide her snobbish disdain.

"Your truck driver brother, does he do anything else for your husband?"

"Good God no!" exclaimed Mrs. Campion. "My brother only has the job because my husband thinks it will keep Waldo, that's his name, from embarrassing us." Her condescension almost overpowered her words. "Waldo is prone to mistakes and has always looked for a fast buck."

"Unlike his sister, who takes her time?" jabbed Scott.

Once more laughing out loud, Mrs. Campion removed her sunglasses and pointed them toward Scott. "You are quite fun, Wyatt." Mrs. Campion folded her sunglasses and theatrically touched them to her cheek. "Waldo is incautious and not often the smartest performer." She paused, presumably for effect. "My husband and I are prudent," she concluded.

"Did Waldo's imprudence involve Mildred Fuller?"

Mrs. Campion wrinkled her nose as if a foul smell had wafted her way. "Ah, the late Mildred. A tacky and tiresome woman." Campion sighed out a lungful of air. "Just like you can't choose your relatives, you can't choose their friends."

"Then brother Waldo...Waldo what?" asked Scott as an afterthought.

"Sleener." The name seemed to catch in her throat. "Our family name, and gladly no longer mine."

"So, what about Waldo and Mildred?" pressed Scott.

"They were maybe an item once." She pondered on the pair. "They liked low-life drinking spots my hired help wouldn't consider."

"How did Waldo look on Mildred taking up with Jackie Martin?" Scott delved further.

"Who knows for sure. But I had the feeling that he, Martin, and

Mildred Fuller were business pals." Mrs. Campion dropped her glasses and moved in on Scott, stretching her arms in his direction. "Talk of them is tiresome. They lack the chemistry we have."

Before she could get her hands on him, Maxwell appeared with the drinks on his tray. Annoyed, she glared at him. "Maxwell, you're so…prompt," lamented Mrs. Campion. She snatched both drinks before he could properly offer them. She handed the tea to Scott. Maxwell nodded dutifully and shuffled off. Mrs. Campion sucked the Lillet from the edge of her glass.

Scott sipped his tea before pressing on. "What business were these pals pursuing?"

"I have no earthly idea." Campion shrugged her disinterest. "Wouldn't you rather like to ask some questions about me? I don't blush at *personal* questions if you like those." She dipped her tongue in the Lillet and drew it gradually between her exposed teeth.

"No doubt you'd give interesting answers," deflected Scott. "I suppose I need to talk to your brother for my answers."

"Waldo isn't that interesting." Mrs. Campion squirmed a little. Talk of her brother seemed to disrupt her relentless flirting.

"I guess I'll find out for myself. Do you know where he lives?"

"Maybe an apartment house near the river." She paused, thinking it over. "No, that was last year."

Frustrated, Scott retorted; "That's the best you've got?"

"Oh, I've got a lot." She beamed. Her innuendo and seduction reawakened.

"About your brother." Exasperation had pulled even with Scott's equilibrium and threatened to beat it to the finish line.

"About us," she cooed.

Scott stood. He set his glass on the nearby table. His summer suit remained pressed and pristine, but Mrs. Campion had managed to wrinkle his reason.

"You aren't trying to leave me so soon are you, Wyatt?" A tone of feigned injury and batting eyes gilded her plea.

Scott left without another word.

* * *

Names and notes stared at Scott from the page. His notepad offered plenty of each on two open cases, but the connections toward a solution remained jumbled. He thumbed the pages to reread a portion when a figure appeared at his office door. Bob Shanks, the bootlegger, walked in when he saw Scott look up.

"Scott, I found your place." Shanks acted relieved at his achievement.

"I see that, Bob. What brings you to visit me?"

Shanks made his way meekly to the guest chair and sat. He took a couple of breaths, before looking Scott in the eye. "I thought of somethin' else about the whore that died."

"Okay. I'm happy to listen." Scott released the pages of notes. He let his empty hands drop into his lap.

"An' I'm happy ta' tell, but I've got another problem I need ta' deal with." Shanks' hands fiddled with the chair arms. "I'm lookin' for help on a matter...and for that help, I will tell."

Scott involuntarily narrowed his eyes and audibly scoffed. "Yeah, figures. So, what is *your* problem?"

"I sold some whiskey to an Indian, who got himself in trouble with the law in Claremore. Then, ta' get outa' trouble, he's named me as the bootlegger, who caused all his problems."

"Okay. What good would I be in this?" inquired Scott.

"I hear yer' in tight with a good Indian lawyer."

"Why would that matter?"

"Figure he could help against tha' accuser." Shanks took a deep breath and exhaled. "Also thought I might need a slick Pinkerton to work out things a lawyer cain't."

Scott studied the bootlegger. It surprised him that Shanks worried over what had to be a recurring occupational hazard. "Were you arrested?"

"Not yet, but they took half-a-case of good Wellers from my place."

"Claremore cops?"

"Yeah." Shanks nodded.

"They don't have any jurisdiction in Tulsa County." Scott reasoned a moment. "I suppose that's why they only took your liquor."

"I figured," replied Shanks. "I worry though they'll get the state boys involved."

"Did they find your refilled Cokes?"

"No. Jus' took the Wellers."

Scott rubbed his chin and mused. "Dump your spiked Cokes in the river. Leave your plain Coke inventory. Without the spiked ones, you're just a fellow who likes Coca-Cola a lot if any lawman asks."

"They still have the Wellers."

"Without a way to prove you are selling it, the state won't go hard on a guy, who held some whiskey for a *friend*." Scott implied the plan for Shanks.

"Friend?"

"Sure. You tell them a buddy left it at your place and was coming back to get it."

"What happens when they ask who my buddy is?" questioned Shanks.

"I'll find one for you." Scott laid it out straight and plain for the bootlegger. "One who just recently died."

Shanks smiled. "I knew you was slicker than a' usual gumshoe."

"I'll run your predicament by Johnny Grayhawk, but I imagine if you dump your inventory quickly, you'll be fine."

"Thanks." Bob Shanks leaned forward. "I imagine you want mah' information now."

"I do."

"The whore tol' me somthin' about the rough guy. She told me the first time I was with her, so I didn't think of it when you came by." He sat up very straight. "I mean it. I didn't hide it from ya' or expect ta' have trouble. Anyhow, she told me this guy that paid extra was classy."

"Dressed nice, like a banker maybe?" queried Scott.

"Not so much that. She said he talked nice and smooth. Real nice was about all, other than her wantin' pills 'cause he was rough. I tol' her ta' stop yappin' 'bout some other guy and use her mouth for what was our deal, and it ended the talk."

"He had a highfalutin vocabulary?" Scott followed up.

"Didn't say it thata' way. I don't think it was the words. More how his voice sounded, I think," explained Shanks.

"Hmmm. Bob, that might help eventually."

"You know, I wasn't recording the whole conversation in my brain," apologized Bootlegger Bob.

"It's fine, Bob. I appreciate your effort coming in." Scott stood to signal the conversation to be complete.

Shanks stood in reply. "You'll talk to yer' lawyer pal?"

"I will, but you hurry home and dump the rebottled evidence, and I will send you a name to be your dead pal."

"Do I owe ya'?"

"Only if you do get arrested. Then, you'll owe Johnny. Just like you wanted to have a clever Pinkerton, I'd like a guy who knows what's what in west Tulsa."

Shanks winked. "Fair 'nough. I'll remember." He departed with a swagger.

* * *

After dark, Scott sat at his familiar barstool in the Tulsa Club. The place hummed. Couples filled the club in twos, fours, and sixes. A smaller number of tables had businessmen dining, drinking, and deal making. The bartender stayed busy making drinks that were illegal by state law but overlooked by law enforcement outside and inside the establishment.

Out of the middle of the room, C. A. Sanborn made his way to Scott and his half-empty Cutty. Upon reaching him, Sanborn looked away a moment into the low light of the tables past the dance floor. He put his hand on the counter and focused away from the din of conversations and rattling dishes to speak to Scott.

"Wyatt, it looks like your questions came in this evening," he uttered in a hushed tone.

Scott looked past him into the crowd. "You're right C. A.," Scott answered quietly. "I just don't know if any of the answers did."

Sanborn smiled at the reply. "Good luck with that my boy." He patted Scott on the shoulder and moved into the club, acknowledging an unseen patron with a wave.

Scott hadn't time to sip his scotch before an elegantly dressed Mrs. Folger approached the bar. John, the bartender, shifted along toward the spot of her advance. She stopped near Scott, but not beside him. She stood erect with regal deportment. Scott sipped his drink. While not intentionally avoiding her, he made no effort to socialize.

"John, would you make me a girlie drink?" She gazed at John. "A Grasshopper would be nice."

"I'll get right to it." The bartender exited through the swinging door behind the bar that connected his realm to the kitchen.

Mrs. Folger focused on the door while addressing Scott. "You won't find what I'm paying you for drinking cocktails in here." More superiority than scorn wafted through her comment.

Scott looked up at Mrs. Folger, then he too focused on the swinging door. "You'd be surprised what one can find at the Tulsa Club."

"You were hired to find that blackmailer's book." She shifted her body to view Scott in the mirror. "I bet you've found nothing but the liquor in your glass," scolded Mrs. Folger.

Scott swigged the remainder of the liquid and slammed the glass on the countertop. Ice and crystal rattled. "I found the ice too."

Folger leaned on the polished wood craning her head more and staring into the backbar mirror. "A strange man called my house...my *house*." With her abrupt revelation, emotion flowed through Mrs. Folger's words. She stirred for the first time and glared directly at Scott.

"Okay, okay." Scott softened his tone. He remained calm. He still focused on the swinging door rather than overtly addressing Folger. "Did you recognize his voice?"

"No." She swallowed hard before resuming her gaze at the door in continuance of the ruse of not conversing. "He wants to meet. He insinuated that if I refused, he'd contact my husband."

"Meeting him is a poor idea for a Tulsa socialite," counseled Scott.

"Then you can meet him." She sighed and leaned against the bar for stability. "You pay him and get the book," implored Folger.

"Did he say he had the book?"

"Not in so many words." She cleared her throat and calmed a little. "He did say he had something valuable for sale."

"Sounds like that's his game all right. Is he calling you to make the arrangements?"

"God no!" She calmed her voice. "I can't risk any more phone calls to my house. The servants or my husband might answer."

"How did you leave it then?"

"He gave me a phone number. I'm to call tomorrow morning at ten," she explained.

"Use a pay phone. The number is likely a pay phone too."

"Yes, unless he's as stupid as you seem to think I am." Equal measures of sarcasm and anger colored her reply.

"No. You're not stupid nor naive. I just like to cover all the bases."

Scott's tone remained calm, and he hoped it would transfer to her.

"Your baseball metaphor meaning you want to be thorough?" queried Mrs. Folger.

"Thorough is good. Cautious is better," explained Scott. "If I know the time and place in advance, I can protect against untoward events."

"Fine."

"I'll call you around eleven. Be near the phone if it worries you," warned Scott.

Again, Mrs. Folger's agitation overcame her coolness as she toyed with her small purse. "I just want the damn book destroyed."

John returned through the swinging door with Mrs. Folger's pale green cocktail. His presence quelled any further conversation about blackmail or the notorious book. Folger perked up at the sight of her cocktail on John's silver tray. Scott watched the transaction in the back-bar's long mirror as she took the drink. She glanced at Scott's reflection. Her reversed image showed no emotion. Neither did his.

"Thank you, John." Mrs. Folger offered a perfunctory smile to the bartender before she started to her table.

With a two-finger wave, Scott prevailed on John for a refill. The proficient bartender produced a bottle and poured Scott's glass two-fingers full before moving on down the bar. Scott rocked the glass swirling the liquid against the diminished cubes. The blended aroma of Scottish distilleries swept up his nose giving his taste buds a preview of the coming attraction.

Before Scott could sample the fresh scotch in his glass, Mrs. Campion swirled up beside his spot. She paused next to him wearing an expensive European gown. Its pedigree paled in comparison to its slinky, revealing design and its risqué cut. There were no shimmering sequins or broad patterns to deflect attention from the essentials of her figure. It clung to her hips with rolled-on efficiency, while it allowed her breasts to dance like forest nymphs under the pliable, flowing cloth.

"You don't want some has-been, silent picture dame, do you, Beef-cake?" She leaned on the bar, which shifted her breasts into a palpably provocative pose.

"Mrs. Campion," he announced with mock surprise. "Here for more Lillet, I suppose?"

"I came for attention and to be seen with my husband." She swept her arm toward a far table with too little light to fully reveal her husband. Mrs. Campion then resettled her hungry eyes on Scott. "Why did you come, my dear Wyatt?"

Scott raised his glass as a visual aid. "For an early cocktail."

"You came too early," complained Mrs. Campion. "I don't really sizzle till later." She bent her knees and shimmied causing her dress to ripple from the asynchronous response of her different body parts.

"Your husband can hear you sizzle even from your table in the corner." Scott continued her metaphor without commenting on her shimmy.

"Don't mind him. Tonight, I'm on the griddle just for you." Her hard sell became harder. She batted her long, fake lashes at Scott.

"Cool things work best in summer." He swirled his drink causing the ice to spin and resonate on the glass. He sipped to complete his theme. He embellished his comment with a sarcastic grin in honor of his sip of whisky.

"Oh, don't spoil my flirtation Mr. Scott," Mrs. Campion whined.

"You'll ruin my evening." She flashed an equally exaggerated frown.

"Better that than your marriage," scolded Scott.

"My husband isn't the jealous type. A world of flirtations won't harm my marriage." She flung her arm out to encompass her world. "His business occupies him; and lately his shady DC pals more than ever."

Scott perked up at her mention of her husband's associates. "Then you flirt on, but if I'm to play along, I need some info in return," replied Scott.

"How may I help, you lovely man?" She tittered with glee as she pressed on with the newly begun game.

Scott took a long pull on his whisky before beginning. "Your husband's DC pals; would they happen to be staying at the Mayo hotel?"

"Correct!" She made a checkmark in the air. "Two more right answers and you win the grand prize." Mrs. Campion cackled and licked her lips, then she outlined her body with her hands inferring it to be the prize.

"I expect you hear little about that business. Where does he fly for them?"

"He goes to South America sometimes. It could be for them."

"I see. I'll change course. What was your brother's business with Jackie Martin and Mildred Fuller?"

"I told you; I don't know." Disappointment at a lapse in the flirting, teasing game flattened her tone.

"Blackmail maybe?" quizzed Scott.

"It wouldn't surprise me." Clearly irritated at the change of subject, she straightened her posture, abandoning her feline pose. "I don't often speak ill of the dead, but Mildred Fuller would do...did about anything to get ahead. I thought her too vulgar to hate."

"But you don't know specifically what they were up to?" Scott took the opportunity to down the final swallow of his drink.

"No. I had no dealings with that nasty woman." Exasperation filled her voice. "And now she's ruining my time with you."

"No, she's not doing that." Scott could not help a smirk slipping out. He stood and picked up his hat.

"You're not leaving so soon Wyatt?" Surprise and disappointment bled into her tone.

"I am." He separated from his barstool.

"But my dear Mr. Beefcake, what about your grand prize?" She ran the outline of her body again.

"Donate it to charity." Scott nodded to Mrs. Campion, then again in the direction of her husband's table.

CHAPTER 15

THE SPY BUSINESS

Scott strolled the Fifth Street sidewalk from the Tulsa Club toward the Pythian Building and his LaSalle parked in front. After dark, he didn't have to plug the meter for the convenience of downtown parking, and thus give his nickel to the mythical fund the city claimed went to fix the streets, which were never fixed. The flares from the refinery across the river provided the background noise for an otherwise quiet night. No one shared the block with him.

As he passed a dark alley, a stocky man wearing a dark suit despite the heat, popped out from the shadows into the sidewalk light. Surprised and a little startled, Scott recognized him at once. It was Pierce, former OSS lieutenant and Fielding's right-hand man. A face, a memory, a person from Alaska, whom Scott wished to never see. The man and his specter immediately soured Scott's night.

"Pierce!" Scott communicated antipathy in his vocal pitch.

"Scott, steer clear of my work," snarled Pierce. He approached

Scott, not unlike one predator advancing on a rival.

"So, your work includes following me?" The question was almost lost in the silo of contempt in which it resided.

"Don't make me laugh. I've been watching someone that matters." Pierce scrutinized both directions down the street. "Someone that needs watching." He glared at Scott. "You...are street clutter."

Pierce's dark suit was cut too tight against his muscular physique to hide the gun bulge distorting his coat. "You won't find much in Tulsa, but even a nitwit could spot an outsider like you packing a forty-five Colt." Scott fired off his verbal salvo.

Pierce reflexively reached toward his gun. "Bright guy detective, I'm not trying to hide anything. We want the little dog to run to the pack. In the big leagues, we calculate our moves."

"Yeah. I've heard from your master. Big plans by Fielding for this small city," scoffed Scott.

"He has information on the guy, and we'll corner him and force him to give up his red buddies," bragged Pierce.

"Your work fits Fielding. He always thinks he knows more than he does." Scott laughed. "Hell, if he stays to form, he'll ruin some innocent idiot while two commies and a Nazi run rings around you both."

Pierce relaxed his tense guard. He let his arms dangle loose and looked straight into Scott's eyes. "I flat don't get what Fielding sees in you."

"Afraid I'll take your place as Fielding's hatchet-man?" menaced Scott.

Pierce shook his head and added a smirk. "That's not what he wants from you. He's got a wet dream about you analyzing commie shit in four languages and helping him become the top dog in the new spy agency."

"You think I'd do that?" Scott leaned aggressively toward Pierce.

"I think you're a fuck-up sissy who ran home after the war," snarled Pierce. "But then I'm not paid to think."

"That's Fielding's singular, wise choice."

The sarcastic recriminations were served with a plate of cold stares. Neither antagonist budged. Bitterness from Alaska boiled on the hot pavement of Tulsa. A blast from the refinery's flare added its commentary.

Pierce broke from the stare-down to snipe away. "You just stick to your bush-league work for your Indian lawyer. You're out of big-league spying as surely as you're out of baseball."

"Tulsa suits me, Pierce. It beats the hell out of Alaska or DC." Scott's eyes dared Pierce for more.

"Then you better get back to your small-town worries and figure out your Mickey-Mouse Tulsa problem." Pierce walked away from Scott. "I've got business, important business." He walked away down Fifth Street the opposite way Scott needed to go. "I'll see ya' in the funny papers...or the obits." Pierce strolled away looking straight ahead.

* * *

The winter gloom could not be eased by the bare ceiling bulb or the one screwed into the wall above the sink and its mirror. Lieutenant Brock fidgeted with his tie while twisting to improve the aspect of his reflected image. Frost drifted from his breath condensing on the mirror and aggravating the view. Frustrated necktie tying caused Brock to rip the faulty knot into two straight strands of cloth. He stared down the two chevron ends in his hands. Captain Wyatt Scott stood in the doorway patiently watching the process even as frost slipped out of his nostrils with every breath.

Brock's moving, dodging, and twisting to view himself brought Scott's image into his line of sight. "Can't get this damn tie with my frozen fingers!" he yelled at Scott. Brock blew on his fingers and shook them. The exasperated actions did not improve the pallor of his digits or the scowl he presented in the mirror.

"You look dandy without the tie. No need to be perfect for California brass – they don't have any sway." Scott stepped into the small barracks room.

"Fielding gives us the evil eye when we're not sharp in front of visitors," argued Brock with a little concern in his voice.

"He likes to flaunt those birds on his collar. It's all about a show when brass meets brass. Fuck'em. Guys with a couple of bars like I have or a single bar like you are expected to get things done and lead men. Full-bird colonels are politicians in khaki." Scott emphasized his statement by tapping his captain's bars.

"I suppose you're right. But Pierce snarls at me like he'll crack my skull." Brock swatted his head with an imaginary club.

"That dumb shit exists to keep Fielding from having to get dirty. Not a thing he does is important to the mission." Scott hacked some snot down from his sinuses. He swallowed not wanting to foul Brock's floor. "Ehh, I just swallowed something more valuable than Pierce."

Brock looked at Scott with his schoolboy eyes. "You outrank Pierce, so it's easier for you to ignore him." His frustration with his fellow soldier and his tie boiled over. Brock pulled the tie from around his neck and threw it on the sink.

Scott moved closer to Brock. "Don't let him worry you." He feathered his tone to be avuncular. "Pierce's just Fielding's yes-man and lackey to worry the enlisted guys. I have no idea if his bite is worse than his bark, but I do know Fielding wants us to crack the codes more than he wants to keep military protocol." Scott crossed his arms and leaned against the wall and door frame. "Just keep up your cipher work. If the turd bothers you, let me know. I not only outrank him, I'm bigger and I'll bury his pug-mug in a snowdrift."

"Wyatt, I am glad to have you around." Brock broke half a smile before he lost it. "This cold, dark hole is miserable enough without a bully."

"Army rules or Pierce's snarl don't mean shit as long as we make progress on Fielding's projects. He needs both of us for him to look good to Bill Donovan and the other brass in Washington," reassured Scott.

"On that subject, I've got a notion on the Russian puzzle." Brock's eyes twinkled. "I plan to gather up some old traffic and test my idea on it. If I get a fit, I'll have something worth more than Stalin's nuts." A tiny smirk crept out of the corner of the young lieutenant's mouth.

Scott noted the change of expression. "You're smarter with puzzles than any of us, but don't get carried away trying to win the next war till we get our butts out of this one." Scott's cynicism had become as cold and bitter as the weather.

"It's a pip of an idea, Wyatt. I'm looking to make an assumption on the spy notion, plug it in, then see if the fit makes sense in the older messages..." He let his sentence trail off. He picked back up with the notion he wanted to convey. "I'd need your help with some of the Russian idioms, but if I get to first base, I'll tell you. I might ask Harris for help too."

"I have confidence in you, but it won't matter. If you make a breakthrough, we'll get stuck working on more of it while Fielding gets promoted out of here." Scott shoved off the wall and dropped his arms. "Save your energy for drinking or shooting pool."

"You're too cynical." Brock touched the tie but left it curled in the sink. "The Russians only like us for killing Germans with them and keeping the Japs out of their backyard."

"Oh?" Scott smirked. "I'm cynical all right. But you, my young genius, are naive. Fielding is working us for his benefit; Russians, Japs, Germans, or neutral Swiss be damned."

"I still think the Russians are worrisome." Brock sighed. "And I'd blow a lot of energy to get out of this iceberg if that's what it takes."

"Got a point there." Scott spread his arms toward Brock. "Get me outa' here, and I'm yours for life." He puckered and kissed at Brock.

Brock laughed. "Wyatt, you're likely to remain your own man. What I'm looking at is a long shot coming down the stretch ten lengths behind. Unfortunately, improving our chances to leave this ball freezer, Russians, or no Russians, is unlikely as long as the Japs don't give up." Brock grabbed the thin chain to the bulb above the sink and yanked the light off.

Scott surveyed his younger friend. "You look fine with no tie. But grab your hat, Lieutenant. You don't want to make the visiting brass jealous of your fine head of hair."

Brock picked up his hat from the corner of his bed. He fit it smartly and militarily correct over his thick hair. He winked at Scott.

Scott nodded back. "That'll do nicely. The bald heads from California won't feel so inadequate around you now."

* * *

A matronly secretary with a bun hairdo escorted Scott through the oversized, double doors into the plush office of Albert Campion. The open curtains allowed sunlight to be thrown across the expansive room. The view from the fifteenth floor of the art deco Adams Building looked down on Boston Avenue and west across the city toward the Arkansas River. Two couches, a half-dozen leather chairs, coffee tables, end tables with lamps, floor lamps, and mahogany paneling with bookshelves decorated the capacious room. Against one wall of wainscoting and marble, a wet bar with dozens of bottles of liquor sat in defiance of the state prohibition laws, and brazenly completed the opulent chamber.

Albert Campion looked up from his massive wooden desk. He smiled as Scott approached but did not rise. Gray flecks showed in his hair despite impeccable barbering and attempts at tinting. His custom, pinstriped suit fit perfectly covering his middle-age paunch. He gestured with his chubby hands and perfect manicure for Scott to sit in one of the chairs fronting his desk.

"Please, have a seat, Mr. Scott."

Scott passed by the first leather chair to sit in the second. Whether the gesture signified anything to Campion or not, his expression did not flicker. Scott settled in, noting that the chair felt softer than the leather looked. He focused on Campion, who had waited to make his next comment.

"Your arrival at my office is providential. I was about to seek your services," proclaimed the air shipping mogul.

Scott eyed Campion. He sought Campion to ask about his brother-in-law, but Campion having heard of Scott and being interested in him twisted the conversation such that he felt compelled to confirm a suspicion. "And your DC friends are okay with you hiring me to help you?" asked Scott with a sardonic lilt.

"Perceptive." Campion pursed his lips. "I heard you are perceptive. Still, I run my own affairs regardless of my business associates." He clasped his hands together on top of his desk.

Other than acknowledging Scott's awareness of Fielding, the cargo tycoon divulged nothing helpful on that score. Wyatt pushed on with his initial purpose. "So, is this affair of *yours* about your brother-in-law?" Scott wanted to set the agenda and speed of the game even though he occupied the visitors' dugout.

"Why...yes." Campion swiveled his chair and leaned his elbows on the desk. "And while I have little faith in Jenk Jones or the Tribune being able to sniff out a cow patty in a rose garden, I worry that Waldo might incite newspaper gossip." Finished, Campion sat straight in his chair.

"At some point, he'll have more trouble than newspaper gossip." Scott jumped to the theme. "Is he blackmailing you too?"

Campion drew back. He studied Scott. He ran his tongue across his top lip but ignored its mate. "No, he is not blackmailing me." Campion bent forward. "Is that his latest conniving scheme?"

"It seems to be." Scott wasn't sure if Campion was unaware of his brother-in-law's felonious dealings or merely being coy.

Mollified with the news, nefarious as it might be, Campion reached for the mahogany cigar case on his desk. He lifted the lid and grasped one. Apparently changing his mind, he dropped it in its row and closed the lid. He took a breath and swiveled in his large desk chair. Scott continued to form his sense of Campion and tried to avoid letting the man's wife color his view. The corpulent man did not sweat nor show signs of stress. Scott sat still watching Campion consider his next words.

"To be frank, I don't give a tinker's damn about Waldo," admitted Campion. "I'd just like to get him out of town before he causes me trouble."

Scott stood. He mulled Campion's comment. He took a hike about the vast office, twirling his hat with his pitching hand. He glanced out the window, surveying the bird's-eye view of his home city. He wandered farther taking in the bar and the expensive liquor brands. Campion watched Scott's sojourn around the office without comment or expression. Other than his eye movement, he barely budged.

"While I don't refuse many jobs, I think I already have a client in your end of the swimming pool." Scott's meandering reestablished him at the chair in front of the desk, but he stood behind it rather than taking a seat. He switched his hat to his left hand, which he counted as his glove side and thus freed his pitching hand – nowadays for his nineteen-eleven rather than a baseball.

"How about you get Waldo out of town before he can harm me or your client?" offered Campion taking a new course to avoid being rejected. Unreservedly proving his insistence, he reached inside his coat and produced a single bill. He stretched his arm, bill in hand, toward Scott.

"Five hundred and no infringement on your client." He looked directly at Scott with the bill grasped between his fat thumb and fat finger. "The amount is enough, I trust?" he added with politeness rather than condescension.

Scott scanned the man's countenance, his eyes, his outstretched hand for any sign of subterfuge. More practiced than most professional card players, he determined Albert Campion to be genuine in his offer. Scott stepped between the chairs and took the bill. "Excessive, but in honor of President McKinley, I accept." He folded the bill and slipped it into his pocket.

"I leave the matter in your professional hands." Campion waved his hand across his desk adding his blessing to the proceedings.

"Then I will encourage Waldo away from Tulsa and any contact with my client," affirmed Scott.

"Fine." Campion concluded the transaction by opening his cigar box once more.

Scott slid past the chair he originally ignored to the edge of Campion's desk. "May I borrow your phone?"

"Be my guest." Campion pushed the black phone to Scott before plucking a fresh cigar from his box. He ran the finely, rolled smoke under his nose. A voluminous inhale and a sigh of satisfaction signaled his appreciation of the unlit tobacco aroma.

Scott aligned the phone toward his body. He withdrew a card with a phone number scratched on it. Having added another commission to his burdens with this obligation to push Sleener out of town, Scott felt the need to complete some previously booked business. He picked up the receiver and dialed the requisite five numbers to reach his party.

CHAPTER 16

HOT DOGS AND PAYOFFS

Crist Economou's Coney Islander hot wiener restaurant was founded in Tulsa in 1926, just two years after the chili covered concoction had been invented at the New York amusement park from which it drew its name. It sold a quick lunch for those on the run or for those who loved the creation. The place served steamed hot dogs with any combination of chili, mustard, relish, and onions that spoke to the patron's palate. The coneys cost a nickel a piece and to wash them down, Cokes, root beer or, for the adventuresome, grape soda could also be had for a nickel. The place thrived as a favorite for families, workers, secretaries, and even businessmen. It happened to be Bugler's favorite too.

Toward the end of the long, narrow strip of the establishment's space, Scott sat next to Bugler in one of nine, one-piece, school desks arrayed along the wall opposite the grill. They served as the only tables and seating that fit the constricted shop. Other diners occupied the remaining seven desks. A woman and a child waited impatiently for some desks to be freed for their use. Two other patrons left with their paper bags full of coneys to go as the proprietor manned his cash register.

Bugler's desktop counted two empty pop bottles and the chewed end of his final hot dog lying on a napkin. Scott's desk bore only a Coke, while his suit coat hung on the chairback. The steaming process used to cook the hot dogs accentuated the summer heat. Even with the overhead fan spinning away, the place felt like a Turkish bathhouse in equatorial Brazil. Scott tended to his half-full, soft drink bottle with little enthusiasm as he listened to Bugler detail his latest adventures.

"So, after that, I took the trolley. Didn't run all the way ta' Sand Springs though. I jus' looped round downtown is all. I like the Sand Springs Line and all, but she costs another dime." Bugler ran into his next story without missing a beat. "And then I saw the four o'clock pichur' show at the Rialto. Dick Powell was a gumshoe like you."

"I'm bigger," interjected Scott.

"Yep. And smarter too. He kept gettin' hit on the noggin 'cause he wouldn't look out," confirmed Bugler.

"Movie detectives don't stop to think much," observed Scott.

"Nope." Bugler agreed. "He got inta' one scrape after another till he got out of 'em near the end of the pichur' show."

"But the movie guys always seem to have pretty looking skirts chasing after them," lamented Scott.

"Yeah, ol' Dick Powell had him one." Bugler snapped to attention in his chair. There wasn't a light bulb floating over him, but his face glowed almost as bright. "Say, that itched my noggin. After the trolley, I saw that looker."

"Looker?" Keeping up with Bugler idioms might require a separate dictionary of its own. Yet, Scott understanding him better than others, gathered that the term meant a pretty woman. Beyond that, Bugler's specificity lost him.

"The one I told ya' 'bout; went inta' Johnny's the other day." A clear explanation as far as Bugler was concerned. "The looker."

"Ruth Brown?" solicited Scott.

"Don't know'er name. Besides bein' at ol' grumpy Johnny's office, she went in the bank and rode that X-calator."

Bugler's memory path twisted, turned, and doubled back more often than a bootlegger on a country road. It was also prone to getting lost down blind alleys and outdated memory lanes. Scott spun a little more toward Bugler to watch for clues as well as listen. "Okay. Go on."

Bugler hopped right into his story like he never stopped. "She gimme' lunch money, but I think it was ta' get shed of me."

Scott could not resist the opening for some good-natured ribbing. "A young skirt gave you the brushoff? Say it ain't so."

"Smart-ass." Bugler gave Scott the evil eye before he continued. "She give me fifty cents. She started at a quarter, but I mentioned that X-calator and she upped to a half-dollar."

"I guess she worried about you having an escalator story brewing up and she figured it was worth another quarter to skip it." Scott poured it on his old buddy.

Scott's ribbing passed by Bugler like a fastball by a blind man. "Got no stories." Seriousness with a twinge of fear fell into Bugler's tone. "That thing worries me sure enough." A sudden memory shifted his look to pensive. "Not her though. That gal jumped right on them movin' steps like the other day when she never looked down and just jabbered away with that dead woman all the way ta' the top."

Scott flinched at hearing the strange news. "What dead woman?"

"The ballpark one."

"Mildred Fuller?" Scott exclaimed more than asked.

Bugler wrinkled his brow. "Mildred sounds like her. But you know who. We run outa' the game early to chase down her boyfriend at your drinkin' club."

Stunned by the odd coincidence, Scott pressed Bugler. "So, you saw Ruth Brown, I mean the looker, talk to the dead woman on the escalator at The National Bank of Tulsa?"

"Yep, all the way up the thing clear ta' where them steps just melt inta' the floor." Bugler appeared to be watching the escalator steps rotate through their cycle and replaying its mystery in his mind.

"When?" Scott moved to clarify this latest information.

"Fore she was dead," answered Bugler without guile.

"Okay. Were the Oilers in town?" Scott went to a time measurement he knew suited Bugler.

"Naw. On the road, Fort Worth. Forgot who pitched, but we lost. Think the guys made a bushel basket full a' errors ta' give'em the runs. Hittin' figured weak too."

Scott took a moment to think and consider. "Weekend series. So, it must've been last Friday." He met Bugler eye-to-eye. "And you're sure the woman on the escalator with Mildred Fuller was Ruth Brown, the looker, you saw at Johnny's office?"

"Yep. It was the looker. Them's not a dime a dozen," proclaimed Bugler.

* * *

Scott leaned against his LaSalle waiting for the appointment he made from Campion's phone. His convertible occupied a lonely corner of the Tulsa Fairgrounds, an obscure, loading area near the animal barns. It saw plenty of action the first week of October during the Tulsa State Fair, but in June, even the pigeons located statelier retreats. Its lack of prying eyes fixed it as today's meeting place. Bugler's revelation occupied at least half his mind, but this rendezvous followed a different purpose.

A little cloud of dust blowing past the side of a show barn presaged a vehicle. A moment later, Mrs. Folger's new Lincoln Continental rounded the barn and stopped parallel to the LaSalle, but remaining several feet distant. She wore another new and different ensemble of seasonal clothes, including a summer hat, but continued with her usual, large sunglasses.

"Mrs. Folger." Scott nodded to her without moving.

Folger looked around before she exited her car. She left the door open and the motor running. Carrying an envelope in one of her gloved hands and no purse, Folger continued to scrutinize the deserted parking area. She stopped short of Scott, too far to hand the envelope.

"Where and when is the meeting?" he asked, disavowing any small talk as clearly irrelevant.

"Union Depot at ten tonight. You're to meet outside where the bags and boxes are kept. I don't know where it is, but I expect you do." Her condescending tone persisted even as her situation appeared more urgent.

"I do. So, he hands over the book for that envelope?"

"Yes." She took a step toward Scott closing the gap between them.

"Does he know I am the one meeting him and not you?"

"He does. I told him I was afraid of being recognized. He didn't like it at first, but he consented when I offered him more money." Folger raised her hand and extended the presumed packet of cash toward Scott.

He pushed off the LaSalle's fender and took two steps to accept the envelope. He felt its bulge and slight heft. He held it examining its contents. Scott stared at Folger; whose eyes remained hidden by the dark glasses. The summer wind ruffled her dress and hat, but she stood fast. Her posture presented calm if not supplementary arrogance.

As the silence grew, she brought her gloved hands together. "I just want the book." Her pitch raised with her plea. "I'll give you another four hundred dollars to get it from him."

"More than fair for a simple exchange." Scott stared at the opaque lenses. His eyes did not relent. "Is that it? He gave no further instructions?"

"No. You trade the money for the goddamn book. The end." Her temper dropped her tone to its normal, low registry. Tension registered in her jaw.

"And it will be a simple exchange." Scott let the statement dangle as the question he meant it to be.

"Yes. That is all," claimed the socialite.

"Then that's what I'll do." Scott stepped away and returned to his convertible. He slid the payment packet into his coat pocket.

"Don't screw it up," added Mrs. Folger. She stood stiff and defiant to both Scott and the afternoon sun.

"Goodbye, Mrs. Folger."

Scott opened the LaSalle's door and slid behind the wheel. Without acknowledging her again, he started the car and drove off. In his mirror, through the red dirt haze thrown up by his tires, he saw Folger standing implacably. This time, she didn't seem to be worried about being seen.

CHAPTER 17

RUTH BROWN

Scott pushed the doorbell button as he waited on the porch of Ruth Brown's mansion. His day had been full as expected, but information and implication accelerated it to hectic. He pushed the bell again as he imagined the maid, Sadie, ambling to the door from some distant recess of the stately domicile. The door opened. Ruth Brown stood there wearing a flowered dress in bright white and yellow. She also wore bewilderment in her eyes.

"Miss Brown." Similar surprise caught Scott. It slipped into his address. "I'm sorry...sorry to bother you at home."

"Mr. Scott." Her quizzical look remained. "You could have called about our date. It would have been perfectly acceptable."

"Yes. You can tell me about that, but I'd like to talk about some other things as well if you don't mind."

Ruth stepped outside closing the door behind her. She offered a hand gesture toward the outdoor chairs stationed on the porch. Scott sat as directed. Ruth sat as well folding her hands on her lap, primly, shyly, and decorously.

"I hope you don't mind talking on the porch. Sadie is off, and I hesitate to entertain gentlemen when I am alone," explained Ruth. On the porch, outside of her grandmother's mansion and its ostentatious displays of wealth, the young woman appeared artless if not out-and-out naive.

"A very reasonable option. I understand and don't mind at all." Scott reassured her with a smile.

"Thank you for understanding." She bowed her head as demurely as a postulant prior to her vow.

Scott took her reaction as his signal to begin asking questions. "Did you know Jackie Martin? He was a B.I.A. agent for the Osage."

"No. Mr. Grayhawk mentioned his name regarding the missing papers."

"How about Waldo Sleener?"

"Who?" Miss Brown gaped at Scott as if he had rattled off a string of Japanese or Russian pornographic idioms.

"Waldo Sleener," repeated Scott.

"I've never heard of him. Did he have something to do with my grandmother?" Perplexed eyes and a blank look stared at Scott.

"Probably not. Just one of those loose ends." Convinced she did not know the last living blackmailer, he moved on. "Did you happen to meet a woman named Mildred Fuller?"

"Not that I recall." Ruth Brown squinted then shook her head.

"Did any strange women approach you in the past couple of weeks?" Scott pressed the subject.

"No." Annoyance crept into Ruth Brown's utterance. "And it's not my habit to converse with strangers." She had been quite patient, but it seemed to be waning. "How does any of this help?"

"Just trying to make everything smooth on your inheritance," lied Scott with a poker face.

"Yes, I hope so." Ruth Brown took a breath signaling her change of subject. "About tomorrow evening, there is no sense in coming early with me. As a Junior Miss, my function is to receive dignitaries prior to the commencement of the actual ball. I won't be free until after nine."

"Nine it is," confirmed Scott as he accepted the change of subject for the moment.

"Wonderful. It's settled then. Please meet me in the ballroom at nine." She clasped her hands on the armrests of the wicker chair.

"I shall see you at the Mayo ballroom." Scott stood.

Miss Brown stood in response. She offered another of her diffident smiles. Her debutante youth fit neither the mansion she now owned, nor the suspicion Scott harbored.

Scott paused on the top step. He addressed her from there. "You know, I liked the photo of your grandmother and her friend. Did Agnes ever visit?"

Ruth Brown lost her smile. "Agnes was my *grandmother's* name." Her emphasis was harsh. "Her friend was Drucilla," added Ruth with a lightened tone.

"Oh, pardon me. I just know her as Mrs. Belcher." Scott covered his intention with both his tone and his phrasing.

Ruth rubbed her hand over her eyelids. She dropped her gaze. Her emotion and her distress seemed genuine as the moisture seeping over her lower lashes verified.

"I'm sorry for bringing up sad thoughts," apologized Scott.

Ruth drew in a deep breath and shook her hair. "I'm just so alone. Without grandmother, things overwhelm me."

"Again, I'm sorry. Thank you for your help, Miss Brown." Scott stepped away to descend the steps. He heard Ruth Brown sniffle. Nothing would be gained by another round of tears and sympathy, so he trooped on without risking additional interaction.

As he strolled to the circular drive, a notion came to him which might allay or confirm his suspicion. He finished the trip to his parked LaSalle. He drove out of the long drive and wheeled away. Down the road and out of sight, Scott parked his Caddy. He climbed out of it and jogged to Ruth Brown's estate. He made his way furtively through trees and bushes along the concrete entrance before he veered away from the curve of the driveway pavement to the garage.

Scott slipped in the unlocked side door of the multi-car garage. Light from the doorway bathed Miss Brown's new, nineteen forty-eight sedan. The huge, prewar touring car beside it had to be that of the late Mrs. Belcher. Scott ignored the touring car in favor of the new sedan.

He bent to examine the nearest tire. Wedged in the treads, foreign fragments required keener examination. Scott produced his pocketknife. He squatted beside the tire. Holding himself steady with his left palm on the tire, he used his pitching hand to jiggle the knife blade into the tread. With it, he pried free a shard of trapped debris. Scott briefly examined the fragment. It was shell. He dug out a second segment, then closed his knife. He dropped it, along with the two sample slivers, into his coat pocket.

Scott stood. He took note of another tire, which had the same telltale pieces in the treads. He moved to the door. Taking care to look toward the house with a chary eye, he slipped out of the door and closed it. He retraced his steps along his previous bush and tree covered route. He needed to talk to Johnny Grayhawk.

* * *

Evie sat at her desk deciding whether to sort the unimportant mail or sneak a peek at the gossip magazine hidden in her lower drawer. Before a decision could be occasioned, the phone rang. She stared it down for its impudence but reached to answer it after the second insistent ring forced her hand.

"Grayhawk Law Offices," she stated politely and professionally.

The voice on the other end came as a shock, but it was unmistakable to Evie. "Dolly, sorry I got tough the other day. But now I need to talk to Scott."

"How did you get this number?!" Evie exclaimed more than asked.

"You told me your law office job. I got a phone book; simple enough," explained the voice that once threatened Evie.

Indignant at his nerve to call, Evie laid into him. "Look creep, Scott knows who you are, and he's booked a room for you at St. John's. And you'll need it for a while after he gets through with you!"

"Don't get edgy. I'm not lookin' for trouble with any of you," pleaded a conciliatory sounding Sleener. "There's stuff he needs to know. Things I need to tell him." His voice cracked with urgency.

Unwilling to believe him, Evie tested the miscreant. "Yodel me your sad song, and I'll pass it along."

"No dice. It's gotta' be direct to Scott. Tell him things are cockeyed, screwy...cops can't do any good; only him." Fear mingled with his insistence.

Evie pulled the phone from her ear. She looked at it as if to try and see the caller through the receiver and discern if the repentant fellow truly was the man who threatened her in Wyatt's office. "He's not around." Evie began to accept his earnestness. "You got a number? I can have him ring you, I guess."

"Not so's I can wait. I'll get him later," sighed Sleener. "Tell him it's important." After a pause, he amplified, "*Real* important."

Another distinct pause ensued. No words came through, no breathing, no sound. Finally, Evie heard the phone click. Once more, she took the receiver from her ear and stared at it. It spoke no more. She wondered if she should hustle to get Scott right then. She eased the receiver onto the cradle. Nothing could be done; no phone number; no address – it could keep. Interrupting without specifics seemed a poor plan at any time, and worse at this moment. She knew when Scott and Johnny played catch, serious matters were at hand.

* * *

In the brick-paved alley behind the Pythian Building, the late afternoon heat had been slightly abated by the shadows of the nearby buildings. Johnny Grayhawk and Wyatt Scott punched the worn leather of their baseball mitts. Still dressed in their business clothes, suit pants, dress shirts, polished shoes, and neckties, the two longtime friends stretched the gap between them to toss a baseball. Scott loosened his tie. Johnny kept his knot intact. Johnny owned the ball to start. He flipped it leisurely to Scott.

"The last time we played catch was after Janet moved to California. Before that it was when you told me about Alaska," Johnny reminded Wyatt about the events leading to their alley-throwing ritual.

Scott appreciated why Johnny mentioned their ball-tossing history. He posited it to find the reason Wyatt came into his office, glove in hand, and commanded the game despite the hot afternoon. He had insisted they play catch that very minute. Johnny recognized the seriousness of their ritual. It far exceeded two former batterymates reliving their high school days by tossing an old baseball back and forth.

Scott caught the ball in his mitt. He examined it residing blithely in the leather pocket. A couple of scuffs showed on the white horsehide, but the seams remained pristine. The red stitching didn't appear thirteen years old, but as he had learned appearances are not truth.

"So, what's up?" Johnny asked without the circumspect expression common to those of his profession.

Scott pounded the ball into his glove before he tossed it to Johnny with a little speed. He had been wondering what to say to him; how to explain what he stumbled into. Finally, he answered Johnny's question bluntly. "Ruth Brown killed Mildred Fuller and Jackie Martin."

Johnny snagged the ball with just his glove hand. "Impossible! Martin killed Fuller and committed suicide." Johnny snap-threw the ball like a catcher's peg to second base. His muscle memory from nineteen thirty-three apparently found all the right steps.

Scott's mitt popped from the game-like velocity. He believed he should speak frankly with sagacity to his oldest and closest friend. "It was murder, Johnny." Scott didn't wind up but pivoted his shoulders and put a little mustard on this throw to Johnny.

"The kid's had problems. She's a little odd, but..." Johnny trailed off. He looked the ball into his glove. He pulled his hand free holding his glove in his armpit. He rubbed the ball belligerently with his bare palms. "What proof is there?" He slid his left hand inside the leather glove and pegged the ball to Scott with equal steam to that which he received.

Scott made the catch before folding the glove around the ball with his right hand. "Ruth Brown told me she had never seen Martin or Fuller. A witness saw her with Mildred Fuller the Friday before the murder." He took up a stretch and made an authentic pitch, a two-seam fastball. His muscles too remembered the process.

Johnny made the catch crouching a little as catchers are inclined to do. He held the ball waiting for convincing details.

"As for Martin, I found lake shell chips stuck in Ruth Brown's tires. A rarity even at the lake," detailed Scott. He stood ready for a throw from Johnny, which did not come.

"What motive would she have?" Johnny continued to hold the ball. The gravity of the indictment required complete attention to Scott's revelation.

"Jackie Martin must have seen something in the B.I.A. records indicating Mrs. Belcher was 'Drucilla' and not Agnes Killingbear. But it took Mildred Fuller's blackmail expertise to move them forward." Scott elucidated the plot to Johnny.

"Who's Drucilla? And without seeing those missing B.I.A. records, why on earth would you think Agnes Killingbear is not Agnes Killingbear?" Johnny threw the ball, mostly with a flick of his wrist, continuing his reversion to being a catcher.

Scott caught it in the webbing. "When I took Evie to Ruth Brown's, I saw an old photo of young Mrs. Belcher with her friend, Drucilla. On the back, the notation said, 'Agnes and me, Nineteen-oh-seven.' Why would Agnes have a picture saying, 'Agnes and me?' It should have been 'Drucilla and me.' Scott toed an imaginary pitcher's rubber. He ground the ball into his mitt.

"I just can't believe it. I'll go to Pawhuska tomorrow and see what I can find in the tribal records." Johnny watched his high school battery-mate prepare to pitch.

Scott wound up and snapped off what the post-war jargon had come to call a 'slider.'

After making the catch, Johnny pulled off his glove with the ball still in it. "This is really hard to believe. I'll check because it's you telling me, but it's damn hard to believe." He stood for several seconds staring at the bundle of glove and ball before walking toward the street.

Scott took the cue and followed.

Johnny called to Wyatt without turning, "You'll ruin your elbow again throwing that damn nickel curve."

CHAPTER 18

Sleener Trouble

Scott ducked into his office to leave his glove. He dropped it in his middle, left-hand drawer where it had rested for over a year. As he shoved the drawer closed, he looked up to see Evie Hall stroll through the doorway. Her measured pace eventually drew her near the desk and beside the guest chair.

"The Campion Cargo creep called and said he really needed to talk to you," she blurted out, skipping any greeting or preamble.

"He's supposed to meet me tonight. Did he say why he was calling now or what was so urgent?"

"No." Evie twisted the chair skewing it from facing the desk to a partial profile. "I'm surprised you're meeting him." She eased into the chair and crossed her legs such that the top one displayed itself from the knee to the ankle. "For what it's worth, he sounded worried, no tough guy yak this time." Her tone softened. "He didn't leave a number or a message, though. Claimed he'd only talk to you." Before looking Wyatt in the eye, she peeked down at her legs making a tiny adjustment to her outfit to display full calves and a flare of thigh.

Her skirt fine-tuning and her flaunted legs went unnoticed by Scott. He shoved a pile of papers to the side of his desk before he looked up to reply. "If he calls you again, get me. Otherwise, I guess he'll tell me tonight."

"Sure. If he calls, I'll get you." Evie stood. She dawdled a moment presumably looking for a longer exchange. When Scott ignored her to open a drawer, she took the hint and left.

* * *

The downtown air in summer always seemed thicker. Around Tulsa's Union Depot, it felt thicker still. The terminal building teemed with travelers and well-wishers seeing them off eastbound and westbound. Lingering arrivals from Kansas City added to the general babble. The southside street entrance maintained incoming streams for the trains and outgoing flows for the cab queue. On the train departure side to the north, porters toted bags out to the platform, while their colleagues wheeled carts of luggage into the depot.

Scott strode along the platform, passing the caboose of a loading train. The static rumble of idle engines mixed with footsteps and pushcart wheels rolling on the platform. As he moved beyond the depot building, the trickle of passengers dwindled to none. A porter passed him, while two cargo loaders moved into the darkness where trucks took boxes and crates for delivery to small towns near Tulsa. He ventured toward the end of the platform and peered into the dim and diffuse light of the storage area.

Fragmentary luminosity etched the stacked boxes and luggage. They stood both tall and short, with edges rough and ill-defined. Scott journeyed into the shadowy labyrinth of waiting cargo. The depot clamor faded as he circled through the lanes that separated stacked goods. His eyes adjusted as his irises flexed wide to their limits. Gray and black ascended as color fell away. A sharp train whistle warned of imminent departure. It was nine-thirty. Scott surmised that scouting the meeting point a half-hour early would be sufficient to prevent surprises. As he circled a corner of stacked crates, he realized differently. Scott confronted the crumpled figure of a man. From Evie's previous description, Scott presumed it to be Waldo Sleener.

Sleener's evening ensemble consisted of scuffed brown shoes, work pants, and a blood-soaked shirt with a hole in the chest. Scott squatted and rummaged through the dead man's pockets, finding a sap and a switchblade. He rolled him on his side where a larger hole in his back testified to the bullet's hefty caliber. His rear pockets were flat, devoid of wallet or blackmail book. Scott eased him down to his death repose. Scott stood. He took a step away and analyzed the scene. The body remained warm. Undoubtedly, the murder happened recently, although not in the last couple of minutes when Scott would have heard the shot. Sleener arrived early and so did someone else.

A gunshot rang out. Its projectile caused flying crate fragments to zip by Scott's ear. The bullet struck far too near him to be accidental. He hit the deck. A quiet moment passed before caution gave way to action. Scott drew his Colt and rushed forward toward the trains and the direction of the shot's report. He sprinted through the stored cargo to emerge on the shadowy end of the platform.

A figure near the caboose fired a handgun into the darkness at an unseen target away from Scott and down the tracks. Scott decelerated to a brisk walk. He saw no return fire from the blackness and nothing else, for that matter, in the void into which the tracks melted. He approached the shooter keeping his forty-five trained on him. The man came into view. Pierce, gun in hand, glared at Scott.

Uncertain about all that had transpired, Scott shouted his conjecture as a question to Pierce. "Did you shoot Sleener?"

"Who the hell is Sleener?" barked Pierce.

Scott used his gun barrel as a pointer toward the dark stack of cargo. "The body over there in the freight and luggage."

Pierce glanced briefly at the shadowed baggage area before replying to Scott. "I shot at whoever took the potshot at you." He nodded down the tracks into the darkness. "I don't know what the hell you're into, but it seems to be rubbing up against my work." Pierce looked beyond Scott toward the platform and the depot building. His head jerked up. He stashed his gun in the holster under his coat. "Cops coming. Scott, I wasn't here. Got it?" Without explanation or another word, Pierce dashed behind the train and disappeared across the parallel tracks into the darkness north of the station.

Scott spun to see two uniformed policemen charging toward him. He raised his gun hand and its empty mate above his head as a pair of staccato whistle blasts announced the train's departure. The cops remained on the platform with their revolvers trained on Scott. Whining, metal couplers pulled taut, jerking the cars into line before the wheels of the caboose grated on the steel tracks. The yellow light cast from the top of the caboose gradually dimmed on his face and body as the two cops signaled Scott to come join them. He complied as best he could with both hands still raised.

* * *

In an otherwise empty corner of the passenger lounge, Detective Art Cleveland sat beside Wyatt Scott. The depot clock had spun past midnight, and the comfort of the wooden benches had not improved. A uniformed officer and another plainclothesman, whom Scott didn't know, stood a few chair rows away watching the waiting passengers. The thin group of remaining travelers no longer gawked at the police detective and his detainee. Uncertainty colored Cleveland's face. Exasperation painted Scott's.

"How many innings do we have to play with no score? I've told you I found him dead," explained Scott for what he knew to be more than the sixth time.

"I know." Cleveland's own frustration popped out. "Just tell me why you were here meeting this Sleener guy."

"Again, I can't Art. It's still a case. I can't divulge the client, and the reason has to do with my client."

"That's not gonna' wash when things get to the DA," warned Cleveland.

"You checked my gun. You know it wasn't fired. I didn't kill Sleener." Scott threw his hands up before dropping them to his sides. "It's pretty clear I'm your best witness and I didn't see it happen."

"You met him," countered Detective Cleveland.

"After he was dead." Scott sighed again from exasperation. "As I told you, I only knew it was him from the description Evie gave me and his two weapons. I never met the guy."

"Never?" questioned Cleveland.

"Never!" Scott rubbed his neck and felt his head. "I'll say he met *me* that night at Mildred Fuller's house."

Cleveland shoved his hands in his coat pockets. He shuffled one way then the other in front of Scott. "Wyatt, this is murder. Another murder you're in the middle of."

"Tangled group of folks. I'm not sure which ones are playing where, but several things are in play." Scott spread his arms with vexation. "Art, if I knew what direction to look, I'd put you on it."

"Muddy mess. If I get bupkis from you, Morgan will blow a gasket," declared Cleveland.

"Art, I know some of it with certainty. I have a notion about the rest. I need to work out a few details to wrap it up."

"Good. Then just tell me what you know, and we'll both be satisfied." Cleveland pulled his hands out of his pockets and fitted them to his hips like a frustrated schoolteacher.

"Loose ends, Art. Loose ends. Meet me tomorrow night at the charity ball in the Mayo," entreated Scott.

"Charity ball?" The transplanted New Yorker shook his head. "Not my spot. I don't know many folks in Tulsa. Certainly not any of the society, rich types like you know."

"It's not really my kind of function either. I got roped into it through Johnny Grayhawk." He stared at Cleveland. "There's something which certainly bears on the Martin and Fuller case. It may even lead somewhere on Sleener."

"Still working the murders that I don't need you reopening," groused Cleveland.

"I'm certain the guilty party will be in attendance. I even think a confession is likely. That's why I need you there."

Cleveland looked toward his milling officers. "I suppose I'll make it if you think it's worth it." He ran a hand through his hair before folding his hands across his chest.

"I'm hoping things will break clean and clear for us all, Art."

"They better," warned the detective. He shifted around looking at Scott then the clock.

"Can I go?" lobbied Scott.

CHAPTER 19

IDENTITY

Johnny Grayhawk was aware of Mrs. Belcher's upbringing in an Oklahoma City area orphanage. Grayhawk knew of her close friendship with another orphan, Drucilla Ward, who died shortly after statehood. He never considered anything but the obvious friendship of two young girls until Scott tossed his bomb-blast theory whereby Agnes Killingbear Belcher was in truth Drucilla Ward. The word of anyone other than Wyatt Scott could not have sent him on this errand of identity proof.

As a lawyer, trusting legal documents seemed the proper plan to follow. As an Osage, Johnny determined to start with an elder who might know more than any piece of paper. He pulled up to the tiny wooden house that sat on the original reservation settlement. The porch faced southeast not respecting the white man's proclivity toward cardinal compass directions over ordinal ones. On the clean, covered porch, George Tosie watched him approach.

George amused himself by watching the world go by and telling stories to the young boys about life before oil and white men ruined things for the Osage. After World War One, he detailed to the B.I.A. about the murders of Osages for their land and oil headrights. He got nowhere since half the B.I.A. were active participants in the conspiracies or bribed to overlook them. He would know who stole what and who deserved their rights if anyone did.

"Hi ho, lawyer," called the thin, wrinkled man.

"Hello, George," replied Johnny. "I came to pick your brain about the past."

"I remember you went to Central High in Tulsa and not Indian school." The old man remarked on Grayhawk's history.

Never sure when George teased or mocked, Johnny just smiled. "I did. Went to college too."

"Yessir. You probably scare'em; an educated red man."

"I do my best." Johnny played along hoping to keep George on his side.

"You bring me anything, Mr. lawyer?" George smiled for the first time.

"I did. I brought my old warrior friend some rock candy." Johnny pulled a paper bag of candy from his coat pocket and handed it to Tosie.

"Well then, thank you." George peeked into the bag. He pulled a nugget out and popped it in his mouth. "Ummm, good candy." He sucked on it before shifting it into his cheek. "So, pick at my brain while it's awake."

"What do you know about William Killingbear and more so his family?"

"Ah. His momma was smart. *He* drank too much," offered Tosie to start. "His momma started buying land around the Osage, mostly in Tulsa County. Later, struck oil on it too." He bit into his hard candy and crunched it to fragments. "He had him a white wife, but she died a year or so after having their baby."

"Agnes," prompted Johnny.

"That was the baby. Francine might've been the wife." Tosie chewed his candy before popping a second piece in his mouth. "Killingbear's momma and his sister died a' the pox in December of nineteen-six. Came after the headrights vote."

"That allowed George Killingbear to inherit his mother's and sister's rights," detailed Johnny from his own research.

"It did, but drove him more to drink. Got so bad he couldn't take care a' his little girl – how she ended up in the orphanage."

"I know he died from the drink. His girl inherited all those headrights and the Tulsa County land. What do you know about her, George?"

"Went to the orphanage in Oklahoma City. About twelve when she went. She and another girl ran away in nineteen-ten."

"Drucilla Ward was the other girl," added Johnny.

"White girl's all I know." George Tosie chewed more candy. "Good candy, lawyer Johnny." He smacked his lips and nodded.

"Glad you like it, George. You know any stories about Agnes Killingbear?"

"Heard she and that white girl ran off to St. Louis...or maybe Chicago." He wrinkled his brow to jostle his memory. "Next thing is a few years later; one comes to Tulsa to be buried and the other comes along with a baby and an old white man for a husband."

"Agnes married a man named Belcher. She had a daughter by him." Johnny identified the written record as he knew it.

"If you say so. I never laid eyes on her after she went to that orphanage," acknowledged George.

"Then you saw her at some point?"

"I did with her aunt and grandmother when they brought her to the reservation. They took care of her sometimes when George first started to drink hard." The old man ran his hand through his black and gray hair. "Thought she favored the aunt more than George or that white mother, but she was clear enough half-breed."

"White skin?" asked Johnny.

"Darker. Half-breed like I said." The wrinkled warrior plucked another candy from his paper bag.

"Hmmm. Guess I need to check things some more." Johnny stepped up and shook George Tosie's hand. "Thank you for your help."

"Welcome, Johnny lawyer." Tosie smiled, bit his candy, and smiled again.

* * *

Johnny Grayhawk plowed through Osage documents at the tribal office. He had previously worn his fingers on government papers at the Bureau of Indian Affairs office with little in the way of information on individual birth or death records. He hoped his brother tribesmen had done better in that regard. B.I.A. apparently loved its accords, treaties, and contacts with chiefs, but held no such affection for the Osage people on a personal basis.

The filing system jumped from subject to date by year with little predictability. Johnny misapplied an hour looking for the maiden name of Mrs. Belcher under Belcher. He switched to Agnes Killingbear, which did yield a few papers. Those included lease agreements with Sinclair Oil and letters from the B.I.A. approving those leases. The morning passed with nothing confirming the identity of Mrs. Belcher nor anything indicating she was not Miss Killingbear.

A change in approach found Grayhawk searching by calendar years. In the nineteen-twelve folders, he found a contract with the signature Agnes Killingbear, rather than her later married name Belcher, even though it was after she married. The script and form seemed to match the ones from the leases signed later. He figured this to be clear enough to conclude Scott's allegation was false, but he trusted his friend's logic and perception, plus he still hoped to find Agnes Killingbear's head-rights papers.

Continuing to sift through the years, Johnny found a sequence of headrights documents. Since that elusive tribal record was the single piece he needed to close the Belcher estate, he dug into them. As he thumbed through the yellowed pages, the archivist, a blue-eyed blonde who had explained her one-fourth Osage heritage on a Swedish grandfather, Osage grandmother, and Norwegian grandparents on the other side, strolled to his side.

"Finding what you need, Mr. Grayhawk?" asked the archivist.

"Still looking, but some things seem to be falling into place." He gave her a quick glance before continuing with the papers. He paused to avail himself of her potential knowledge. "Are all of the headrights filed by year?"

"The early ones certainly are. Certifications only became important after the Allotment Act of nineteen-oh-six. It is still run by the B.I.A. and part of the Washington DC regulations."

Johnny gave the young archivist a sharp look. Certain he didn't want some blonde pushing the national agenda for his people, he focused on his current objective before further words incited him. "Okay. What I really want to know is the best location to find such papers."

"Most of them were in the early twentieth century years. Nineteen-six through eight." She rattled off the dates with the snobbery of a librarian explaining the Dewey Decimal System.

"Fine. Then I will plow through these as I have been." He stared at the blonde woman.

She stood motionless and blank until apparently realizing his unstated message. "Well, I will leave you to your search." She stepped away, then departed, the room of stored and largely forgotten information.

Nineteen and six began Johnny's new search. Page after page of the same official-looking papers with different individual names along with the certifying signatures of Osage leaders passed through his hands. One almost slipped by, but he pulled it from the discards and slid it on top of the unread stack. Agnes Killingbear showed as the daughter of her father, George Killingbear, and thus one of the two thousand, two hundred twenty-nine registered Osage. Johnny examined the signature. The penmanship was far more practiced and elegant than the previous ones he had viewed. He scrutinized the old paper searching it for an ambiguous second signature or fabrications among the official endorses. The document displayed everything he might want to close the estate – everything but matching handwriting.

The fluid cursive, compared to the scrawl on the Sinclair documents or the nineteen-twelve tribal document, screamed at an identity switch. As problematic as Mrs. Belcher being an imposter would be for Johnny, denying the truth would be harsher. Having found what, he hoped he would not, he had two phone calls to make. He would call his longtime friend and tell Wyatt his conjecture seemed correct. After that, he would call his client, Ruth Brown, and let her know that her grandmother was not a Killingbear and thus she was not the rightful heir to any Osage headrights, Killingbear land, or oil.

CHAPTER 20

THE CHARITY BALL

Well-heeled couples arrived in front of the Mayo Hotel in Yellow cabs, Checker cabs, and by chauffeur-driven, deluxe automobiles. Men in tuxedos or tails accompanied ladies in summer gowns from Tulsa's finest women's shops or in haute-couture designs as overpriced as New York's houses could manage and still sell to the Oklahoma gentry. Scott, outfitted in his tux, lingered in the lobby on the lookout for Cleveland. He debated with himself about having left his gun at home, hoping he would not rue the decision. As he waited, he observed ball patrons filter in through a process that seemed reflexive. They trickled through the lobby, formed clusters, and loitered, watching for additional friends to arrive. Interrupting the unidentified flow, the first familiar character, Albert Campion, came through the door. Wyatt stepped toward him.

"Making the rounds, Campion?" Scott grabbed his arm.

"I came to fulfill my civic obligation." Campion glared at Scott's hand on his arm.

"No bereavement regarding your brother-in-law," chided Scott. "Or remorse about killing him?" he added plying for the reaction.

"What? I'm no murderer, and I wouldn't hurt my wife." He jerked his arm free of Scott's grasp. "She's home bawling her eyes out over Waldo."

"From talking to her, I didn't think she cared so much about her brother," ventured Scott.

"Well, she does!" Campion tendered disdain to Scott, served up on a chubby face crimson with indignation.

"I am sorry for her, then." Scott studied Campion up and down.

"I thought you were working for me and not against me, you ass!" Exasperation with a sprinkling of hurt seasoned his proclamation.

"I'll work for you and others as long as none of you get in the way of the truth."

"That is fine by me!" Campion started to leave, then stopped and delivered a last thought. "Some truth may be beyond your comprehension and outside your resources, buster."

"Oh, I'm aware of some of the games swirling around town." Scott cracked a sarcastic snicker. "I suppose you think that if all else fails, Fielding can bail you out because he knows all the government angles."

Campion imparted a mordant expression to Scott. He started to speak, but apparently thought better of it. Dismissing Scott entirely, he shook his head before shuffling off toward the elevators. Scott watched as even the corpulent mogul melted into the mingling multitude of black formal wear.

Scott continued to lurk in the Mayo lobby waiting for Cleveland. Formally dressed ball patrons coursed in and drifted by conversing, beholding, or simply contented to be seen. Pierce, in dark clothes and a jacket, came down the hotel stairs moving against the flow of the ball crowd. Scott noted him and hoped to avoid the distraction he might cause, but Pierce had his scent and detoured toward him, leaving Wyatt stuck with the confrontation.

Eyeing Scott's formal attire, Pierce snarled, "Monkey suit; fits your style, Scott." He waited for a reply which did not come. "I've got the country's business now, but if you're around after eleven, you can be my new hobby."

"I have business too. And don't dream that you'll have any different outcome than being dropped in the Alaskan snow no matter how many spy tricks you've learned." The quiet tone could not hide the taunt of their war past and Alaskan feud.

Pierce stepped aggressively close to Scott. As the pair glowered at one another, Detective Cleveland walked up to them clad in a simple, dark blue suit. "So, Scott, is your gangster pal here a protégé of Sleener?"

Pierce glared at the interrupting newcomer as Scott replied. "No detective. Pierce is a bad memory from my war days in Army Intelligence."

The CIA man returned his stare to Scott, pursing his lips as he did. Cleveland gave him a second scan. Ignoring Cleveland, Pierce's glower did not waver from Scott.

"I'd introduce you formally, but I think he's on his way to save the republic," offered Scott, with equal parts sarcasm and derision.

The two men stared at one another until Pierce scoffed his annoyance. He left, bumping into Cleveland as he departed, and marched toward the street doors. Scott and Cleveland watched him bounce through the crowd toward the street.

Smirking at Scott, Cleveland commented on the departing spy. "A serious fellow...and he carries a big gun like you."

"About all we have in common," replied Scott.

With the tension of Pierce's presence gone, the pair observed the throng thicken and grow. Cleveland's informal dress did not raise an audible buzz even as it stuck out like a blue dot on a black leopard. For the most part, the gala goers ignored him, although he did draw some glances and a few disdainful scowls from the dowager and diamond necklace set. "So, I'm here, Scott." He scrutinized the now congested lobby before eyeballing Scott. "Conspicuously underdressed and out of place, I am here."

"Thanks for coming, Art." Scott tapped him on the shoulder. "Police tuxedos are far too confining, so don't give it a second thought."

"Yeah, funny," Cleveland scoffed. "Well, you told me you would give me what you have on the murder cases. So, spill it."

"I have reason to believe Ruth Brown murdered Martin and Fuller." Scott dropped the information like a cold bomb from an invisible plane.

Disbelief grasped Cleveland, while his respiration paused a moment. "The granddaughter of Agnes Belcher, the rich old lady that died a few weeks ago?"

"The same."

"Farfetched, but I'll bite. Why?" quizzed Cleveland.

"Blackmail. Her grandmother was not the true heir to their Osage oil rights, the land, or the Tulsa County land and its oil fortune," revealed Scott.

"Operating on more than a hunch, I hope?" grilled Cleveland.

"Johnny pulled the orphanage records and the headrights records kept by the Osage. He confirmed the identity switch this afternoon. The real Agnes Killingbear died. Her friend Drucilla Ward took her identity by forging some later documents. I figure Martin found the switch after the old woman died. Then the pair blackmailed Ruth Brown."

"Good motive. You have any evidence?"

"I know Ruth Brown met both Martin and Fuller despite her denials. There's a witness for Fuller, and physical evidence for her being at Martin's cabin." Scott laid out the essentials of his case to the detective.

"Just meeting them is flimsy," argued Cleveland.

"Art, she's a kid not a seasoned criminal. My hope is she'll confess. If not, I know you guys checked fingerprints at both locations, take hers and you'll have your evidence."

"Okay." Cleveland ran his hand across his chin. "And Sleener's murder?" His expression pressed to tie the cases together.

"Have to see about that one," admitted Scott. "I'm working on it."

"A different gun killed Sleener," reminded Cleveland.

"I know. I saw the hole in him."

"So, this little heiress shot him with a different gun? Or did you dig up her helper that took care of Sleener?"

"That murder is murky. She had a motive, but I can't see how she could pull it off. The other two fit with tangible evidence."

Cleveland considered the information with narrowed eyes and a skeptical expression. "You got me here to show me, so show me."

Scott, glancing toward the door, spied Mrs. Folger, and the presumptive Mr. Folger as they entered the lobby. He refocused on Cleveland.

"Art, I have another issue before I confront Ruth Brown. Wait here till you see me go to the elevator, then follow in a couple of minutes."

"Okay." Cleveland browsed around. "You're sure about this, Scott? This spot is full of Tulsa elite. It might get messy if you go confronting folks here."

"It'll be fine, Art." He nodded his certainty. "I'll see you in a little while. Just follow me upstairs when I walk by." Scott left Cleveland alone among the formally attired assemblage of Tulsa society.

Cleveland edged away from the doors, shifting east toward the elevators. He pulled out his pack of Camels and fidgeted to withdraw one. Before he could finish the process, a buxom woman in pink satin bumped his elbow, sending the pack on a trip across the lobby. Rather than pursuing the cigarettes, he faded back until the wall stopped him.

Scott witnessed Cleveland's travail before he edged his way through the throng, closing in on the Folgers. The pair bore toward the elevators, but they, like the entire throng, were impeded in that direction by the shortage of elevator space. As they crossed the lobby, Scott maneuvered behind Mrs. Folger.

Into her ear, he whispered an imperative. "Excuse yourself! We need to talk." He moved on without hesitating.

Mrs. Folger stopped and halted her husband. "Clifford, I'd like to powder my nose. I'll meet you at our table."

"Of course, dear." Mr. Folger withdrew his hand from his wife's arm.

The Folgers exchanged polite smiles before he continued the slow shuffle toward the elevators at the east end of the lobby. Mrs. Folger paused for a moment before gliding north. The fashion-forward socialite and blackmail victim progressed past the wide, marble staircase to the furnished section of the lobby.

She reached the seating area of the hotel near the grand stairway to the mezzanine. The chairs were arrayed back-to-back with two double rows. Scott sat in a chair in the second double row facing the lobby and the front door. Mrs. Folger meandered to the farthest row and sat one seat down facing the stairs and away from Scott. A cautious dance of deception proceeded without music.

"Well?" asked Folger under her breath.

"What did Fuller have on you? It puzzles me." Scott spoke to the empty space in front of him.

"I told you, I won't be compromised," Folger reaffirmed her position.

"You're already compromised," countered Scott. He stood up without glancing toward Folger. He reached in his tuxedo jacket. "I've got your payoff money. Sleener wasn't able to accept it." His sarcasm rolled across the chairs.

"Keep it. It's your pay for when you do find the book." Mrs. Folger craned her neck looking to either side. Satisfied there were no eaves-droppers, she continued. "I'm counting on you. I'm sure you can retrieve it."

"That's a fool's errand," growled Scott. "I've no reason to look for the book." He swung enough to drop the envelope over Folger's bare shoulder and onto the tiny clutch in her lap.

Surprised, Mrs. Folger jumped slightly before making a full recovery and concealing the envelope with her white-gloved hands. She shifted in her chair unsnapping her purse and sliding the envelope inside. Despite her need for discretion, she turned partway toward Scott.

"Why would you say that? You had reason enough in your pocket before you dropped it in my lap."

"Because you have it. You have the damn bankbook." Scott twisted to glare at Folger. The difference in elevation precluded eye contact, but the tone rang clear.

"That's silly. How would I have it?" Surprise and relief blended in her voice.

"By taking it from Sleener after you killed him."

"I'm not a killer," argued Folger.

"You're the second person to tell me that tonight – must be a fad."

"In my case, it's true."

"In your case, it's more refined. Truth is a rare coin these days."

Mrs. Folger jerked around once more offering her back to Scott. "Just because you know I must be beyond discreet, given my social standing, does not mean I will accept your abuse."

"Social standing? You mean power and money." Scott's disdain for the pampered and privileged could not be missed.

"The power and money that can be raised against you if you publicly slander me, yes," threatened Folger.

"I believe it's true. Proving it is out of my current reach." Scott sat down in his chair, leaving him once more facing away from Mrs. Folger. "The aristocracy has always made its own rules," opined Scott.

"It does," agreed Mrs. Folger. "And the proletariat always suffers." She stood and straightened her ballgown. "I'll be joining my husband now." She strode away with flecks of superiority trailing from her designer shoes.

Scott remained a moment. He deliberated about Folger. No evidence indicated her involvement in the killing, at least directly. The gun seemed too big for her to handle. She might have hired it done. Yet, all the other blackmail victims had the same motive. The report Evie gave him on Sleener's call indicated concern. For all he knew, Sleener worried about another partner in the blackmail scheme.

While Folger's attitude bothered him and Sleener's death perplexed him, Scott knew his cogitation abetted his avoidance of his principal task. He dreaded confronting Ruth Brown. He stood and trudged to his perceived duty. He passed by Cleveland, who signaled he saw him. Scott made it to an elevator and crowded in with Tulsa's privileged.

Scott departed last from the elevator car, more from procrastination than politeness. Big-band music filled the floor. He strolled along the hallway, whose outer wall consisted of windows reflecting the inner wall that bounded the ballroom. It also conveyed the reversed images of the ballroom doors and the ball patrons flowing through them. He turned from the window likenesses and passed through the grand ballroom's double doors. A few feet inside, Ruth Brown stood waiting for him.

She wore an evening gown not outclassed by the older, more sophisticated of the Tulsa crème de la crème. It was layered delicately and fitted with the tiniest of straps to not test her bosom as the gown's upper support. Miss Brown carried a purse in a complementary pink to her dress. Open-toed high heels completed her ensemble while adding more than an inch to her modest height. She closed the gap to greet him.

"Mr. Scott." She extended a delicate, gloved hand.

"Miss Brown." He took her hand and bowed slightly before releasing it.

"Ruth," she corrected. "And Wyatt, I hope." She smiled up at the much taller Scott.

"Fine. Ruth, are you finished then?"

"My obligations are complete. I'm yours, but I could use some air. Let's go to the terrace." She took Scott's arm and led him from the ballroom.

"I'm not sure you realize your situation." He began to ease into confronting her.

"I realize I'm with the beau of the ball." Ruth blushed slightly as she glanced at Scott.

He hoped his ad hoc plan would evolve into something reasonable without embarrassment or danger for either of them. Hankering for things to work out, Scott let her lead. The pair made their way to the stairs and climbed the one flight to the observation deck with its predominantly southern and slightly western view of Tulsa. Scott opened and held the heavy, glass door for young Miss Brown.

Terra-cotta tiles covered the deck's expanse. A smattering of potted plants and outdoor furnishings populated it. An ornate wall that was the continuation of the building's exterior rose four feet above the deck. Beyond the wall, skyscrapers, stars, a slip of moon, and the June night provided the backdrop. Unseen insects or roosting pigeons aside, the pair had the space to themselves.

Scott let the door close as Ruth coasted along the tiles. Away from the ritzy crowd of over-jeweled necks and off-the-shoulder gowns revealing sagging cleavage, Ruth Brown remained a child. Her young face soft in the moonlight, she appeared harmless despite her murderous transgressions. Scott knew the score and he had to call it out.

"Johnny Grayhawk called me," blurted out Miss Brown still facing away from Scott. "He told me he was bound by attorney-client privilege concerning what he found, but you were not." She spun to confront him.

Scott halted. Stunned by her sudden and overt declaration, he did not reply. The whole story being known without him having to detail it for her, put him at ease. He could focus on convincing her to leave quietly with Cleveland and him.

Ruth opened her purse. "Here. Forget what you think you know about my grandmother and me." She withdrew several five-hundred-dollar bills and raised them up for Scott to see.

"President McKinley. I'm getting to know him quite well these days." His try at humor came with a sigh of relief that bribery was her reply to possible exposure.

She extended her hand and stepped towards Scott. She smiled with no hint of guile. Every feature cast naive innocence. If he didn't have the evidence and almost certainly knew her to be guilty of murder, he would never have imagined it.

"I'd also have to forget about Fuller and Martin." Scott made no effort to reach for the bills. From her expression, he surmised that she fully expected him to accept her bribe.

Ruth Brown continued to hold the bills in her outstretched hand. She looked around the deck. It remained empty. "This isn't enough?" She waved the bills. "Okay. When I get my inheritance, I'll give you more." Scott's muteness seemed to increase her distress. "I'll leave Tulsa. You won't have to think about it," she pleaded. She widened her eyes and broadened her girlish smile. Her expectation of him taking the money appeared to be the only outcome she had envisioned.

"I can't let murder go." Scott stated his position calmly without exposition or pretense.

"That woman threatened me," justified Ruth.

"How?"

"She threatened my future and my dreams."

"You killed her to keep what really wasn't your grandmother's or yours and compounded it by killing Martin." Scott recited her shallowness to her.

"You don't know any such thing," she rebutted.

Scott decided to detail it for her, after all. He hoped she would see the hopelessness of her argument. "Johnny found the headrights forgeries. Jackie Martin must have found them too. Your grandmother was Drucilla Ward not Agnes Killingbear. He and Mildred Fuller blackmailed you. The motive is clear." Scott kept his eye on Ruth. She stood with a lost expression and a gaping mouth, while she wiggled the currency. "I recovered evidence that you went to Martin's cabin, and there's a witness, who saw you meet with Mildred Fuller. I'm sure the police have your fingerprints from both scenes and only need to test yours for the match."

"They were blackmailers," she argued. "And so-what, I met them." She licked her lips and swallowed saliva along with her glob of fear. "That doesn't mean I killed them." She added denial to her case.

"You did."

"No." The gravity of the problem finally seemed to creep into her eyes. Panic swam in her welling tears.

Scott moved very slightly toward her. "Look, Johnny can get you a top-notch criminal lawyer." He softened his expression. He tried coaxing the young murderess with his eyes.

"She was going to ruin my life." Ruth continued rationalizing to Scott.

He kept his tone soft. "Plead guilty with extenuating circumstances." He inched closer to her. "Blackmailers that come with shady pasts will look like they got what they deserved."

Ruth shifted. She stuffed the bills back in her purse and pulled out a small-caliber, chrome pistol with a pearl grip – a girly gun. She let her purse drop. "No, I'm not going to jail. That woman was a nasty cow."

"She was," agreed Scott.

Brown waved the gun toward Scott. He remained calm, his eyes sympathetic.

"I'm not going to jail for her!" Ruth Brown slid toward the exit but stopped abruptly. Detective Cleveland approached the glass door oblivious to the scene outside. Ruth fired in the direction of the door missing Cleveland by yards. "I'm not going to jail." She tipped her gun toward Scott, then the door.

Cleveland burst through the door with his revolver in hand. Ruth shot again at Cleveland, missing badly once more. He dived for cover behind a large pot with an elephant ear plant.

"Don't shoot, Art!" screamed Scott in an effort to protect the unstable girl.

Ruth flipped her aim toward Wyatt. He hit the deck. She fired wildly once more. Ruth Brown flitted along the wall like a trapped sparrow.

"I'm not going to jail! I'm not!" Ruth discharged two rounds with no aim. She ran madly away from the pair and toward the west end of the observation deck.

Cleveland abandoned his cover. He gave chase. His leather soles slipped and skidded on the ceramic floor, but he maintained his advance. Scott scrambled to his feet and pursued her as well.

She flailed and darted screaming; "No jail!" Not a drop of sanity emerged in her eyes, and none prevailed in her actions.

"Ruth! Ruth!" shouted Scott trying to get her attention and hoping to break her maniacal trance.

"No jail! No jail! No jail!" Ruth Brown dropped her gun as she raced toward the roof deck's west wall. "No...."

The two men dashed after her. The young woman's intent stood clear. As she closed on the west end wall, Scott dived for her feet making a shoestring tackle. Ruth tripped and crashed headfirst into the wall. Her face battered, teeth lost, nose broken, and out cold, Ruth Brown remained alive. Cleveland reached her, while Scott pushed to his feet.

"Good God! This kid is nuts," exclaimed Cleveland.

"Yeah. A real Carmen Sternwood," replied Scott.

Cleveland looked bewildered. "Who?"

"You need to see more movies, Art."

Cleveland gave Scott a quizzical look, then holstered his revolver. "I'll try to see a movie tomorrow. Now, I'll go call an ambulance." He headed toward the terrace door, pausing to pick up Ruth Brown's little gun.

Scott crouched near the battered young woman. He looked her over, noting the damage and hoping her brain would recover at least from the concussion. Uncertain how to treat her injuries, he stood and walked to the west wall that Ruth Brown intended to fly over. He peered down. Saturday night bustle played out on Cheyenne Avenue. Farther west, the refinery smoked and flared, oblivious to rich and poor alike.

A thin crowd of ball attendees pushed onto the deck. Their whispers produced a murmur that Scott caught. He glared toward the noise. The faces and figures in evening dress kept their distance. None of them registered in his memory.

He assessed the repercussions. There would be Osage claims on her grandmother's illicitly gained property. Ruth would lose the land, oil, and money. Although, it wouldn't matter now if she had it. The mental hospital in Vinita will care for her just the same. He wondered if the tribe would get the land and money or if some distant Killingbear relation would reap an unexpected windfall. Either way, Johnny would get some of the work.

It remained warm even at ten. He would go home and cool off. He'd let Cleveland sort things out. That was his job. Tulsa paid him for that. It didn't pay Scott a dime and it didn't owe him a thing. He paid his taxes and kept his obligations. Since the war ended, Scott and Tulsa had a quiet, simple deal; both went about their business ignoring the other. He wanted to consider Darlene's murder and Queena's frustration. He needed to dig at unanswered questions.

CHAPTER 21

The Babe Is Dying

With no new information on the missing whore, Mary, or the murdered one, Darlene, and only unfounded doubts about Mrs. Folger and Sleener, Scott had no concrete business to pursue. This afternoon, he chose to listen to the broadcast from Yankee Stadium as they celebrated the twenty-fifth anniversary of its opening. It was a national radio broadcast before the regular Yankee's game. The fans came or listened not for the anniversary or the game; they sat in the seats or played their radios to hear Babe Ruth, the Bambino. Naturally, Bugler could not be kept away from baseball history.

The pair listened in Scott's office – Scott behind his desk and Bugler half in the guest chair with both elbows on Scott's desk and his noggin a foot from the radio. Mel Allen described the setting, the crowd, the lovely day, and all the officials arrayed on the field. Allen reported that the ceremony included the Yankee organization retiring Babe Ruth's number three jersey, never to be worn again by a Yankee player. Scott recalled the first jersey retired, the late Lou Gehrig's number four. He thought of both men in Japan when he threw batting practice for the barnstormers. Contrasting personalities, but both great ballplayers. Allen introduced the Babe to a thunderous ovation. Ruth stepped to the mic and thanked everyone in a raspy, sick voice that the world knew came from the throat cancer that ate away at his life.

The rattle of Ruth's voice disturbed Bugler. "Don't think the Babe'll be 'round much longer." The grizzled, old fan shook his head at the thought.

"No. Cancer is vicious," Scott replied.

"Yep. I'd rather get run over by the trolley," declared Bugler.

Scott chuckled. Bugler did not seem to understand the humor, but he grinned in response to his pal's merriment. The Babe continued his thanks, but the tone and timbre of his sorrowful voice transported the actual words of his speech beyond their meanings.

The squeak of the office door alerted Scott to scrutinize its movement. The door swung open. Former OSS colonel and current CIA functionary, Fielding strolled in. He made his way to the far end of Scott's desk and a few feet distant from Bugler and the radio. Scott watched his progress with hawk eyes and taut limbs.

"I'm leaving town, Scott," he announced.

Bugler instantly shushed Fielding and pointed at the radio where the broadcast continued to emanate. "Yankee Stadium. Retirin' the three," explained Bugler.

Fielding glanced at Bugler but wasted little time before glaring at Scott. "I read where your heiress was insane as well as a fraud." More than a sliver of reproach slipped into Fielding's declarative sentence.

"Haven't had time for the papers. There's baseball history going on today." Scott blunted Fielding's veiled inquiry into his investigations with the saga unfolding on the radio.

"I see your point." Fielding smirked. "In Tulsa, it's news when a rich girl goes crazy. Not much interest though in a prostitute killed and another one missing. Just who cares – a local cop or two; other hookers; maybe a small-time PI?" His mockery made; Fielding glanced at the radio as Mel Allen continued his broadcast to the entranced Bugler.

"House that Ruth built. Have some respect Fielding," rebuked Scott. "It's a memorial as much as an anniversary. Even in your misanthropic soul, there must be a little spot for the game and its greatest player."

Fielding reacted by peering down at him. "Yes. Twenty-fifth anniversary of Yankee Stadium. You pitched there in thirty-four, right?"

"Yeah, twice." The ghosts the pair shared had nothing to do with Yankee Stadium, his career, or anything to do with baseball. Any chitchat from Fielding carried the resonance of duplicity. Wyatt had no interest in prolonging the exchange. "Why are you here?" He narrowed his eyes. He could see through Fielding. Inside his suit, he existed as a natural bureaucrat angling for promotion.

"I dropped by to tell you what you're missing." Fielding slid around the desk and bent to Scott's level. He whispered quietly in Scott's ear. "We're moving in on a little commie."

"I thought that was J. Edgar's job," replied Scott even though he knew it to be the FBI's responsibility to deal with domestic spying.

"He only finds them when they wear signs." Fielding did not hide his contempt for the smug FBI Director. "And we only give them to him if we want trials." Fielding detailed the interagency conflict when it came to the American spy game. Fielding righted his posture. "I plan to find the whole rat's nest operating out of here."

"A little too much hyperbole, Colonel." A smirk of skepticism swept across Scott's mouth. "Why would commies give a damn about Tulsa?"

"Right now, one seems to be buzzing around Douglas Aircraft." Fielding shrugged his shoulders. "Why the others are here is still a puzzle."

"You really believe there's a spy ring in Tulsa?"

"There is something, Scott. I expect to be back in Tulsa soon."

"It will be here," replied Scott glibly.

"You could come on board and help root it out." Fielding finally stated his true purpose. He eschewed his usual detached manner replacing it with a tone of consideration and hope.

Scott could not figure out why the spy bureaucrat remained so dogged in his pursuit after being rebuffed repeatedly. He swiveled his chair to challenge Fielding. "No! Still no." Scott left zero room for uncertainty in his declaration. "I'll leave Tulsa's phantom commies to you."

Fielding smirked and made his way to the door, while Babe Ruth rasped out his thanks and farewell to the fans and the Yankees. The CIA operative stopped with his hand on the knob. He put his hat on before smiling at Scott. "I'll show you a couple of commies in the flesh on my next visit."

"Colonel, you have a safe trip." Sarcasm dripped off every word.

"And don't forget to pack up Pierce and take him with you," added Scott.

Scott stretched an arm past Bugler's face and spun up the volume on the radio. Fielding left. Bugler's attention never wavered during Scott's exchange with the espionage commander. He stared at the radio as Mel Allen took to the microphone after Babe Ruth concluded his poignant farewell. As with Lou Gehrig's tragic death years before, baseball fans did not expect to see the Babe again.

Wyatt found it melancholic that the great men with whom he toured fourteen years ago were dying off. He roamed from Bugler and the radio to stare out his window. The sun shone bright on the city street. Scott's Tulsa had moved through June fine despite would-be commies, Babe's impending doom, and a whore-killer among its denizens. Scott hoped the rest of the summer would resolve things more serenely. They say there is always hope. They also say there's a sucker born every minute.

CHAPTER 22

Life Goes On

The wind blew Scott's hair as he drove the LaSalle down Riverside Drive. Water covered some of the sandbars, but the river had dropped noticeably from the heavy rains of late May and early June. Poor ol' Arkansas rarely had a pretty side. Raging, roiling, flooding most Mays or early Junes only to be more sandbar than water by July. Nothing in size compared to the Mississippi, but more dangerous because folks didn't respect it or fear it.

The pretty day, the top down, green scenery, and the rhythm of the LaSalle diverted Scott's attention. He rolled by the Denver Avenue intersection calculating he might chance Houston or push to the end of Riverside and veer onto Seventh Street. From behind, a shrieking siren jolted him from his motoring serenity. In the rearview mirror, a motorcycle cop grew larger and clearer. Scott pulled over as any reasonable citizen would. The cop pulled around beside him and stopped even with his door. The officer put his right foot down for balance, while leaving the motorcycle idling. He squinted into the open car to gawk directly at Scott. He scrutinized Scott's face for a moment then inspected the LaSalle as if he might want to buy it.

"You Wyatt Scott?" asked the cop.

"Yes. What's the problem, officer?" The diplomatic and polite Wyatt Scott garnered better results than the confrontational one. He understood this well even as he tried to calculate whether or not he was speeding and why the cop called him by name.

"I need to take you to Mohawk Park to see Detective Cleveland," stated the cop flatly.

"You followed me across town?"

"Naw. Cleveland put out the word on your car. Hard to miss this bright buggy." The cop gave the LaSalle another long survey down its side. When he concluded, he brought his foot back on his bike and revved the cycle's motor. "Come on. I'll lead the way."

He took off without his siren. Scott followed close behind. Maintaining the motorcycle's pace, he still wondered what Cleveland wanted and why he would select Mohawk Park as their meeting place.

Reaching the park grounds and making their way to a picnic area, the officer pointed for Scott to steer into the parking zone. As he followed the directive, two black-and-whites left the site. He switched off his engine and assessed the scene. A hearse bearing *Coroner*, another black-and-white, the motorcycle cop, and an unmarked sedan occupied the other spaces. The tail-end door of the hearse sat open in anticipation of its somber cargo. Two men in white coats conveyed a stretcher with a white sheet presumably covering a body. As they approached the parking lot, Scott left his LaSalle walking in their direction.

Arthur Cleveland, Scott's frustrated detective contact and provisional friend, ambled toward the parking area. Since his longtime family buddy, Mike Barton, retired from the force, Scott held little regard for Tulsa's older detectives. He believed in Cleveland and trusted him but categorizing them as pals was a step too far. Scott shifted toward the hearse and the destination of the coroner's attendants. Cleveland quickened his pace and veered to intercept Scott prior to him reaching the two men.

"Thought you should see this since you're working for Queena Capps." He pointed at the sheet as he pulled alongside Scott.

"You got a whore snitch? I don't give out who hires me."

"I got snitches all right." Cleveland smirked. "Though you working for Queena Capps is news like the sun rising in the east." Cleveland slowed as they neared the stretcher. "Figured you'd want to know first-hand on this. I also hope you can help me with what you know." He signaled the two attendants to halt.

"I know there's a young girl missing from the May Rooms," confided Scott.

"That's a start." Cleveland nodded toward the stretcher. "Think we found her. One of the patrol cops that got here first recognized her as a hooker they tried to process, but she got bailed out easy enough."

The pair converged on the two men and their solemn cargo. Cleveland moved beside the apparent cadaver. Scott swung around to the other side. He watched as Cleveland pulled the sheet back to reveal blonde hair and a once pretty face decaying more on one side than the other.

"Could be Mary. I never saw her, but she's supposed to be blonde and nineteen." Scott looked from the girl's poignant figure to Cleveland. "What can you tell me, Art?"

"Family goes on a picnic to Mohawk Park. Dog runs into the woods. Starts yapping like crazy, dad goes to see what's the matter, and lo and behold there's a body." Cleveland shook his head about the circumstance of the discovery. "I let the family go. The father was upset, but the mom shook like a leaf – thought she'd upchuck. They don't know anything. Just a bad memory and a ruined picnic."

"You see her where she lay?" questioned Scott.

"Yes. Clear she was moved into the trees, not killed there."

"How was she killed?"

Cleveland re-covered the dead girl pulling the sheet over her head. He gestured to the bearers, and they loaded the corpse into the hearse. "Coroner hedged, but made it clear enough she was strangled. He put it about ten days ago."

"Timing fits for little Mary. Was she attacked too?"

Cleveland glanced around without looking Scott in the eye. "No rape if that's what you mean. Her French frillies were still intact even though her brassiere was on the ground." Cleveland hesitated. He peered at his shoes. He kicked at the gravel in the parking area. He rubbed his chin. Finally, he stared at Scott conveying a sense crueler than the words to come. "She was beat, cut, tortured maybe."

Scott shuddered slightly at the unexpected brutality of the murder. "Tortured?"

"Knife cuts on her breasts and nipples."

"Wow. Gotta' crazy son of a bitch, Art."

"Yeah," corroborated Cleveland. "I can't imagine it."

Scott's mind ran off without permission. He pictured a scruffy man in work clothes on top of Mary. The amorphous man pressed his thumbs against her airway and tightened his grip around her neck. Her brassiere was twisted and tossed on the ground beside her. Her blouse lay open. Her breasts, slashed and bloody, heaved from her diaphragm laboring for air. Doomed, Mary's mouth formed a scream that her constricted throat could not release. Her wide eyes were big, blue marbles of terror.

Scott jerked his head trying to shake the involuntary vision. He looked at Cleveland. "Sadly, I *can*."

The detective stared quizzically at Scott before his duty tugged him back. "You have any suspects from Queena?" Don't hide behind that client shit, I need everything I can get." The police detective pressed Scott.

"She doesn't know much. That's why she hired me." Scott looked Cleveland directly in the eyes. "I'm poking into some long shots. I can't say I expect much, but occasionally long odds pay off." He looked toward his LaSalle. He took a step toward it.

Cleveland grabbed his arm. "Scott, I need you to work with me, not against me."

Scott glared at his held arm then at Cleveland. "Art, if I get evidence, I'll run straight to your office."

Cleveland let loose his arm but glared at Scott. "Do that. And when you do, run *fast*."

* * *

The nineteen thirty-five calendars would flip to May the next week. A bright, brand new baseball season was underway. A dozen games into it, the Athletics found themselves in the middle of the pack. Their second-year pitcher, Wyatt Scott, started his third game of the season two days before. Going into the game, his record stood at one and zero with a win and a no-decision. In the third inning, something popped in the elbow of his throwing arm, forcing him to leave the game. The trainer in the clubhouse calculated the injury to be a tendon, but he suggested, and Connie Mack agreed, Scott should see a doctor, a specialist in fact.

With his shirt behind him, Wyatt sat bare-chested on the exam table of Doctor Kershaw, the specialist recommended by the Athletics team physician. The gray-haired Kershaw manipulated Scott's arm. He bent, then straightened, then bent it again. He ran his index finger along the outside of Scott's elbow. He repeated the maneuver with his thumb. The doctor bent down to within an inch of the suspect elbow. He stared at the joint and squinted for added measure. He straightened and eased Scott's elbow to rest on the exam table.

Doctor Kershaw adjusted his glasses before looking at Scott. "Tendons. They're bad."

Apprehension seized Wyatt's face like rigor mortis claims the dead. "Tendons, Doc? How bad?"

"Ripped. The whole connection is loose as a goose." The old man's expressionless facade conveyed no supplementary details.

"The trainer said it was a tendon – take a while to heal." Scott pleaded a case thin with expertise and piled high with hope.

"Um hmm."

"That it? What you're thinking too, Doc?" The question contained a dash of optimism and a cup of fear.

The old doctor crossed his arms. "You have any tingling in your fingers?"

"Yeah, a little. I figure it'll go away."

"It will...eventually."

Scott shifted on the table. In an almost unconscious act of filial comfort, his left hand caressed his right elbow. "So, what's it look like? Is the whole season shot?"

Kershaw dropped his arms to his side. "You've torn your ulnar collateral ligament." His tone was flat, his discourse scientific. "Your elbow will eventually heal enough to function satisfactorily."

Youthful optimism took over Wyatt's thought. "Good. When?"

The old doctor stepped in front to look Scott directly in the eyes. "By the end of the summer you should be able to do most simple things. You still will not be able to put pressure on the elbow."

"When do I start throwing again?" Young Wyatt Scott stared at the doctor, anticipating a date that he was sure would be too distant for his liking.

"Son, you might be able to throw a ball in a year...but you will never pitch again." Avuncular sympathy flowed with the dire news despite the bluntness.

"What do you mean?" Shock constrained his reaction, but confusion covered Wyatt Scott's face.

The aged specialist cleared his throat. He took a breath. "When it finally heals, your ulnar ligament will be so scarred that you won't have control, you won't have much speed, and your curve will hang like a towel on a clothesline."

The candid assessment slammed a hammer into Scott that brought him to rage. "God Damn! Nothing can be done?"

"No, son. You're young. Better think about a career," advised Kershaw.

"Fuck me! Thought I had one."

"I'm sure you did, but not now; not baseball anyway."

Sullen and lost, Wyatt rubbed his right elbow. He looked at the door hoping someone would come through and alter the prognosis for his future. In the sullen moment, his jaw dropped, and his mouth froze. When his eyes fell once more on the doctor, they blurred his image from their thick mist cover.

Doctor Kershaw remained all business as he started for the door. "Put on your shirt. I'll call Connie and tell him personally." He stopped for a moment and sized up Scott one last time. He seemed to flip through a mental Rolodex of comforting clichés before settling on one. "Buck up, son. You've many years ahead of you." The statement hung in the air between the two. There was little salve in its truth. The old doctor departed without another word.

It took Wyatt ten minutes to put on his shirt. One minute included draping it around his upper body, while it took another minute to properly button it. Desolation obliged the balance of the time.

* * *

Late in the day, an uncommon occurrence took place in the parlor of the May Rooms. Not a creature stirred; nary a john nor a painted lady could be found. Bereft of visitors and working girls, the salon resembled an empty theater set more than a functioning cathouse. The situation occurred due to the presence of Detective Cleveland in

Queena Capps' office and a recent discovery too late to make the morning's Tulsa World but would become sensational news for the evening edition of the Tulsa Tribune.

Miss Queena Capps kept a mindful eye on Detective Cleveland. The transplanted New Yorker wore no hat, and his wrinkled suit cost him added disfavor with the madam. He busied himself writing with a pencil in his notepad. She disliked police in her office whether on government business or collecting bribes. Queena shifted her weight left and right imparting her mounting agitation to one foot then the other. Art Cleveland and Queena Capps had no tangible dealings before, but he knew of her reputation and that of the house. She didn't know Cleveland, but she knew cops, lots of cops.

"Queena, if you don't play square with me, Morgan will shut you down. That won't bother me one bit, but I'd rather get to the bottom of these killings." Cleveland stopped writing long enough to stare at Queena.

"I told you; I didn't know she was dead. All I knew was she was gone." More than defensiveness resided in her tone. Sadness swirled through it, and remorse hung on top like oil on water.

Cleveland cocked his head with sarcastic disbelief and an eye roll not unlike Groucho Marx. He let his stare speak for him without the need for words.

Queena caught the gesture and the body language. "I mean it! I liked the kid. She came to me from a friend in Kansas, Lawrence, the college town." She pleaded her case by way of history and geography.

"Sure. She was a coed and you're a protective auntie to these girls." Cleveland's sarcasm chafed crueler with his New York accent.

"She was a working girl like all of them. And Mr. New York cop, we simple Okies look after each other." The inferno behind Capps's hazel eyes blazed. "In fact, if you find the bastard that killed Mary, give him to me for ten minutes, and you won't have to worry about no damn trial." Passion and fervor flew from Queena that would've shocked her friends and acquaintances of longstanding. Cleveland, not being one of those, stood impassively.

Before either could continue the spat, the office door opened, and Carl Jefferson came in followed by Wyatt Scott. Scott approached the pair. Carl eyed Queena seeking direction. She tilted her head, gesturing for him to leave. Carl obliged, leaving Scott with the madam and the detective.

"What's going on?" quizzed Scott.

"For starters, Miss Capps here hasn't told me all she knows. I told her the rough end to that young girl of hers, but she can't seem to get my story." Cleveland set his jaw showing Scott his resolve.

"Tell me about it, Art."

Cleveland tapped his pad with his pencil. As a prelude to his story, he inhaled air and exhaled frustration. "It's about Mohawk Park. It's about the girl."

"Mary," interjected Queena before Cleveland had a chance to finish.

"Yes. I told Miss Capps about Mary."

"And she was more than murdered." Queena flushed. Her nostrils flared. She had hatred popping out of her face that her makeup couldn't contain.

Scott stepped close to Queena. "Yeah. I know. Art called me out to see the scene." He almost reached out to her, but the cold hatred pulsing in her veins told him to stand still.

"She had cuts, bruises, things done to hurt her." Queena's mouth quivered. "Cruel, nasty things to places no one abuses." A moment of pain showed through her hatred, but she retrieved it to spew more vitriol. "The fucker!" blurted out the madam.

Scott took a breath. He looked toward Cleveland. "Okay, Art. What is the problem between you two? Queena surely wants this guy brought in," reasoned Scott.

"Scott, so you know, the problem is Mrs. Capps here, if she can be believed, says she did not send Mary out on a trick. Says Darlene, our dead, flying whore, set up the john for the young kid. You can imagine my...skepticism." After explaining his thinking to Scott, Cleveland narrowed his eyes to indict Miss Capps.

"I said Darlene may have set it up." Queena explained and pleaded at the same time. She extended her arms palms up toward Scott. "Wyatt, I honestly don't know how it happened. Mary went to eat. I expected her to come back to her room."

"I remember. You told me." Scott took in the stories as well as the sentiment and animosity displayed by both parties. The room dripped with distrust. He nodded to Cleveland.

With Scott deferring, Cleveland followed on. "Okay. I'll switch stations. Our suspect, this guy, whoever went with him, have a name?"

Queena shrugged her shoulders. "John. They're all named John." The exasperated madam recapitulated her story. "Darlene never breathed a word about any date or about Mary. Couple a' days later, Darlene goes out the window. Mary's not in her room. Tulsa Police play Keystone Kops. Clear enough?"

"I'm not buying it!" Cleveland, obviously perturbed by her comic reference to his fellow officers, stared daggers at the madam. "Somehow Mary got in the car with the wrong john and ended up dead. Darlene, with a thousand miles on her whore meter, also turns up dead. And innocent ol' Queena Capps doesn't know the john or anything about any of it." Cleveland invaded Queena's space looking down at her rigid jaw. "Now, you are the director of this double-murder drama, who did these girls meet?"

"I've told you; I don't know. And if you ask again, I still won't know. So just swallow your whistle, copper." Queena stood her ground and sharpened her glare.

"You think Darlene set up Mary's date?" Scott jumped in to simmer the boil. Neither party had communicated through the last several sentences.

With Scott easing the tension, Cleveland pulled away a couple of steps giving the madam room to move. Queena paced. She weaved a few feet, for once without a cigarette, but her mind seemed elsewhere.

"Queena." Scott reminded her of his question.

"I told you, Scott, rumor around the house was she wanted to be Queena's competition." The madam focused her attention and her anger on Scott. "You bastard men think you know women, but you barely understand your peckers."

Scott took out an option to stare down Queena. The pause was short before he eased his posture and relaxed his face. He restarted his questions. "Darlene aside, what was Mary's talent?"

"Being young and pretty." Queena raised up and narrowed her eyes. "And being blonde, not beauty parlor blonde, real blonde where the drapes match the carpet."

"Beyond her natural talent," dismissed Scott. "Did she ever work in the rough trade?"

"I don't deal in that." Queena looked from one man to the other. "I don't care what a pervert wants, but that stuff is dangerous." She thought a moment. "Maybe Darlene did on the side."

Cleveland watched now. His skepticism regarding Queena Capps seemed to hold firm, although he left the jousting to Scott. His look revealed curiosity about the path Scott started down. He folded his arms and cocked his head.

"You say that why?" Scott asked Queena.

"She's had bruises before. And Queena knows if God don't, Darlene never had a boyfriend, rough or sweet."

"Darlene comes up with a john, who likes to play rough, and Mary ends up in the woods," hypothesized Scott. "Not sure how to make the switch, but it plays for Darlene to be the next victim to cover up the killer's contact with Mary."

Cleveland jumped in hearing this new speculation. "How do you know Darlene came up with the john let alone he liked to be rough?"

"Deductive reasoning and detective work, Art. I do that." Scott couldn't resist teasing Cleveland on his profession.

"Okay gumshoe, what's it give us?" Cleveland remained perturbed.

"Darlene cooked up a date for Mary that went wrong. She knew the guy and either threatened him or he thought she would. He tosses her out the window to be sure. We find the john Darlene kept to herself, and we've got the killer."

Cleveland looked to Queena. "Any chance of Darlene trying to book a rough trick on her own since you don't condone it?"

"Sure. Darlene is hard. Money is all she knows."

"Was," corrected Cleveland.

"Yeah, was," sneered Queena.

No useful information was being exchanged despite both Queena and Cleveland wanting to find the killer. Scott dug for some evidence he figured Cleveland possessed. "Art, did you get anything from the coroner?"

Cleveland pivoted toward Scott. Dealing in police information lowered his tone and calmed him. "He confirmed strangulation." He dropped his arms and relaxed his posture. "The coroner detailed a litany of bruises, cuts and all the horrible things I told you at Mohawk Park."

Scott grimaced. He had seen awful things. The war proved the unimaginable to be actual. Nothing should shock him, but evil did disturb him. "Crazy guy still fits. That it?" asked Scott.

"Her last meal was rhubarb pie." Cleveland shrugged.

Scott narrowed his eyes. "Rhubarb Pie. Hmm…Thursday."

"What?" replied Cleveland.

Queena regarded Scott like he had lost his mind. Cleveland glanced at Queena. Neither spoke seeming to be searching for meaning in Scott's non sequitur.

Scott stepped toward Cleveland. "Let's wrap this up. We've all got things to do. Art, are you charging her?"

"Not up to me in the end. Seems unlikely the DA will press. I may be new in town, but I'm quite sure the path from the courthouse to the May Rooms is festooned with greased palms. I'm not ready to kick that beehive."

"Best policy all around," declared Scott.

"Scott, I told you, you better keep me in the loop on anything you come up with on these two murders. I've got too many stacking up on me." Cleveland scowled at Queena Capps. "You too Miss Capps." He sighed and shook his head as he closed his notebook.

* * *

On the rooftop of a Tokyo building overlooking the city, Moe Berg took photos of nineteen-year-old Wyatt Scott. Reluctant and bored, Scott posed in a new suit, modern in style and contemporary for nineteen-thirty-four. He bought the suit in Philadelphia, with some help from a few Athletics teammates, explicitly for the barnstorming tour. Less formally attired than young Scott, Berg wore simple slacks and an all-stars jacket, meant as a warm-up to be worn at the baseball games. His appetite for snapshots seemed endless to his rookie pal.

As Berg wound his camera film forward a notch, Scott complained. "Moe, I thought we came to play baseball, not make all these sightseeing tours."

"Barnstorming, kid. It's supposed to be a holiday." Berg checked the photo number on his camera. "Sightseeing is part of the pay." Berg raised the camera to his eye and swept it in a very wide arc obviously passing Scott. He panned over to Scott again before passing him in the other direction.

He settled the lens closer to Scott's angle. "Kid, move a little to the right." Berg waved his hand to his right. Scott understood and moved to his left. "Good. Okay. Good. Hold it there." Berg snapped a photo;

rolled the film forward; snapped another, rolled, snapped, rolled, snapped. He looked up from his camera. "End of the roll," he announced.

He rewound the film while continuing to scan the skyline. Scott stood watching the veteran catcher and part-time tourist work with his camera and exchange the exposed roll of film for a new one. Noting the pause in his modeling duty, Wyatt left his spot and made his way to Berg to vent his feelings.

"Moe, sometimes I feel peculiar going on these excursions with you. I'd like to spend more time with the guys."

"Believe me kid, they don't miss an Okie, wonder-boy pitcher who, strikes them out at B P." Berg offered Scott a good-humored ribbing along with his analysis of how veteran players feel about young baseball prodigies, him or any other.

"I dunno. They're nice guys. They always say 'hi' to me. Lefty and Gehrig even know my name." A smile of pride popped up on Scott after his revelation.

Berg completed his reload. "Let's get one with you over there." Berg pointed ninety degrees from where he just took the previous series of photos. Scott dutifully moved as Berg shifted to account for the new position. "Connie Mack brought you along. The guys respect him, so you get the trickle down."

"We're all ballplayers. They understand."

"Don't kid yourself about ballplayer collegiality." Before raising the camera to his eye, Moe offered Wyatt a little more insight. "You can't expect hugs and kisses; you're barely beyond a rookie. Remember, eighteen months ago, you were a high school kid." Berg peered into his camera again. "This time, why don't you look out over the city…sort of candid photo style." Berg spread his arm out to illustrate.

Scott twisted his body away from the photographer and looked across downtown Tokyo toward the harbor. It was a beautiful vista. The dots of people below and the contours of ships paled against the bay and the sky that dipped to meet it.

Berg clicked a single photo before lowering his camera and addressing Scott. "Our trip's a sepia-tone memory."

"What?" Wyatt spun to hear Moe Berg's homily.

"We're making history," intoned Berg. "Just-around-the-corner history, deadly serious down-the-road history, and the fuzzy distant kind where your grandkids laugh at your clothes." Berg clicked and rolled through several more shots arcing far left and right of Scott.

"Moe-san, please no photos."

Neither American had noticed that Hiroshi Ishikawa, the official Japanese government guide for Berg, had joined them on the rooftop. Hiroshi was thirty, clean cut, and well-dressed in a new, high-quality suit tailored in Tokyo by the Japanese proxy of a British Savile Row establishment. He looked at once dapper and professional.

Ishikawa stepped quickly and directly to Berg. He halted in front of him ignoring Scott and his posing. He stood expressionless as if carrying out the cliché of Eastern inscrutability. However, his right hand tapped his thigh betraying some lack of patience. Scott watched without full comprehension. Berg stood easy and relaxed.

"The Japanese Imperial Government welcomes you to tour and take pictures, but you must stay with your guide. There are sensitive locations that our beloved Emperor and his Imperial government believe should not be photographed. Please, for the security of Nippon and your protection and safety as well, follow the rules." Hiroshi bowed politely to Berg.

Berg made a bow to Ishikawa. "Hiroshi-san, you're just in time to take a picture of the two of us." Berg extended the camera to Hiroshi.

Hiroshi narrowed his eyes at Berg before he snatched the Leica from the American catcher's hand. He opened it, and pulled the exposed film from the reel. He stuffed the loose film and the remainder of the unexposed roll in his side coat pocket, then handed the empty camera to Moe Berg.

"Darn it, Hiroshi, you've ruined the kid's memories," scolded Berg as he took the camera.

"I will get him many beautiful photos of Tokyo," replied Hiroshi flatly.

"But Hiroshi-san, he won't be in them." Berg took a new box of film from his pocket. He methodically withdrew the Kodak film roll from the box. With the fresh film removed, he placed the empty box in his other pocket with the previously exposed roll. Berg popped the new roll into his camera, pulled the leader of the film across the shutter plate, and threaded it into the take-up reel. All this under the watchful eye of Hiroshi. Scott watched the uncomplicated process thinking it was nothing more. The layers of forethought and the cleverness of Moe Berg would not find Scott's consciousness for nearly ten years.

"Here." Berg closed the camera case and handed it to Hiroshi. "Take a picture of the two of us, then I'll take one of you with the kid."

Hiroshi reluctantly took the newly loaded camera. He glared down at it like a filthy animal he had been forced to safeguard.

Berg waved his arm to Scott. "Come on, kid. We'll pose in front of the wall. Hiroshi and the Emperor can't be worried about that."

Scott walked to the stairwell wall to join Berg. Hiroshi fiddled with the camera to understand its exposure settings. He twisted the lens' settings twice before putting the camera to his eye. When Scott arrived at the wall, Berg fussed with his jacket.

"Do I look all right?" he asked Scott. Berg glanced at Wyatt, before refocusing his gaze onto Hiroshi.

"You look as you always do, a baseball player," remarked Hiroshi.

Berg pulled down on the bottom of his jacket to make sure. "That's good then. How 'bout the kid?"

"Young Mr. Scott is very presentable. He looks like a gentleman and does your country credit." Apparently satisfied with his exposure setting, Hiroshi brought the camera to his eye for a final appraisal of his composition. He gripped the camera ready for word from Berg.

Moe clasped his arm around Scott's shoulder. Hiroshi pivoted the camera and fastidiously focused it. He snapped the photo with a grinning Berg and a confused Scott staring at the lens.

"Take another, just to be sure," cautioned Berg.

Hiroshi obliged. This time with little fuss and indifferent execution.

"Thank you, Hiroshi-san. Now you must pose with Wyatt so he can show his family his new friend and your true Nippon hospitality." Berg dropped his hold on Scott's shoulder. He stepped to Hiroshi, held out his hand, and received the camera.

Hiroshi held his spot for a few seconds. Relenting, he trod hesitantly to Scott. The short journey took a painfully long time with Hiroshi circuitously meandering his way there rather than steering a straight line. Once he achieved the same depth as Scott, he stopped.

"Good." Berg waved his arm at them. "Move together." The reluctant subjects indulged him. "Great. Why don't you shake hands?" The annoyed guide grasped the hand of the befuddled young American. "Perfect! Say cheese." Berg clicked the shutter on his half-smiling subjects.

"Moe-san, we must be going," urged Hiroshi.

"Do we have more sightseeing?" Berg put the cap on his camera and snapped it into its leather case. "I promised young Wyatt we would visit Tokyo Harbor. He's from Oklahoma, you know. It's all dust and cowboys with nothing like the great achievements you have."

Moe Berg grinned. Hiroshi bowed perfunctorily, while annoyance crept into his smile. Ten years before he would come to understand the politics, Wyatt Scott just watched.

CHAPTER 23

A Cultured Voice

"Back in the day ballplayer?"

The image of a Tokyo rooftop, fourteen years prior, popped like a bubble. Berg and Hiroshi disappeared into the ether. The familiar voice of Mamie White broke Scott from the memory sparked by the photo of him standing with Hiroshi. He stepped away to see his favorite diner proprietor. She stood in his office doorway wearing her waitress garb and soft-sole shoes. An exceptionally nice lady, Mamie always stocked a smile for Scott. She wore that customary smile as she maintained her grip on the doorknob.

"Playing hooky from the diner?" joked Scott.

"Ten o'clock even Joe can handle."

Scott walked to his desk and offered Mamie a seat with his upturned palm. "Always happy to see you if this visit is social. If not, do you need me for something?"

"Maybe." Mamie stood her ground, making no move toward the

chair. "I think I need to tell you something." She shoved her hands in her apron pockets. "Wyatt, I need to tell you about the dead young girl in the paper. The one they said worked as a strumpet."

Ready to sit before Mamie spoke, the surprise of the subject left Scott standing. "I'm all ears, Mamie."

She considered Scott, still awkwardly poised between standing and sitting. "That girl came in a week ago Thursday," began Mamie. She motioned him to sit.

Scott obeyed, sliding into his desk chair. He paused a moment, then decided to let Mamie in on what he deduced from talking to Cleveland. "Yes. I know she came in that Thursday, and she had rhubarb pie."

Mamie screwed up her face at the surprising remark by Scott. "Yes, I believe she did. Don't recall you being there to see, but you're right she had a piece of pie."

Mamie changed her mind about the chair. Or maybe, she did not want to converse about whores from across the room with the door wide open. Either way, she shut the door and made her way to the guest chair. After she sat, she scooted it closer to the desk.

Mamie took a breath. "I came because of that young, little girl. What I saw, what I think I saw, did not start with her."

Scott pulled his pad from his front drawer. He grabbed a sharpened pencil out of his desk holder. "Take your time. Tell me any way you want, Mamie."

Appearing a little more at ease, she settled in her chair. "The older one, the vulgar one that got thrown out of the window, she came in now and again after dark. Just took coffee, that one. She wasn't rude but detached. I doubt she knew I was there. It was clear she was a..."

Mamie fumbled for a word her moral integrity could stomach. "...well, one of *those*." She sighed before starting again. "Each time she met a different man, working men in work clothes or maybe a clerk. Then, one day, she meets up with this fellow who wore a suit. He had some class, even meetin' a floozy, he dressed respectable."

Scott cleared more space on his desk shifting the phone to the side. "Sounds like what I know about her. What did the guy look like?" Scott readied his pencil. He twisted the scratch pad to better center it in front of him.

"Brown hair. Decent suit. Average guy." Mamie considered another moment before concluding. "Nothing special 'bout his looks."

"Did you hear anything they said?" quizzed Scott.

"Not really; a word or two, but I think it was all prostitute code not real conversation."

"Probably so," agreed Scott.

Mamie looked sorrowful. Her brow furrowed and her eyelids drooped low. Her genial smile might have been stashed in her purse, but for now, she no longer wore it. "My concern, my comin' to see you, is that same guy met another one, a young working girl – her first time at the diner. I never saw her before or since. After I read about the dead girl at Mohawk Park and saw her picture..." She hung her head. The retelling seemed to weigh on her. "...I figured it was her." She delivered the last phrase quietly and an octave lower. "In fact, now I'm dead sure it was that little girl."

"You're right to tell it, Mamie, but why not tell the cops?" Scott tried to be consoling, but he had to ask the question.

Mamie straightened in her chair. She held her chin high. "I thought about telling them, but cops think older women are busybodies when they talk about that kind." Wide ovals replaced the drooping slits of her eyes. Her scorn for police department effrontery swept away her despondency.

"I'll look into it and pass anything important along," assured Scott. "The police are looking at this. I'm working on it too, but independent from the police."

"Good. Then I was right to come to you. You're a square shooter and a good guy, Wyatt. Some of those Tulsa detectives come in the diner. I wouldn't trust some to find a lost dog." Mamie straightened her dress in preparation to stand. A second thought made her stop and lean forward again. "The man, the one that met the Jezebels, he had a real nice voice; a cultured voice."

Scott made a quick note. "Like a British accent or a college professor type?" asked Scott digging for elucidation.

"No, not snooty. Nice sounding," assessed Mamie.

"Nice like Ronald Coleman?"

"No. Not *that* nice. Mostly clear, precise, like a classy pitchman," corrected Mamie.

A new path unfolded for Scott. "You ever listen to KTOO Joe at night?" questioned Scott.

"I go to bed by eight-thirty. Barely listen to Fibber McGee. I get plenty of gab from my cousin Joe." She grinned. "I wouldn't sit up late at night for Ronald Coleman reading passages from the Good Book."

Scott cracked a smile at her preference for sleep over the eloquent actor. "The guy you saw with the girls – you'd recognize him?"

"Sure. If he comes in again, I'll call you." Mamie scooted her chair and stood. She wiggled her torso and rolled her shoulders loosening them after dropping their metaphorical heavy load on Scott.

Scott nodded to her and rose to his feet. "Thanks, Mamie."

She donned her Scott-smile once more. "Peach pie today – tasty in the summer," she advised.

"If I miss lunch, I'll grab a slice at dinner."

Mamie walked out of the door waving her right hand without looking back.

Scott scribbled a note on his pad. He added a second line. He considered some options. He doodled. He thought. He doodled Evie's name.

CHAPTER 24

Whoring Up

Scott waited in his office with Queena Capps. He relaxed in his desk chair. Queena paced and smoked. Arrayed on the outer edge of his desk were lipsticks, rouge, eye shadow, makeup brushes, eyeliners, a white washcloth, and a makeup pencil. Hanging from his coat tree, a short, shiny, and wantonly garish dress embarrassed his traditional fedora on the other peg. A pair of long, black, high heel pumps waited under the apparel, daring any Pythian Building packrat to steal one of the faux jewels that adorned them.

"You sure about this, Scott? He won't try anything on her?" asked Queena between a small puff and a deep pull on her cigarette. Her smoke haze hung heaviest away from the door and nearest his wall of memories.

"Just trying to smoke him out." Whether the phrasing came from a subconscious reaction to Queena's habitual puffing or just followed the lexicon, Scott did not analyze his response. "Joe'll be too surprised at

Evie's appearance at his radio station to consider any plan."

Queena angled herself toward Scott with her empty hand on her hip. "Still." Her accusatory glare hit stronger than words.

"I've told you, Queena; I'm driving her and waiting in the LaSalle. *Anything* seems iffy or she takes too long, I pull the nineteen-eleven and shut matters down."

The madam merely smoked in reply.

Footsteps in the hall, followed by the door opening, signaled the arrival of Scott's new undercover operative. Evie Hall carried enough in the caboose and possessed tastefully sized bosoms sufficient to confirm her as a grown woman. Yet, her good figure could not dispel her girlish glow or eradicate the innocence her freckles betrayed. She was the expression of every man's ideal daughter and the hoped-for wife of the young fellows who believed The Saturday Evening Post knew the manifestation of the ideal, guileless girl. She didn't bear the remotest resemblance to a prostitute.

She swirled in smiling like the young woman she really was wearing the professional clothes of the woman she claimed to be. "Howdy. I'm here to make ready for my performance." She halted to peer directly at Scott. "And to make those promised sawbucks."

Queena dropped her cigarette butt and crushed it on the floor. "Okay, hon, let's get started on your hair and makeup." She walked to the guest chair and tapped it.

Evie made her way to the chair and sat. Scott stood and tugged his chair around to the front opposite the guest chair before fighting through the smoke to his wall of memories. Queena scooted Scott's chair next to Evie and plopped down in it. She took Evie's head in both hands and swung it left and right. Evie smiled at Queena. Queena scowled at Evie.

"Okay, missy. If you're agreed with this, I will make you into a bawd that ought to be arrested for showing herself in daylight." Queena reached for the eyebrow pencil and began streaking lines across Evie's unadorned brows.

"This dress-up gag will be cookin' with gas," declared Evie.

"Shush, girl. I need you still." Queena scowled a moment, then found Scott. "You got an ashtray? I'll need a good smoke to do my best work."

Scott slipped behind his desk. He opened the top, right-hand drawer that housed his backup thirty-eight revolver. Deep in the drawer, behind the pistol, Scott grabbed a glass ashtray and set it down beside Queena. She nodded her approval. He slipped off to his photo memories and out of the way.

Finished for the moment with her pencil and placated by the ashtray, she moved on to an eye shadow packet and dipped her forefinger in it. Evie closed her eyes in anticipation. Queena swiped one lid with the blueish cosmetic then the other. She admired her work but dabbed both lids again to perfect her design. Satisfied with the eye shadow work, Queena broke for her cigarette. Firing it up, she moved away from Evie and blew the smoke farther.

Evie glanced at Scott and tossed a daring grin his way. He caught her out of the corner of his eye. He paid no heed to her impish enthusiasm, allowing the creation of whore-Evie to continue without comment. Queena noted her head movement and pulled it to square with the light. She nestled her Lucky into the ashtray where her lipstick ring proclaimed her ownership, while its smoke floated to the ceiling. The makeup artist madam wiped the eye shadow finger on the washcloth. She selected an eyelash brush and darkened, fattened, and vulgarized Evie's lashes. Her eyes darker than any brunette's, Evie began to resemble a vamp character from a silent film.

Not able to contain her enthusiasm, Evie blurted out, "How my I doin'?"

"Oh, you'll be a street-whore in no time." Queena opened a rouge case. "I'll redden those cheeks like Santa Claus in a blizzard."

Evie beamed her appreciation. Scott shook his head as much at the simile as the proceedings. Queena applied the rouge with the assurance of a professional makeup artist, which she could claim in the world of girls-for-hire. She smeared and dabbed with precision. She scrutinized her work as she retrieved her Lucky Strike from its spot on the ashtray. A deep pull and exhale gave her time to make her decision. A quick puff and the cigarette found renewed rest in the ashtray. A rouge brush broadened and quieted Evie's cheeks from obscene to merely garish.

A whim seemed to catch Queena as she grabbed her pencil and imparted a dot on Evie's chin. "A beauty mark is prewar and out-of-date, but johns see them as calling cards." The madam lightly grasped Evie's jaw giving her head a spin to the right and then to the left. She maintained her loose grip while her eyes scanned and re-scanned her young canvas.

"When do I get to see?" muttered Evie.

"When I'm done." Queena dropped her hands to her side. "I'll do your hair last." She accessed her collection of strong cosmetics. She grasped a lipstick cylinder and pulled off the cap. Her twist of the base produced a vivid, deep red shaft. Queena let a short and a sharp cackle slip out before truncating it and resuming her professional attentiveness to detail.

Evie, eyeing the lipstick, whistled. "That's some wacky red."

"Stop talkin' and pucker up. I need to paint this on thick and precise," announced Queena.

Evie puckered her lips. Scott moved to check the progress of the endeavor. He gawked but made no comment. Queena paused for another drag on her cigarette. After propping her smoke gently on the ashtray, she homed the lipstick in on Evie's mouth. A stroke along the left upper lip, then one along the right, and a dab in the middle of the lower lip completed the procedure.

"Purse your lips together and roll them." Queena demonstrated her command.

Scott watched as the generally innocent, classy-dressing, Evie Hall morphed into a caricature prostitute with a mouth that could be spotted in the centerfield bleachers by a nearsighted home plate umpire. Evie smacked her lips as if trying them on for the first time. She wrinkled her nose before running her tongue along her upper lip. Queena assessed her work in progress. She reached for her dark pencil, held it a moment, then set it down. Satisfied with her creation to this point, she cracked a smile.

"Time to do up your hair, hon." Queena selected a comb and a brush as her tools. She left her chair and circled behind Evie. She took a length of hair from the top, middle of her head, stretching it up high. Evie sat still as Queena pulled the comb from the scalp to her hand holding the ends. Satisfied, she ran the comb up and down violently, fast teasing the strand. She repeated the process with new strands, while Evie grimaced persistently during the hair-pulling process.

Puffed up and far uglier than Evie's normally styled hair, the scraggly result triggered a mitigated, but apparent sigh from Scott. Queena caught the sound and shot Scott a glare as she circled to her chair. The young secretary as her canvas, the artistic madam brought her tools to bear for the final additions. She deepened the almost sable eyebrows another shade darker.

Another review prompted Queena to toy with her pencil, but it never made it off the desk. "I think your face is done and your war paint complete."

Evie squirmed. "Let me see!" She frowned toward Scott and pleaded to Queena. "Give me a mirror, dang it."

Queena unsnapped a compact with a mirror and handed it to Evie.

Evie grabbed the compact and twisted it from side to side to glimpse her visage. "Oh, my Lord." She laughed before she reined it down to a giggle using her hand to cover her mouth.

"Don't ruin your lipstick," admonished Queena.

Evie dropped her hand and sought approval from Scott. "What do you think?"

His thoughts were too obscene to voice. He needed her to provoke his suspect, but the creation being produced gave him pause. Scott forced a smile while he worried about the result. He walked closer to Evie to view Queena's masterpiece of whore horror.

Evie widened her grin. Miss Capps, imperious as Queen Victoria posing for her regal portrait, sat silently awaiting praise. Scott revolved partway around Evie. He nodded a few times.

"Well?" An impatient Queena searched for her well-deserved praise.

"Yeah, I gotta' be on active duty looking like this," jumped in Evie. "Spill! Tell us how guys will look at me."

Scott cleared his throat. "They'll think you're a working girl all right." He wasn't sure they wouldn't worry about her being crazy, but other men's urges and delights were not a subject of his conversations.

"She's perfect for stalking your man." Queena stood and stretched a little. "He'll bite at her, or he don't bite at all."

Evie stood also. "Wowser. He'll make me an offer, and I'll play coy."

"Don't get carried away. Just try to get him to meet you," scolded Scott.

"Now, you need to leave, so I can get her into her outfit." Queena and Evie looked at the bright red, noticeably-short dress hanging on Scott's coat tree.

Evie started with a grin before graduating to a laugh. "Glad it's summer. My legs would freeze in that thing during winter."

"Shoo Scott." Queena flung her arms out toward the door.

"Got it. I will sit on the stairsteps till you call me." Scott left. Queena shut the door. He could hear Evie's girlish giggles about the dress fitting despite the wall and door. He sat on the top step wondering whether his ploy would work.

* * *

Radio stations are lonely places at night. No one noticed Evie Hall, dressed like a lady of the evening, sashaying down the empty corridor of the KTOO radio studio. She had spent more than an hour being floozied up by Queena Capps. Twenty-five years in the business had given Queena the expertise to transform a twenty-year-old virgin into as worldly looking a prostitute as any john might expect. Evie's eyelashes fluttered long and lush calling attention to the dark and copious mascara that set her eyes deep in their sockets. Thick, scarlet lipstick stood out even against her heavy makeup. The crimson summer dress with bare shoulders fit as tight as any skirt, conforming to her body like wrapped wax paper. Its hem stopped too far above her knee, displaying her pretty legs while barely covering her garter snaps. Long, thin, high heels raised Evie two inches taller while their open-toe design exposed her red-polished toenails through her hose. Any semblance of subtlety regarding Evie's occupation did not escape Queena Capp's handiwork in Scott's office.

Evie completed her swaying-rear waltz down the carpeted hall. She arrived at the third broadcast room where she pressed her hands to the glass. She could see the radio personality she sought talking into his microphone. He looked much like his publicity photos, making it certain this disc jockey was indeed KTOO Joe. Evie rapped on the glass.

KTOO Joe left his turntable and came to the door. He opened it to the width of his body but kept his grasp on the knob. An average looking man and well under six feet tall, he would blend into any crowd. He sported brown hair, brown eyes, and brown shoes. He wore navy slacks and a white shirt with brass cufflinks. Edging out an initial look of annoyance, an expression of superiority pasted Joe's face. He took time to scrutinize Evie up and down, incorporating leers, sneers, scoffs, and smirks in his inspection.

"I'm working," he declared in a clear and resonant voice. He narrowed his eyes showing disdain for the interruption. "This is a live broadcast." He leaned on the door handle angling his body. As he contemplated Evie's youth and physical appeal, which shone through despite the camouflage of her makeup and attire, his stern countenance slackened.

"Just give me a sec," solicited Evie. She dropped her head down and her eyes up adding a hint of innocence to her otherwise trollop facade. "I didn't know how else to reach you."

"I've got maybe a minute on that platter, so what are you after?" His melodic voice made his question seem profound and more significant than it was.

"Business honey." Evie switched her pitch to worldly and professional. "I was Darlene's new girl till she flew out the window. So now, I'm my own girl." She smiled with pride.

"I don't know a Darlene and I'm not looking for a whore." Joe switched from defensive at the start of his sentence to demeaning at the finish. He began to close the door.

Evie stiff-armed it. "Yeah, ya' did. You knew Darlene. You knew her, and I know how you like to get your kicks." She gave him a corner-mouth grin to show she understood everything about him and Darlene. "Don't bother me as long as you don't touch my face." She looked Joe straight in the eye. The young woman had nerve in reserve and grit in her pocket.

"What doesn't bother you?" quizzed Joe.

"Playin' rough," Evie replied without hesitation. "I can take it...if you pay up for it."

Joe blanched even as his eyes narrowed. He pushed the door wide and let loose of the handle. He took in all of Evie, viewing her in the new light of her disclosures. He glanced around at the record revolving on the turntable. The needle glided toward the center and its end of play. "Wait a second. I have to change platters."

Joe shuffled back into his broadcast room and fussed with his equipment. He brought the needle up and let the old disc whirl. He started a second disc spinner with its vinyl pre-mounted and dropped the needle into place. A new song flowed from the speakers. Joe placed the spent record into its sleeve.

With Joe busy and not looking her way, Evie stepped from the door and took the moment to calm herself. She pulled and tugged on the strange clothing to reset it. The character of her outfit never challenged her sensibilities, yet the same could not be said for its touch. The feel of the garments bothered her from the cramps in her toes to the draft coming up the short dress. She pushed down her discomfort determined to see the job through as much to please Scott as to claim the double sawbuck.

His record changing and time check complete; Joe slid to the doorway. He considered Evie's body without the pretense of admiring her ensemble or hiding his purpose. He did not salivate, but his eyes evaluated her like a wolf evaluates a rabbit. His leer persisted while he nodded ever so slightly.

Evie caught the message and responded. "So, no face. You get an hour at your place or a hotel. No cars, no outdoors." She laid out her ground rules. She spoke flatly, bluntly and with the tone and timbre of experience.

"If I do enjoy such things, you don't look old enough to have much experience," countered Joe.

"Better than you've ever had. Young, firm, and I got plenty of experience, but it'll cost," replied Evie with as much moxie as she could muster.

"How much? How much will it cost me?" arrogance and condescension flew out with the words like spittle from a sibilant stutterer.

"Fifty." Evie put her hand on her hip, pushed her jaw out, and dared him with the high quote.

"Fifty!" Shock registered on Joe. "Whores run ten dollars."

Sure of herself after shocking him, Evie displayed more confidence. "Not for what you want, Buster."

Regaining his sophisticated demeanor, Joe bargained. "Okay, but Darlene charged thirty for it."

"I told you what I charge. I'm an upgrade, the deluxe model." Evie ran her hands along the sides of her body to emphasize her point. She threw in a little body wiggle. Full in on the high price and hard sell, she licked her lips aiding her closing argument. "It's fifty."

Involuntarily licking his lips in reply, Joe mulled the statement. While his face didn't sweat nor did his trousers bulge, it became apparent that something wanton stirred inside him. He took another long, slow view to fully gauge Evie's attributes. The young, solid product evidently sold Joe. "I get off in an hour and a half."

"Just because I'm up-for-grabs doesn't mean I got no jobs." Evie straightened her angled pose. "I'm working regulars tonight." Her salacious sales pitch complete, she allowed the businesswoman to emerge. "I'm lookin' to fit you in between chrome-domes and oil boys." The slang was pure Evie, but it seemed to fit a young prostitute's view of her clientele. "Tomorrow fills the bill if you can finish playing before ten.

That's when the bankers come out and a girl can't afford to miss a try at a banker." She slid slightly as if to leave. "Meet me tomorrow at Joe and Mamie's Diner. You know the place?"

Joe moved a little into the hall. He glanced both directions to see if anyone shared the corridor with them. Seeing no one, he nodded in the affirmative. "When?"

"Eight-thirty. If it works for you, sweetie." Evie leered and licked her lips with dramatic slowness. "And don't forget the cash," she added from her business side.

"Eight-thirty is aces by me, babe." An unsettling smile spread on his lips. "What is your name, sweetheart?"

"Sweetheart will do. Otherwise, it's whatever you want it to be." Evie ostentatiously bit her lip and walked away. After two steps, she twirled around toward Joe. "Better change your record, Joe." She batted her eyes and strolled away from him with her newly perfected butt sway finalizing her performance.

* * *

The next evening at Queena Capps's office, Evie Hall had once again been transformed from clean cut girl to hardcore prostitute. The new outfit continued the short hem, summer weight design, while Queena had dialed down the makeup to overdone from gaudy slut. Still, the young secretary appeared harsher and nastier than any of the May Rooms' true working girls. A cocktail dress six inches shorter than risqué covered Evie and clung to her just like the over-tight ensemble of the night before. She requested simpler shoes, but only managed to get

Queena to close the toes and cut the heels down an inch in selecting the new pair.

Queena sat admiring her second transformation of Evie. Not a canvas for her art, Queena saw honey for her flytrap. She turned to Wyatt Scott, smiling at her accomplishment. Scott sat passively through the process. He saw young Miss Hall once more become that which she was not. Tonight's program presented greater risks and a wider range of possible misadventures, all of which worried him. Yet, because the collaboration managed to secure the meeting he wanted, where he wanted, he saw no reason to interfere.

Evie strained to view the mirror, but it eluded her. "Okey-Dokey. Do I look like a professional sharecropper now?" The previous night's dress rehearsal only whetted her appetite for continued vamping. She moved to the closet door that concealed Queena's long mirror. Evie opened it and viewed her new persona. She admired her temptress look, twisting to note her face and chest, then bending to view her legs and rear. Evie practiced slouching and looking down her nose.

Scott shifted from watching Evie's vanity showcase to catching Queena's eye. "You don't think it's too much?"

"A hardcore john will want a hardcore whore," replied Queena. Her voice of experience convincing Scott and creating a broad smile on young Miss Hall.

Evie chimed in. "I like it this crazy." She pivoted to see Scott. "If my folks see me, they'll never recognize me." She reported back to the mirror to model once more. It in return, reported her slutty reflection.

Queena rose and approached the seated Scott. "Wyatt, you take her out through my closet door to the kitchen. Carl can let you out into the alley and your car." She made it sound more than reasonable. "No sense taking any chance of her being seen on the street out front."

Scott knew of Queena Capp's secret passage, but never saw it put to use. He stood and moved to Evie's side near the closet. He touched her shoulder to bring an end to the alter-ego narcissism that had swept her up. She broke free from the mirror's hold to peer at Scott.

Queena entered her closet and pulled her clothes to one side. Behind the clothes rack, she slid a bar to unlock the false wall and pushed the hidden door out of the way. She stepped out of the closet clearing a path. Before she waved Scott and Evie through, Queena added to her earlier instructions. "Scott, tell Carl to come see me after he lets you out. I need him to get some things ready for me."

CHAPTER 25

Danger and Justice

The popularity of Joe and Mamie's Diner extended far beyond Wyatt Scott. A regular clientele sustained it during the war, while returning vets and oil company hires brought new business through the door. The aroma of home cooking wafted in the air from bacon and eggs in the morning, to fried steak at supper, and hamburgers in between. It did close early, as nine o'clock figured to be a late night for most of Tulsa's diner patrons.

A young couple talked more than chewed at one table. A pair of obvious pump-jockeys, oil rags and all, swallowed meatloaf, and mashed potatoes, while swilling low-alcohol beer, which by statute Oklahoma deemed to be non-alcoholic. Another two working men ate at the counter, scraping bread across their plates to sop up gravy. At the counter, but near the register, Wyatt Scott stirred and toyed with his cup of java. The trolloped-up Evie Hall waited at a window table sipping coffee and toying with cherry pie.

KTOO Joe came through the diner door. Dressed in bland sports clothes without a hat, he did not measure up to the suited, local businessmen, nor did he fit in with the working men. Joe stepped in, closed the door behind him, and stood. He charily scanned the room finding Evie before he stirred. She watched him until he made eye contact. She held her gaze a beat then peered down at her plate and cut a bite of pie with her fork. Joe stepped smartly toward her.

At the counter, Scott made eye contact with Mamie. She investigated Joe's features. She stared and squinted with the intensity of a hawk. Her stare of investigation grew dark with disdain and sharp with conviction. She glared toward Scott and nodded her recognition that it was indeed the man who met Mary. Scott tossed a dime on the counter before whirling on his stool. The front door opened during Scott's process of spinning around. A granite-faced Lieutenant Morgan stalked directly toward Scott.

Joe reached Evie. He stopped beside the table near her chair. He investigated both ways for eavesdroppers before offering a terse imperative. "Let's go." Having made no pretense to small talk or civility, he leered at his human commodity.

"I've still got pie left," protested Evie.

"If you want your money, come on now." Joe was implacable.

Evie took a quick sip of her coffee before standing. "Leave a half-dollar for me would you, Joe?" she asked sweetly. She peeked toward Scott at the counter seeking reinforcement.

"Pie and coffee runs twenty cents," countered Joe. He slapped a quarter on the table. Malevolent ferment and puerile impatience quaked through him rinsing out in shaky hands and a tapping foot.

Morgan reached Scott, who tried to glimpse around him to mind Evie. Morgan rammed his finger into Wyatt's ribs. Scott glared into Morgan's eyes knowing the Tulsa detective's timing could not be worse. To view Evie, he broke from his stare and tried to peer around the lieutenant.

"PI, I'm wise to you and your game," scolded Morgan. "You and your Indian lawyer are pretty cozy with Queena Capps." He dropped his finger from Scott's chest.

Scott put his hands on Morgan's shoulders and physically shifted him to observe Evie and her would-be customer. The detective flashed surprise at Scott's action but did not retaliate. As Wyatt twisted to view the proceedings, KTOO Joe took Evie by the arm and escorted her to the door. He halted jerking on Evie's arm in the process.

"You sure you understand?" Joe leered down at her. An ominous coldness dripped from his eyes.

Evie smiled at Joe hiding clenched teeth and a stomach full of butterflies behind her bravado. His icy expression did not waver. She glanced toward Scott making eye contact with him once more. This time, the reality of her predicament weighed on her face. Scott caught Evie's distress even as Morgan kept up his harangue.

"Cleveland thinks you're on the up-and-up, but I got my doubts," declared Morgan while shifting to his previous spot and once more impeding Scott's view.

Joe pulled Evie's arm. "Did you hear? You know the deal." He whispered the second part with a sinister insinuation. His grip was forceful and his tug insistent.

Playing every bit the part, she hired on to do, Evie cocked her head and replied coolly, "I know the deal. You got my fifty?" She seized his grasping hand with her free one.

Joe released his grip and jerked his hand free. Staring indignation at Evie, he reached into his shirt pocket and showed the tops of two twenties and a ten. "You get the money when we play." He shoved the bills down in his pocket. He opened the door, holding it for Evie. She paused, then continued her performance by strolling out. Her butt-wiggle, having been practiced and perfected, sold the sham likely for those gawking from the street as well as KTOO Joe.

Witnessing the encounter conclude far faster than expected, Scott snubbed Morgan's comments and ignored his authority. As the diner door closed behind Joe, Scott shoved Morgan's hand away. "Morgan, I need to go."

"If there's any going, it'll be to the station," growled Morgan as he stepped over to block Scott's way.

Morgan's head blocked Wyatt's view as Evie disappeared down the street. "I'm telling you, Morgan, I *have* to go!"

"Then you'll go in cuffs, Scott!" Morgan reached toward his back pocket.

Scott dodged around him. Morgan grabbed Scott's arm. He pivoted toward Morgan, his fist clenched for visceral combat. Mamie, conscious of the entire play being performed, abandoned her station behind the counter. She scrambled directly to Morgan, physically interceding between the cop and Scott. Her effort forestalled any further escalation in the clash.

"Lieutenant Morgan! I'm about to close," advised Mamie, her tone more fretful than reproving.

Scott jerked his arm free and dashed toward the door. Morgan grabbed at him, but Scott's pace bested the detective's reflexes. Morgan seemed to contemplate his next move, having been bowled over by those of Scott.

Mamie threw a new choice at him based on his predictable behavior. As she stood with her hand on her hip smiling at Morgan, she made her point. "Table or stool if you want your usual pie."

More interested in peach pie than scolding Scott, Morgan abandoned his pursuit and moved toward a stool at the counter. Scott reached the door and threw it open. Mamie made her way back behind the counter and pulled out a cup and saucer. Scott tore down the street after Evie without closing Joe and Mamie's door.

Two blocks down from Joe and Mamie's, Evie jogged to keep up the urgent pace set by KTOO Joe. Lamp poles, with satellites of swirling insects, provided islands of light in the downtown darkness allowing Evie to verify her path. The pair skimmed in and out of the circles of illumination as they hurried along the street. Evie twisted her head to check behind her, but no one followed. Those butterflies had multiplied and prospered in her stomach. The whole swarm flitted and flew from top to bottom and side to side threatening to burst out along with whatever measly morsels she had eaten that evening.

Evie halted her quick march catching her breath and another quick glimpse around. Joe continued a few strides before sensing her failure to keep up. He pivoted and trooped back to where she stood. A tiny burp slipped out instead of the words she intended. Evie swallowed to calm herself before trying again.

"Where are you parked, Joe? This is some walk to get to your buggy."

"Up and over," growled Joe. Agitation flickered in his eyes. "Come on!"

"Okay but take it easy." Evie started moving with a slow and measured pace. "There's no hurry, Joe. You're not on the meter yet."

He didn't reply or change his expression. He tipped his head forward and waited for Evie to start off. Three steps in, Joe picked up the pace again and glared at Evie to keep up. They promptly made their way to the corner. Without a word or a signal, Joe pressed his shoulder against Evie forcing her to the right. She staggered a little in her high heels before righting herself. She slowed her pace as they approached a sedan. Evie stared down the street from where they rounded the corner. A distant car's taillights diminished as it sped away. No human could be seen, let alone Wyatt Scott. The night felt warm, but Evie's sweat was born of fear.

Joe reached his car. He pulled the passenger door open while the lagging Evie continued to approach. "This is it. Get in," he ordered.

Evie moved toward the seat but grabbed the top of the door. "Sure, but there are rules." She looked Joe in the eyes. "Even you johns have to play by the rules."

Annoyed by the delay, Joe snapped sharp with his reply. "Okay, but for fifty, it's going to be extra rough."

Headlights split the darkness down the street as a new model sedan made a crossing at the intersection half a block ahead. Evie's heart raced with hope. Joe watched with caution and distrust. It passed by a streetlight revealing a passenger in the backseat, but no other detail before it rolled out of sight.

After the car passed, Evie scrutinized the deserted street and lifted her ears. None of the distant sounds reverberated with rescue as an undertone. Her short dress and bare shoulders were not ventilation enough to cool the nervous heat flowing through her skin. She took a breath. She calmed just enough to continue the ruse and exhaled her answer. "Fine. Remember the agreement, nothing on the face."

"For a young chippie, you've got a lot of sass," sneered Joe.

Drawing on all her fashioned moxie, Evie played the role. "I've got a lot of everything, Joe. You got a room?"

"Sure. It's nice and quiet too." He looked across the car door at Evie. "No one will hear us play, so you can be as loud as you like." Joe spun and surveyed the street. Apparently satisfied with its emptiness, he completed his thoughts. "Get in. We'll see how long that sass lasts when I get to work on your sensitive spots." Devoid of passion, he served up menace with a side of cruelty.

With her skin on fire, her stomach in flight, and no help in sight, Evie drew up an off-the-cuff plan. She raised her arm and pointed behind Joe. "A cop's coming our way!" she warned loud and shrill. When he turned to look, Evie bolted down the street. Seeing no cop, Joe raged and ran after her.

Her lead shrank as she neared the middle of the block. She veered across the pavement making her way east down Sixth Street. The move gained her a few more feet, but she would not outrace him another block. With Joe cutting the intercept distance by angling across the street, Evie seized on the intersectant alley as her escape route.

Sparse light spilled into its shadowy corridor, but she dashed through the darkness seeking the thoroughfare at its end. As she ran hellbent for deliverance, the road bricks' uneven surface took a toll on her pumps. One heel snapped, then the second, slowing her each time. Evie ran hard. She ran fast. Joe ran faster.

Scott sprinted full tilt through the empty streets pointing east along the presumptive path Joe took Evie. He wasn't tired or hot yet fear and frustration poured sweat down his forehead. Veering south and seeing nothing but empty roads, he maneuvered east on Fifth Street heading toward Detroit Avenue. He contemplated whether to continue to Elgin or move south again. He did not contemplate what might happen to Evie, he wouldn't let himself.

Joe caught Evie and pinned her against a brick wall. "If you're trying to make me beat you harder, I don't need motivation," snarled Joe. Saliva spilled from the corner of his mouth. A preying wolf on the dark alleys of Tulsa, he bared his teeth. He dug his fingers into Evie's bare shoulders.

The game no longer safe, her role played out, Evie scrambled to think of a way out. The nearest door was steel and locked against burglary. Her injured feet didn't want to kick. Her eyes teared. She slouched a little and pled the truth. "You got it wrong. I'm not really a whore."

Colder than Siberian snow, Joe replied, "Doesn't matter now." He coiled his right fist and drove it into her solar plexus.

The air driven from her lungs; Evie gasped. Her legs buckled. She slid down the wall scraping tiny swaths of skin along her spine and pulling her short outfit farther up her exposed legs. The brick alley stopped her slide imprinting its pattern on her rear and jarring her tailbone. This second jolt instigated a quick succession of coughs.

At Detroit, Scott spontaneously charged down it. A new sedan, with a chauffeured passenger and a driver up front, crossed Sixth Street traveling west. It was the first car he had seen in blocks, but it didn't contain Joe or Evie. His leather soles clacked against the concrete reinforcing his fear with every beat. As he neared Sixth, he weighed his next move. He craned his head left to look east. Pockets of lamplight dotted the way for blocks. No signs of movement and nary a parked car disturbed the view. Scott swung to look west. While that direction also showed no life, a parked car swayed his choice. He rounded the corner still running full tilt down the middle of the road.

Joe kneeled to stare Evie in the eyes. He leered savoring his control. Without hint or warning, he slapped Evie, reddening her right cheek. In what seemed like a change of intent, he cupped her right breast with his left hand. Evie jerked her head down to scrutinize the transgressing appendage and its role. His digits worked toward her nipple with the apparent intent of eroticism. Upon reaching their objective his forefinger and thumb squeezed and twisted with such force and cruelty it made Evie whimper.

"Owww! You shit!" yelped out Evie.

Joe laughed. "Get used to it!" He slapped her, this time pulling his left hand from its sexually cruel toil to wallop the right side of her face.

"You won't get away with this. People know I'm with you," shrieked Evie.

"I doubt that my slutty little toy." His dismissal of the notion carried equal weights of logic and arrogance. He ran his hand along her exposed thigh once more stopping and pinching her flesh rather than seeking the center of her sex.

"Damn it! That hurt!" cried Evie. She could feel the blood run to the injured flesh and the inevitable bruise start to form. "People do know I'm with you, KTOO Joe, and you'll get caught!" Even knowing this to be the case, Evie began losing hope that she would be rescued. Mustering her courage more than her strength, she swung her arm with fingers curled and nails flaunting.

Joe jerked away avoiding the slash across his chin. He grabbed both her arms then shook her. "You're just going to make it harder on yourself." He enjoyed another sneer at her expense. "Even as lonesome as this spot is, it's too public. You need to be allowed to scream at the top of your lungs." Looking left and right down the dim alley, he tipped off his plan. "I've got knives." The pitch in his voice and the glint in his eyes shifted in reaction to his declaration. "You'll be the center of attention. We'll see what sensitive parts make you bawl the loudest." Some spittle dribbled out of the corner of his mouth.

Still pinning her with his left hand, Joe punched Evie square in her cheek and jaw. Her eyes drooped and closed. She slumped, tilting to her left from the blow. Her short garb pulled to the side exposing her garters and panties. Her back slid down the wall scraping the skin but slowing her fall and easing her head's contact with the bricks. Joe scooped her up, slung her limp body over his shoulder, and carried her down the alley.

Dazed and groggy, Evie stirred enough for Joe to notice. He halted in the alley just short of the street. He pulled her from his shoulder and held her up. Joe sneered and bared his teeth again. "I plan to do things you've never seen in your nightmares." His usually eloquent voice found a tone that could chill boiling water. He grabbed her up, again carrying her like a flour bag to the end of the alley. He looked both ways before scurrying across the avenue with Evie.

Down the way from the parked car, Scott saw a dim blob emerge from an alley. He slowed to a trot trying to decipher the image. As it broke into the circle of light from a streetlamp, he saw KTOO Joe hauling Evie over his shoulder. Relief, adrenaline, and anger propelled him into overdrive. He tore down Sixth forcing his wingtips to bow like never before.

Intent on making it to his car with his prey, Joe did not see Wyatt Scott racing to intercept him. Just as Joe made it to his car, the flying steps and flashing image of Wyatt Scott registered. Realizing the rendezvous was indeed a setup, Joe callously dumped Evie on the pavement. "Ya' bitch whore!" he screamed in the process. He darted across the street and toward the same alley where he caught and abused Evie.

Scott reached the dazed and groggy young girl. "Evie! Evie!" He bent to check her and rubbed her neck. She opened her eyes and smiled in recognition. Still stunned, she garnered the wherewithal to motion for him to go after Joe. Scott followed her directive and sprinted across the road into the alley following her attacker.

Joe ran like a kid who didn't play sports and a man who sits on the job. The high school sports star and professional ballplayer ran with wider strides and twice as many per minute as the radio announcer. At the halfway point of the alley, Scott's natural speed continued to narrow the gap. Joe sucked wind and scurried with fruitless motion. Scott closed in; his fist, by this time, clenched to strike.

A few steps short of the alley's end, Joe swiveled his head to see Scott ready to overtake him. From the opposite street at that end of the alley and with no sound or warning Carl Jefferson materialized. Joe twisted around to see him looming but could not stop before he ran into the chest of the immense man. A single jab in the forehead from his enormous right fist, dropped Joe, unconscious, into his arms.

Scott slowed as he approached Carl. "Carl. Nice timing." Scott smiled. "I can take that slug off your hands." Scott stopped a few feet in front of the big man, who held the limp KTOO Joe like a rag doll he'd won at the fair. Carl said nothing and made no move to hand the villain to Scott.

From the same corner where Jefferson emerged, Queena Capps strolled into the alley with a large caliber pistol in her hand. Dressed in black and in a modest style contrary to her normal flamboyance, Queena looked menacing. As she walked, she held the gun up and minded Scott. She stepped to Carl's side. "No, Scott," she said flatly. "He's mine."

Eyeing her gun and calculating her intent, Scott reasoned with her; "May not be the best plan, Queena."

"It's the only plan, Scott." Her tone crisp and clear, her voice all business. "You're not going to make trouble, are you?" she warned.

Moral ambivalence propelled Scott a step forward but tempered his plea. "Let me get the cops. Besides, folks saw him leave with Evie."

"Sure. Folks see things. They never remember what they saw." She smirked.

"Queena!" Scott made a step forward. Still holding Joe, Carl shifted to counter him.

"Scott, you're a good egg. Let it go," advised Queena.

"Lot of danger in this." Scott tossed his hand in Jefferson's direction. "Not just for you, but Carl too."

"We can take care of ourselves." Queena motioned with the gun beyond Scott and down the alley. "Take off."

"He's famous. Folks will wonder what happened to him," argued Scott.

"Sure. They'll wonder where he went." Queena paused looking at Joe's limp figure hanging from Carl's arm. She stepped from the alley's mouth and scanned the street. Resolve, marinated in hate, flared in her eyes. "And they'll wonder a long, long time." She came over to Carl's side keeping the gun trained on Scott.

Scott played baseball by the rules. He played at life by most of them. Like an umpire having to decide between strike or ball for a pitch on the edge of the plate, a person must decide about life's plays on the edge. Scott made his call and held his tongue.

Again, Queena waved her gun toward the far end of the alley and Evie's location. "You go take care of that little girl. Carl and I will take care of this sack of shit." Queena redirected the gun barrel toward the street behind them. "Take him to the car." Carl accepted the command and hoisted Joe like Joe had done Evie, though Carl did so with greater ease and even less care. He strolled away bearing his burden and disappeared from the alley. Queena remained, keeping Scott at bay, and still brandishing her weapon.

"Queena..." Scott started to offer counsel, but she cut him off.

"This isn't your side of town, Mr. PI. Go on. See to her. See to that kid." Queena held her pistol while she backed away.

Scott moved on toward Evie.

Queena stopped before she left the alley. She hollered to him. "Scott."

He halted, spinning around to see what Queena wanted.

No longer pointing her gun, she held it against her hip with her elbow out. "The little gal's got moxie, but I better not see her whored up again." Queena spun around and left the alley tracing the path Carl took.

Scott hurried out of the alley and ran across the dark, deserted street. A tiny breeze swept down it and across his forehead. He noted the evening's heat for the first time as he reached Evie. She hadn't moved, but as he bent down to see her, she blinked her eyes and looked up at him. Some droplets of relief dripped into the bucket of guilt he carried. Scott stooped close. Her whore ensemble was stained, her blouse torn. Smeared from the corner of her mouth to the edge of her jaw, the war paint lipstick impersonated blood. Her deep mascara had run from perspiration and tears, creating charcoal streaks on either side of her nose. The rouge on one cheek had been replaced by a swollen bulge.

"How are you?" Scott panned her body for injuries then settled on her face.

"Not sure." Evie raised her head. "How do I look?"

"Knot on your jaw another on your cheek. They'll bruise," Scott replied honestly if incompletely.

"Damn!" Evie rocked forward to a sitting position. She rubbed her bruised jaw. "Owe, damn it *is* swollen!"

Scott reached under her arms and helped Evie to her feet. "The LaSalle's down the block. I'll get some ice before I take you to the office."

"Thanks." Evie wobbled before righting herself.

Scott held her steady. He stared into her eyes. She blinked and nodded. Satisfied with her sentience, he guided Evie down the street.

"Where's the son-of-a-bitch creep?" asked Evie as she wobbled a little.

"You don't need to worry about him." Scott deliberated before completing his answer. "He won't be a danger anymore."

Apparently satisfied or at least not wanting elucidation, Evie squeezed tighter on Scott. He kept the pace steady encouraging her with his grip. He got her through the next block knowing they were close to his car.

As they rounded the corner and caught sight of the LaSalle, Evie perked up. She stopped long enough to look at Wyatt. "You better make good on both those sawbucks."

A little surprised, but pleased at her attitude, he replied, "Well earned." Scott shook his head and hugged Evie just a bit. "They're yours."

THE STORY

Scott changed the plan and brought Evie and her real clothes to his apartment where he could soothe her wounds with ice and iodine. He felt rueful bringing her there, but short of the hospital and questions, which neither of them wanted to field, the Sophian Plaza seemed like the ablest venue. She raised her blouse and performed like a stoic when Scott swabbed tincture of iodine on the scrapes along her spine. After tending to her wounds, he supplied her with freshly chipped ice in an ice bag to reduce the swelling on her jaw, cheeks, thigh, and arm.

With her bodily injuries tended, she rested in Scott's easy chair while he employed a bowl of soap and water to cleanse away her streaked mascara and gaudy, smeared lipstick. The young lady he appreciated gradually emerged from Queena's whorish mask even if a little worse for wear. After cleaning her face and patting it dry, Scott refilled the icebag. Evie eased it against her swollen cheek.

"That Joe guy was certifiable," blurted out Evie. Except for a whispered 'thanks' and one 'ouch' when Scott dabbed her facial bruises with cotton balls soaked in alcohol, she had said nothing since they crossed his apartment threshold.

Scott, who had been on his way to pour himself a Cutty, peered at her. "He is!" He completed his trip to the bar and the console unit next to it. He pulled out the scotch bottle, setting it next to a glass. He ignored the phonograph side of the cabinet and switched on the power to the radio. "Would you like some music while you ice those bruises?"

Evie pulled the ice bag down for a moment. "Frank Sinatra would be sharp." She grinned at her choice and returned the icebag to her jaw.

Scott sucked air through his teeth at her choice of crooners. Not that he hated Sinatra, but big band, jazz, and lady torch singers all rated above the pack of songsters classified as crooners. He grabbed the bottle and poured three-fingers into the glass. He took a quick swig for consolation before tuning the dial in search of Evie's skinny dreamboat singer. The dial made it to the end without encountering Sinatra. He spun it the other way quickly producing static and pops of sound along the path. Near the end of the spectrum, Scott paused long enough to hear the announcer declare Frank Sinatra would lead off after a commercial break.

"Got your guy coming up after we hear about something we don't need." The advertisement did not make Scott a liar. It droned on about Geritol and the iron-poor blood that he at thirty-three and Evie at twenty doubtless had. He started to rejoin Evie when she stopped him.

"Hey. How about one of those for an injured doll?" She did not smile or hint she was joking. Evie held the ice to her jaw and held a stare on Scott.

"Didn't think a nice, underage girl like you drank," replied Scott.

"It's Oklahoma. Just as illegal over twenty-one."

She had the facts right. If Scott thought of her as a girl before tonight, he had no such right after what transpired. "Scotch is a little bitter, more an acquired taste. Anything else strike your fancy?"

"I'm not too gone on what's what except all the fancy cocktails I read about in magazines." She broke a little grin. "What would a gumshoe's babe drink?"

Scott didn't want to venture down that road and answer such a loaded question. He mused a bit about what he could concoct that she'd keep down and not overdo. As he ran through a mental list of drinks and mixers, most of which he did not stock, he recalled the bottle in his kitchen courtesy of Bob Shanks. "I'll get something special from the kitchen."

Frank Sinatra began to croon at Evie. She slouched a little on the sofa. Her head swayed slightly with the velvety tones. She shut her eyes. Scott left the room hoping she'd find serenity from the song and solace in her dreams.

In the kitchen, Scott pulled the spiked Coke from his cabinet along with a glass. He rummaged through a drawer for the bottle opener. He popped the cap letting it bounce and flop on the countertop. He let the cola concoction settle a little, then poured the glass half full. Digging in the modest freezer portion of his new refrigerator, Scott withdrew the chunk of ice left from his earlier chipping. He used the icepick still on the counter to chip four decent pieces free. He dropped them into the glass before tossing the reduced ice hunk back in the freezer. Wyatt figured the cola would be familiar, while the light bourbon mix would give Evie enough alcohol burn to satisfy her urge.

He entered the living room to find Evie had switched the icebag to her knee. Sinatra sang ardently, finishing with his lover's plea. She opened her eyes and grinned as Scott brought the drink to her. She took the glass and guardedly sipped.

"Oh. It tastes like Coke." Surprise registered in her response.

"It has a kick in it," reassured Scott. "It's the latest in bootlegger wares. Can't tell a nickel Coca-Cola from a spiked-up one till you down it." He paced back to his scotch next to the radio. Emanating from the console, Peggy Lee's voice replaced Sinatra's. A positive change in Scott's opinion.

Evie sipped again. A quick swallow and she shifted to a gulp. This time the alcohol scratched its way down her throat. She throttled a gasp quickly converting it to a cough. "I think I like it."

"You have whatever you want, Evie Hall. You're a woman and a stronger one than most I have met."

A smile bloomed on Evie that threatened both ears. "Thank you, Wyatt. I'm glad you finally realize that." She took a normal drink. She plopped the icebag on her lap to change hands for her drink. She regripped the bag and brought it to her cheek.

"You're welcome." Scott took a big pull on his whisky. He relished the burn and the flavor. "Now we need to get you into some real clothes, and get you home to your folks."

The reality of her parents jolted the new sophisticated, highball-drinking Evie. She jiggled the glass rattling the ice. "Yeah, they'll probably be wondering where I am."

"I'll call them." Scott pointed to Evie's left where the closed door guarded the room next to the kitchen. "Your clothes are on the gue-stroom bed."

Evie eased up from the couch. She dropped the icebag on the coffee table. She limped a little as she made for the door. Keeping her drink, she sipped along the way.

"Drop your undercover disguise on the floor. I'll toss those things in the trash or burn them myself."

Evie flashed a sassy grin. "Sure, I won't need them again?"

"Not in this life!" Scott pointed with his whisky glass. "Get in there and change into the Evie Hall I can explain to your parents."

"Gotcha' boss." She saluted adding to her sarcastic reply.

Scott refilled his glass and sat on his couch. He sipped the whisky considering the errors he had made that evening. He should've brought Cleveland along for backup and a law presence. Queena outplayed him from the jump. He thought he was finding the killer for justice despite the disinterested police. She wanted him for vengeance. He didn't feel the least bit remorseful on account of Joe; he would've burned in the chair in a few months anyway. Scott worried that Queena would get Carl in trouble. Any hint of a body and a Black man's involvement would spell sad news for him. Scott gulped down the remaining tawny fluid. He looked at the glass. Scott admitted to himself the foremost trigger of his vexation was letting Queena exploit him.

After two minutes of self-recrimination, Scott called Evie's parents to tell them they would be right over. He explained that Evie's tardiness came about due to late research work for him. He apologized for not calling sooner. They were about to head home from the supper he bought her for a job well done. He explained how Evie was in the ladies' room of the restaurant and asked him to call to ease their concerns.

When Evie emerged in her own clothes, she showed little of the evening tumult. With just enough makeup to cover her bruised cheek and jaw, she looked like the twenty-year-old girl she had been only a few hours past. She smiled at Scott, which made him feel ashamed, but he had to do something scotch-breath, guilty-eyes, and all.

"Here's three tens." Scott held out the bills to Evie. "You earned a bonus for outstanding work."

A little surprise registered on her. She recovered quickly taking the bills and smirking at Scott's munificence. "I'll take it!" Evie stuffed the bills in the new purse she got from her Vandevers job.

The pair left the Sophian Plaza and drove the LaSalle toward the Hall's modest home. On the drive, Scott and Evie concocted a wonderfully creative story for her parents to cover any holes in his original story. It seemed, a dog ran in front of the LaSalle and Evie screamed for Scott to stop, which caused her cheek to hit the dashboard when he slammed on the brakes. This coming on the way to Evie's folks' home after their nice dinner at Bishops, which Scott had alluded to during the phone call. He allowed in the telling why Evie's work proved indispensable in solving his case. It worked well enough on Mr. and Mrs. Hall, but Scott had to tell Johnny Grayhawk the truth and take a ten-minute lecture the following morning.

* * *

After a day of dodging cops, phone calls, and Johnny's repeated, fatherly admonitions against endangering Evie, Scott sipped pure coffee while lounging in his bathrobe. A lot of sun remained outside his west-facing window. He thought about closing the drapes, but he liked looking at the river or at least the trickle between the sandbars. Scott slouched in his chair and slurped more coffee. He felt improved. Nat King Cole's dulcet tones, rendering *Nature Boy*, floated from his radio. Scott liked it. The previous perky song, *Buttons and Bows* by Dinah Shore, scraped against his mood.

His uncertainty and remorse over endangering Evie had been mitigated by time and perspective rather than the overload of scotch consumed when he finally made it home the previous night. His headache seemed much better. So much so that despite a bad night and long day after, he decided not to waste an aspirin on it. A knock on his door postponed any thoughts on his situation and the questions he didn't want to ponder.

On the other side of his apartment door, Scott beheld Queena Capps in a wide summer hat and wearing a long, seersucker sundress. She looked more like a grandmother dressed against her age than a madam running prostitutes. Struck by an image he never dreamed of Scott searched for her lost scowl and a Lucky Strike that had to be lingering somewhere unseen and smokeless.

"Well, are you going to invite me in, mister?"

Scott stepped back from the door still questioning what manner of hallucination alighted on his threshold. "Miss Capps," he managed to grumble as he slogged several steps backwards into his living room.

Queena strolled in scrutinizing his abode with a slow pan from the kitchen door to his bedroom door on the opposite end of the apartment. Repetitive head nods signaled the madam's approval of his stylish apartment. She tapped the radio in time with *Toolie Oolie Doolie* by The Andrews Sisters, which Scott had not noticed, but now reinflamed his headache.

Looking from the radio to his liquor cabinet, Queena scoffed at Scott's manners. "Aren't you going to offer a lady a drink?" She set her purse on the edge of the cabinet.

Scott bit his tongue on his immediate thought about 'lady' and Queena. He pointed at the cabinet with glasses on top. "Pick your poison, Queena. Bottles are inside."

The madam bent to open the cabinet then squatted to view the selection. Rye being her choice, she grabbed the bottle and pulled out the corked stopper. An ample pour seemed to satisfy her, although she left the bottle on top rather than consigning it to the confines of the cabinet. She swirled the whiskey before taking a sip. "Not joining me?" she challenged Scott.

"Too much yesterday. I'm on the wagon at least till tomorrow." Scott's headache approved of his decision.

Queena quaffed more than half the drink in a solitary swig. She set the glass on top of the cabinet next to her handbag. "As much as I love social visits and always wondered about your apartment, I came to pay you for your work." She opened her purse without picking it up. She withdrew a white envelope and extended it toward Scott.

He walked to Queena and took the envelope. Without looking inside, he rattled off his rates. "Forty a day and expenses."

"Ha." Queena laughed. "There's two grand in that envelope. More than forty days and expenses. I told you I'd pay a lot more if you delivered."

Scott looked in the envelope. He spied a thousand-dollar bill in front leading ten little hundreds in a phalanx of cash. "I'm not taking hush money."

"Bonus. Just like I told you." Queena grasped her glass and downed her remaining rye. "What are you worried about? That Joe guy run off. He left town."

"You expect me to believe that?" Scott narrowed his eyes staring holes in Queena.

"I don't expect anything from you. I'm just telling you what happened." She held the glass an inch above the cabinet and let it drop. The sharp ring punctuated her statement. "You can tell the cops or your priest what you want."

Scott eased his stance a little and slipped a hand in his robe pocket. "Personally, I don't care what happened to Joe. He had a date with Old Sparky anyway and if there's a hell, he'll have a firepit for a bed. But I do worry about Carl. Any hint of him being involved or maybe a body being found does worry me."

"I said the Joe fella' run off. Carl will say the same. We don't know where and we won't know for the cops, you, or any other snoopy folks."

Scott couldn't buy it. His skepticism overflowed. "Things will heat up when they find his body."

"Oh, they *won't* find a body. There is no body." Queena grinned. "He ran away, remember?"

"I don't like it," asserted Scott.

"Like it or not. That's your choice. The money will spend on rent or groceries – spends on whores too, if you ever pay'em." Queena beamed at her barb.

"You just be damn sure poor Carl stays clear of this!" barked Scott.

She glared at Scott. "I take care of Carl. He takes care of me." She grabbed her purse. "I'll see you when I see you." Queena threw open the door and marched out, leaving it open.

Scott drifted to the door and shut it. His headache paled next to his frustration. He squatted down at the liquor cabinet. Cutty Sark called his name. Four fingers, and then some, filled the glass. He sat in his chair beside the floor lamp next to the window and looked across The Arkansas. With July just starting, June had been more than he wanted. He hoped and wished for a quiet July and August. Of course, hopes were often dashed, and wishes rarely came true in Scott's Tulsa.

THE END

Join the community of readers! Visit my website (slchalmers.com) for behind-the-scenes insights, history of the times, and photos. After that, pop over to Amazon to leave your review. Your feedback means the world to me!

Follow on X – Slchalmers@WyattScott1948

SCOTT'S TULSA II is coming in the first quarter of 2026.

www.ingramcontent.com/pod-product-compliance
Lightning Source LLC
Chambersburg PA
CBHW020059310726
48970CB00002B/393